FREE LOVE

Also by Annette Meyers

The Groaning Board
These Bones Were Made for Dancin'
Murder: The Musical
Blood on the Street
The Deadliest Option
Tender Death
The Big Killing

ANNETTE MEYERS

FREE LOVE

THE MYSTERIOUS PRESS

Published by Warner Books

A Time Warner Company

Copyright © 1999 by Annette Brafman Meyers
All rights reserved.

 Mysterious Press books are published by Warner Books, Inc., 1271 Avenue of the Americas, New York, NY 10020.

Visit our Web site at www.warnerbooks.com

 A Time Warner Company

The Mysterious Press name and logo are registered trademarks of Warner Books, Inc.
Printed in the United States of America
First Printing: October 1999

10 9 8 7 6 5 4 3 2 1

Library of Congress Cataloging-in-Publication Data

Meyers, Annette.
    Free love / Annette Meyers.
        p.   cm.
    ISBN 0-89296-694-7
    I. Title.
PS3563.E889F74   1999
813'.54—dc21
                                                                99-14589
                                                                CIP

For Olivia Baron Brown

Acknowledgments

My thanks to the wonderful people at Mysterious Press/Warner for the love, nurturing, and support they've given this book. To Sara Ann Freed, truly an editor for all seasons. To Bill Malloy, Susan Richman, Susanna Einstein. To Honi Werner, designer, for the ravishing cover and design.

Thanks as well to my matchless agent, Stuart Krichevsky, who stirs the pot with finesse.

To James Leach, archivist of St. Vincent's Hospital, who generously gave me his time and a tour through his old photographs.

To Marty for his clarity and insight, and for being surprised.

And to my niece and nephew, Jennifer and Tom Brown, for letting Olivia come out to play.

FREE LOVE

When I die
I hope they will say of me,
She was always at the boil,
At a constant rolling heat
Beneath the surface
  Fulminating,
  Roiling,
Bubbling anger, love, pain,
  Outrage, joy,
Thrown by the process every which way.
  Alive.

—Olivia Brown, 1920

Chapter One

$\mathcal{I}$t was the kind of rain that didn't honor an umbrella, for it came down sideways, with sudden frigid gusts of wind. Anybody out in it was sure to get a good soaking. Flooding came on quickly, as the old streets of Greenwich Village were ill equipped with drainage, and the walks, courtyards, and alleys were rife with shallow dips where water accumulated quickly. Which is why no one found the body until the rain let up and we ventured abroad again for something more sustaining than the food of love.

Having rehearsed at the Playhouse through the previous evening, we'd gone to Chumley's for our usual nightcap. It had rained so relentlessly for three days, the courtyard leading to Chumley's was underwater. And Chumley's itself looked more deserted than usual, though we knew there was no less activity.

But that night we were more inclined toward lovemaking, and so we happily bypassed the speakeasy and waded our way to Bedford Street. It was well after midnight. We stayed home in bed reading poetry, smoking and making love, even sleeping, through the night and most of the day.

After dark, when we finally came out again, our first stop was the Waverly on Bank Street, where I could indulge my craving for meatloaf and mashed potatoes and chocolate pudding. Prohibition being what it was, the Waverly served no spirits. And we'd already polished off the gin in Whit's pocket flask. Our spirits needed spirits. Arm in arm, we ambled down Commerce Street past the Cherry Lane Theatre to the dim courtyard that led to Chumley's.

And that's how Whit and I ended up being the ones who found her.

We thought it was a red blanket bunched up in the pool of filthy water that filled the courtyard. I never bother with stockings, so though it was cold, I took off my shoes to wade through the mess. Of course, Whit had some choice things to say about dirt and germs—a fair enough lover, but such a prig. I never listen to anybody about the way I choose to live my life, so I certainly wasn't going to pay much attention to his "rules and regulations," as I like to call his pronouncements.

It was a mistake; the water was cold and slimy. Still, there was no way I was going to impart this and have him say "I told you so," so I took my time sloshing through it. Oh, prig or not, he probably wouldn't have gloated because he's a better person than I am.

As I was having this whole debate with myself, I tripped over something, arched back to stop my fall, and sat right down on my derriere in the mess next to the soggy blanket. Whit turned around and laughed. I was not amused. I held up what had brought me down. It was a rather elegant, albeit sopping, high-heeled shoe.

"Get up out of there, Oliver," Whit said in that supercilious way of his.

He reached over to give me a hand, and I couldn't help it, I gave him a mighty tug. He landed right on top of the sodden blanket.

There she was, wrapped up practically like a mummy. Only wet strings of hair could be seen from one end; from the opposite, long bare toes of one foot and on the other foot, the water-logged mate of the elegant high-heeled shoe that had tripped me.

We pulled her out of the still water onto somewhat drier pavement, where pinpricks of light leaked from Chumley's darkened windows. I suppose it was the wrong thing to do because the coppers like to have things left intact, as they were quick enough to tell us later, but at the time we weren't thinking too clearly. It was a shock finding a dead body practically in your backyard. And then too, there was little light and we were a bit drunk. We didn't notice that we were stained by her blood.

"Shouldn't we open the blanket so she can breathe?" I set her other shoe down beside her bare toes, my thoughts fluttering about the poem taking shape in my head.

"She's dead," Whit said, but he loosened the blanket anyway, and we saw that she had been strangled with a red cord. "Damn," he said. He looked away, then moved away. Chumley's had no telephone. "I'll get a cop."

Whit went off; a moment later I heard him retching in the darkness. I lit a cigarette and kept watch over the poor creature, once a living, breathing girl like me. I struck a match and looked at her again. Her face was blotchy with makeup, smeared with dirt and death. She seemed vaguely familiar and yet not. She lay as if asleep in the blanket.

Not strangled, I decided. Strangulation leaves the eyes popping and the tongue protruding. I'd seen our stable boy after he hanged himself in the barn when he was fourteen.

What Whit and I'd both thought to be a red cord was the slash across her throat. She'd bled to death, her blood mingling with the rain and filling the courtyard where the dip in the cement formed a valley.

Before long, Max and Mary appeared, then Rae with Merrill and Emma, and Edward Hall. Edward has such a quick mind. I felt a mild twinge of regret we were no longer lovers. He went right into Chumley's and warned them that we were bringing the cops for the dead woman. And quickly, with much groaning and carrying on, all the booze was cleared away and out came the teacups. Pretty soon, everyone was standing around outside looking at the dead woman.

"Does anyone know her?" I asked the assembly.

Someone held a flashlight close to her face. Under the dirt her skin was sheer, white and bloodless. Her lips were blue.

"Poor mouse," a man said.

"Seen her around once or twice," another fellow said.

By then my teeth were chattering. I stubbed out what was left of my cigarette. I'd been sitting far too long on the cold, damp cement, my wet skirt wrapped about my bare legs. I felt a hand clasp my shoulder.

"You are soaking wet. You can't sit out here like this. You'll have pneumonia."

He was tall and slim, to my liking. His dark hair hovered near his collar, shaggy, as if he cut it himself. He knelt beside me close, so he was looking into my eyes. I tasted the gin as his breath brushed my lips. I'd seen him before, at Chumley's, around the Village. He'd been in the War and spoke French with ease. I tried to remember his name . . .

"Andrew Goren," he said. "Come inside and dry off."

Of course. He wrote in a clean, honest style. "I read one of your stories," I said. "You're very good." I let him lift me to my feet. The cement felt rough on my soles. Well, no wonder I was cold. I'd dropped my shoes when I fell.

He brought me into Chumley's, where the chess pieces from the interrupted games awaited the players' return. For the moment the entertainment was outdoors, not in. We sat near the fire, and we drank gin from teacups, smoked.

"I read your poem 'Hay and Straw' in *Vanity Fair*," he said. "I liked it. I admire your work."

He had hot eyes, deepest blue, almost black. Count Dracula eyes. I bade a silent adieu to Whit, for I'd decided then and there Andy Goren would be my next lover. "I've lost my shoes," I said.

"I'll carry you home," said he.

Oh, love, I thought.

Outside, we heard raised voices. The police had arrived. He rose.

"Where are you going?"

"I have to talk to the police. I'll be back for you."

"Did you know her?" I asked.

"She was my wife," he said.

Chapter Two

Of course, this was a case of the best-laid plans, for the man who saw me home to Bedford Street as dawn came stealing over the Village was a thick-chested, respectful Irish cop by the name of Brophy.

"I'd like to ask you a few questions, Miss, if you're up to it," he said.

I told him that after I'd bathed I would be happy to do so.

I was elated to find Mattie, my companion and housekeeper, home at last from Boston where she'd been helping a young cousin to birth her second child in as many years. Mattie's presence quite obviously did not displease Brophy, who, after a brief explanation of what had occurred for Mattie's benefit, settled himself in our tiny kitchen for a cup of tea, while I excused myself for a quick bath. When I returned, clean if not refreshed, he and Mattie were laughing together over their tea, quite companionably.

"I'm ready," I said, "to answer your questions now, Detective Brophy."

Brophy's pleasant face was a mass of freckles, his red hair closer to orange, as mine was closer to brick. "How long have you lived here, Miss Brown?" He paused to dip a piece of Mattie's shortbread into his tea. The saucer was full of crumbs and liquid.

"Mattie and I have lived here since April last," said I. "This little house came to me from my great-aunt Evangeline Brown." What I did not tell him was that Great-Aunt Evangeline was the black sheep of the family because she had chosen to live in Greenwich Village in an open relationship with another woman. It was only after she died that I even knew of her existence.

"How well did you know this dead woman?"

"I didn't know her at all. We—Whit and I—found her by accident. Anyone might have."

"The poor girl," Mattie said. "Do you know who she was, Detective Brophy?"

"She's—" I began. Brophy was looking at me expectantly. I shrugged. Hadn't Andrew Goren identified her as his wife?

"You said you didn't know her," Brophy said, as if I'd let him down.

"I don't. I thought I heard someone say he'd seen her around. So I assumed . . ."

Mattie's sharp look made me realize my mouth was hanging open. I shut it. Well, wasn't that interesting. I had assumed . . . a grave error.

Detective Brophy took his leave somewhat reluctantly, I could see. While my Mattie in deep blush showed him out, I began to feel the exhaustion that I had been fighting these last hours and adjourned to my bedroom where Mattie had changed the linen and removed the empty wine bottles. I crawled between the fresh sheets, searching my tired brain for the right words to describe . . . the death of a young girl . . . death's red collar . . . and immediately fell into a deep sleep.

This new life of mine in Greenwich Village had not begun twenty-four hours before or even twenty-four days before.

Two years earlier I had thought my life was over. I'd gone through a prolonged period of physical and mental devastation caused by the death of everyone who was dear to me. Everyone but Mattie, who had nursed me back to a modicum of health.

The Great War had taken the life of my dear fiancé, Franklin Prince, and the dreadful influenza epidemic in 1918 took the lives of my guardian, Mr. Avery, and my beloved teacher, the poet, Miss Sarah Parkman.

I had been orphaned at an eary age and became the ward of Jonas Avery, an elderly bachelor who, though kindly, knew nothing of bringing up a girl child of some precosity. So it was well that Mattie Timmons, Mr. Avery's housekeeper, took charge of my care. Though not much older than I, Mattie had been on her own for many years and was clearly a mature and responsible person. She was also warm and loving, exactly what an orphaned waif, such as I, needed.

Franklin was my best friend. Three years my senior, he was the boy next door, the son of Dr. Prince, our family doctor. We'd grown up together. Actually, he had grown like a weed, as they say, while I remained tiny. He taught me to be fearless, to run like the wind, climb trees, play baseball, and later, much later, to make love.

When the War began in Europe, Franklin was at Cornell, studying to be a doctor like his father. He and a slew of other boys went off to Canada to join up, learn to fly, certain America would be drawn into it before long. We became engaged before he left. Six months before the Armistice in 1918, Franklin's badly damaged plane went down over the English Channel. Lost. A hero, they said, presenting his father with his medal.

> *Clear and cloudless was the sky,*
> *Not turbulent the sea.*
> *Men go to War to play, not die,*
> *Oh woe, oh woe to me.*

My education was put into the sturdy hands of Miss Sarah, a friend of Mr. Avery and a graduate of Vassar College, who had taught at the Emma Willard School until her sixtieth year. The formidable Miss Sarah was a suffragist, called upon often to speak for the Cause. She saw me as fine clay, and convinced that women would most certainly get the vote, she devoted herself to giving her avid pupil a classical education equivalent to that of a young gentleman.

Through her connection to Vassar, Miss Sarah had become acquainted with the poet Edna St. Vincent Millay, whom she greatly admired. So it was under Miss Sarah's tutelage that I came to be inspired by Miss Millay and began to write my poems.

Shortly after my recovery I received a visit from Mr. Bernhardt, my late guardian's attorney, himself a man of some years, who brought with him a full accounting of my financial status. Though modest, it would be adequate for me and Mattie so we would not want of the basic necessities. It was thus the news came to me that my guardian had made me his heir, which in itself meant little, for Mr. Avery had, it seemed, been an inveterate player in the stock market and because of losses had dipped into my principal.

The beautiful old house, shaded by ancient oaks, in which I'd spent my formative years, had become a costly burden. I had no memory of any home but this. As a child, I had run up and slid down its splendid balustered staircase. My favorite room was the wood-paneled library. On the soaring shelves were a multitude of books accumulated by generations of Averys. Many a day had I lain on my stomach in front of the fire, reading the fables of Aesop. I'd traveled with Odysseus on the wine-dark sea, sat with Estella and Pip at Miss Havisham's table and accompanied a Yankee to King Arthur's Court. It was here Franklin knew to find me when he finished helping his father in the surgery.

Everything now would have to be sold, and I resigned myself to a more financially circumspect life. Or, as I told Mattie later, with a very serious face, we could both, of necessity, become nuns.

"Of course," Mr. Bernhardt suggested, "You might consider selling the house on Bedford Street."

"What house on Bedford Street?" I asked, quite confused.

"The house on Bedford Street in New York," he said, obviously unaware that I had no knowledge of such.

"A house in New York? On Bedford Street? I know nothing of this."

"It belonged to the sister of your grandfather, Oliver Brown, for whom you are named," he said. "Miss Brown passed on while your guardian was ill, and I received a letter from her attorney in New York, notifying me that you are her only living relative and, therefore, her heir."

"New York," I said, feeling the first tingle of curiosity since my illness and my terrible losses. "Bedford Street. It sounds lovely, but would it be more costly to live there than to stay here in Albany?"

Mr. Bernhardt, being of a very conservative bent, looked aghast. "You must not consider such a move. New York City is not a place for a gentle young woman alone."

"Is the house not inhabitable, then?"

"Quite the opposite. I understand the house is in fine condition and will bring a fair price on its sale, the only question being—"

In my excitement I did not at first assimilate the words, "the only question being," in Mr. Bernhardt's reply. I said, "Perhaps Mattie and I could travel to New York and inspect the house and the area before we make up our minds."

"I hardly think—"

"Forgive me, Mr. Bernhardt, but I am quite overcome with all the news you have presented to me. Please tell me about my grandfather's sister. I had no idea that I had any living relations, and I'm sorry to learn she has passed on."

"I know little about her," he said primly. "The house, however, comes with its own trust fund and a codicil."

"A trust fund? For a house? This gets better and better."

"Your great-aunt, Miss Evangeline Brown, left a sum of money in trust for the care and upkeep of the house and the salary of a full-time housekeeper."

I was overjoyed. "Why, Mr. Bernhardt, my great-aunt, whom I never knew, will provide a home for Mattie and me. This is wonderful news. We will put this house on the market at once and Mattie and I will begin a new life in New York."

"As you wish." Mr. Bernhardt wore the sourest of expressions. I am certain he did not know what to make of the new generation of young women and our desire to exercise control over our own lives. "But," said he, his thin lips set in disapproval, "I have not told you of the codicil."

Oh, dear, I thought. He was about to burst my bubble. "Yes, the codicil."

"There is a tenant in the house, on the ground floor. He has a private entrance."

"Yes, I see, a tenant. Well, if I am to live in the house, the tenant will have to move."

"That, my dear child, is the codicil. The tenant—an odd, nocturnal man who seldom makes his appearance in daylight and who has equally odd nocturnal visitors—he is the codicil. According to Miss Evangeline Brown's will, he is to live there for his lifetime."

"Oh, I see. Well, that shouldn't matter. Since he has a private entrance, and is, as you say, nocturnal, I shall see little of him, and the rent will be extra money for our coffers."

The old gentleman looked positively triumphant. "I'm afraid," he said, "there will be none of that, as he is to live rent-free so long as he remains in the house."

"Well, then, so be it," I said most cheerfully, for I looked at the tidings about my new house as a gift from God, as well as from my unknown (to me) great-aunt Evangeline. "Still, it is a very odd arrangement."

Little did I imagine just how odd it truly was, nor that it would change my life as I knew it forever.

Mattie and I arrived in New York on a particularly lovely spring day in early April and were filled with awe by the magnificence of Grand Central Terminal. Light streamed down on us from a lofty skylight, and everywhere one looked, there were well-dressed ladies and gentlemen in traveling clothes, porters following with mounds of luggage and trunks.

Mattie took charge at once, summoning our own porter, and soon we, too, were surrounded by hatboxes and satchels.

"We must wait for the trunk," Mattie said, still fussing over my health, which I had quite regained.

"I beg your pardon, but would you be Miss Brown? Miss

Olivia Brown?" A tall, amiable young man, very properly dressed, stood before me.

"I am. And who might you be?" I had become very direct since my recovery.

"Thomas Jenner, at your service, Miss Brown." He tipped his hat, giving me just a glimpse of unruly dark hair. "I am charged with delivering you, your housekeeper, and your luggage to No. 73½ Bedford Street. Your attorney, Mr. Lyon Bernhardt, made the arrangements."

So it was that Mattie and I, with our guide, Mr. Thomas Jenner, directing the driver, were ensconced in a livery cab piled high with everything we cared to bring with us from our old life to our new.

I shall never forget our first ride down the celebrated Fifth Avenue in magical sunlight. I had never seen so many automobiles and people all intent on going somewhere. I was dazzled by the beauty of the city, as was Mattie.

"This is Madison Square Park," Mr. Jenner said, pointing to a charming treed area as we rode by. "And the Flatiron Building, which you can see looks as it is called. And the Ladies' Mile."

We passed Union Square and the beautiful homes and tall buildings of lower Fifth Avenue, then Washington Square with its great arch. Mattie and I were quite overwhelmed, and were relieved when Mr. Jenner tapped our driver on the shoulder.

"Between Morton and Commerce Streets," he said.

We found ourselves in the heart of Greenwich Village, where small shops and brick town houses stood side by side on the winding, narrow streets.

Our driver stopped before a small three-story house of red brick with peeling white trim. Shrubs filled a handkerchief-sized area in front, guarded by a black ornate wrought-iron fence. A fine oak door with brass trim led to a small vestibule.

The two large set-in windows on the ground floor obviously belonged to the flat of my tenant-in-perpetuity, and I admit to being very curious, particularly since those windows were shuttered.

I raised my eyes to the two floors that would be my new home and I was most inordinately pleased. Who would not be?

On the second floor, three tall windows, and on the third, four windows, taller still.

Our escort saw to the unloading of our luggage and produced a shiny brass key from his inside pocket, while our livery driver waited impatiently to receive his payment and be gone.

And I? I fairly danced in the vestibule of my new home. Then stopped. There were two doors here. Which door was mine? Not the door to the right, surely, for the brass plate set beside that door finally informed me of the identity of my tenant-in-perpetuity. It said: H. MELVILLE, PRIVATE INVESTIGATIONS (CONFIDENTIALITY ASSURED).

Chapter Three

*T*he doorbell woke me. I hoped it wasn't Whit. He'd been making noises about moving in. He'd asked me to marry him, and I'd put him off, saying I'd think about it. But I knew I wasn't going to marry him. It wasn't just Whit, with his tiresome pronouncements. Marriage gives a man too much control of a woman's life.

I stretched, luxuriating in the comfort of my bed, the clean smell of the bedding. My room lay in sepia light, the curtains drawn. Drifting, I had no sense of time. I got up, wrapped myself in my dressing gown and put a fresh page into my typewriter. I sat down at my desk.

When Mattie brought tea and scones a short time later, I had the first line. Well, almost.

"Stop and eat something," Mattie said, setting the tray down on my desk. "You're nothing but skin and bones."

I set my work aside. Sometimes it's better not to force it. The right words are always there in my mind, hiding. When I least expect it, they will come. "Who was at the door?"

"Someone left a package for you. I'll bring it up."

"No, it can wait. Detective Brophy rather likes you, I think. And you like him."

Mattie blushed. "He's a married man."

"He told you?" I turned on my desk lamp. The glow cast a fuzzy glaze on my writing paper. The words, crossed out and otherwise, bled into each other.

"No. And don't you be telling me to ask him." She bustled about the room, making up my bed, emptying the ashtrays. "You had some telephone calls. Edward Hall called twice. And Whit stopped by. I told them all you were resting. As you should be."

I found I was ravenous. I made short shrift of the scones, wiped my fingers on the napkin and leafed through the letters that Mattie had placed on the tray. The one from *Vanity Fair* produced a check. Always very welcome. I handed it to Mattie. The rest were bills, a complimentary letter about my poems from a professor at Amherst, an invitation to read my poems at a women's club tea in Greenwich. I lit a cigarette and offered it to Mattie. She took it and I lit another for myself. We smoked, smiling, sharing the intimacy of the smoke. I was glad she was back.

The doorbell interrupted us. Mattie went to answer it, and I moved the tray to the floor and returned to my work. She knew not to disturb me.

> *How fragile is the air we breathe:*
> *When we are young there is no sorrow.*
> *How brittle is the life we lead*
> *As if there is no morrow.*
> *Why who's afraid of jeopardy?*
> *We thrive on our supreme creation,*
> *For peril's youth's necessity,*
> *Its darling drug, exhilaration.*
> *And so we gambol with our fate*
> *Consumed by motion, more by chance.*
> *Abandon mind? There's no rebate*
> *But death, who'll take us in mid-dance.*

I had no idea of the time when I stopped. My final couplet wasn't coming to me. I read my sonnet through with all the crossings-out, then retyped what I had to a fresh page. Without the final couplet.

Numb from sitting in one place, I opened my door. Voices rose from below. I combed back my hair with my fingers and tied my gown around me. Wafting up at me were bouquets of roasted chicken and potatoes. I came down the stairs in my bare feet.

Detective Brophy was sitting at the kitchen table, a bowl of soup before him. His coat was open, but his face was shiny with sweat. When he saw me he scrambled to his feet. "Good evening, Miss Brown," he said.

"Sit, please, Detective Brophy," I said, grinning at Mattie. I tucked my tongue in my cheek. "I hope we aren't keeping you from your family."

"The job often has me out at night, Miss," Brophy said. "My mother always leaves my dinner for me."

"Really? You live with your mother then?"

"I do, Miss."

"Never married?"

"Olivia!"

Mattie still calls me Olivia, though to my Village friends, and to myself, I'm Oliver. My lips twitched. Mattie's face was the color of a summer plum.

Brophy barely held back his smile. "No, Miss. I'm the youngest of seven. All the others are married."

"How nice to have such a big family, Mr. Brophy. Mattie, am I too late for supper?"

Mattie pointed to a chair and while she ladled out a bowl of parsley-flecked chicken soup, I smirked. I couldn't help it. It was obvious that Brophy was smitten.

"Detective Brophy came by to ask a few more questions about the poor dead girl," Mattie said, looking daggers at me.

"Ask away, Mr. Brophy." Mattie's soup was heavenly.

"Well, Miss, this morning you gave me to believe someone knew the dead woman, but no one has come forward and identified her."

"Oh, dear," I said. "Maybe I was wrong. I was so upset, what with finding her and then having her blood all over me." I was not wrong. I was sure that Andrew Goren had told me she was his wife. Why hadn't he told the police?

"We had one of our artists do a drawing of her as though she were still alive. Perhaps if you saw it you might recognize her." He wiped his mouth, reached down to the floor, and brought up an envelope. I was struck by the fact that he was avoiding eye contact with me.

I heard Mattie gasp when Brophy removed the drawing from the envelope, but I didn't understand why until I saw it for myself. Without all that muck on it, the girl had a narrow face with delicate features, a high forehead, pale eyebrows over green eyes, a sensual mouth, and long red hair.

She could have been my sister, if I had one.

In short, she could have been me.

Chapter Four

"But I'm very much alive," I protested. "As you can see for yourself."

"You have no sister?" Brophy asked.

"No sister, no cousin. No living relative. Can't you use things like fingerprints to identify her?"

"Her fingerprints would only come up if she had a prior record. Someone is already checking this out, but it takes time."

It was a conundrum. I was not frightened, as Mattie was, but it did make me uneasy. Detective Brophy left the drawing with us, at my request.

Sending poor Mattie off to bed with a glass of hot milk, I returned to my room to think. Perhaps it was time to tell the police about Andrew Goren. And yet, I hesitated. He was a writer, and so attractive. He would certainly have a good explanation . . .

I felt in my pocket for my cigarette case and holder, lit up, and smoked in the semidarkness. A girl who looked exactly like me had been murdered. Was it too far-fetched to think that there had been a mistake, that perhaps I had been the target? I put out the cigarette in a glass ashtray and left my room.

Old houses have definite personalities, marked by how they

settle on their foundations. My house sighed rather than creaked, as the house in Albany had. It sighed softly when I paused in front of the enormous oak hat-and-umbrella stand in my front hall. A gaily wrapped package with a large ribbon bow sat on the marble-topped table section of the stand. Mattie and I had quite forgotten all about it.

Mattie was not a night creature. She slept normal hours while I was often out late with my friends, either at Chumley's or Columbia Gardens, another saloon, not far from the Provincetown Playhouse. I'd come home in the wee hours and, if I was alone, I would write or play the piano. But frequently these days I was not alone.

My house gave another soft sigh as I stared at my image in the mirror in the center of the hat tree. The unknown dead woman was my doppelganger. It had terrified Mattie and, in all honesty, unsettled me. The woman in the drawing had already been identified by several people as the poet Olivia Brown. Except for the hair, which was quite long, as I had worn mine before in celebration of my newfound independence, I bobbed it.

My shawl round my shoulders, I picked up the package as an afterthought, and went downstairs. In the vestibule, the light from the lamp overhead was dim, and the brass nameplate on my tenant's door was in shadow, but I knew he was home and still awake by the ribbon of light seeping from under the door.

I set my package at my feet and gave his bell a firm twist. A hoarse sound followed, and I waited.

I'd met Harry Melville the very first night I was in my new house. Awakened by strange noises from the street, I'd come downstairs to find that the lock of my tenant's door had been removed, leaving a gaping hole. I peered into the hole, but it was black as tar inside. I held my lamp near the hole and was rewarded with such a fierce growl that it took my breath away. Then the door swung open inward and a voice said, "Douse that bloody light."

I was so startled I froze, and he ordered me to come inside. And I did. His voice was resonant, yet not unfriendly. His accent was quality American with a faint undertone of something else I couldn't quite catch.

The room I entered was large and wood paneled, but everything else in it was wrecked, including the shredded mattress of a Murphy bed. A carpet of feathers from the empty pillowcases lay on the floor.

My host was bent over the fireplace, coaxing a fire from one lonesome log. When he straightened and faced me, I saw a man in his middle years, broad of shoulder, though not much taller than I. His hair was fine and pale, almost to his shoulders, and on his forehead was a lump the size of a walnut and a bruise that had broken the skin.

"Oh, my," I said, "You've been hurt."

"Comes with the territory." He stared at me and laughed full out. "You must be the old girl's niece."

"I am," I admitted, "Olivia Brown."

"Green eyes and red hair run in the family, Niece," he said, looking me over thoroughly. "Take a seat." He gestured toward the sofa, on which were piled papers and folders of every sort, in no particular order. He did not clear a space.

I moved a snarl of loose papers carefully to the floor and sat. "You are H. Melville, Private Investigations, then?" I said. "My codicil."

"The very same." He removed a bottle of scotch whiskey from a desk drawer, poured some of the liquid onto a handkerchief, which looked none too clean, and placed it over his bruised forehead, wincing as he did so. He lifted the bottle to his lips and took a long drink. Then he offered the bottle to me.

Still being a little uncertain about the rapid changes in my life, I refused. I would not today.

"Your loss," he said. He set the bottle down and lit a cigarette. "Vangie could put it away with me, swig for swig." He seemed amused at my expense, his coal-black eyes showing no pupils.

"Vangie? You don't mean Great-Aunt Evangeline?" I said, astonished that he could be so familiar about her.

He took another long drink and squinted at me. "This was her business," he said. "She brought me in and trained me. We worked together for fifteen years until Miss Alice died and Vangie's health started to go."

I was by now totally confused. "You mean Great-Aunt Evangeline was a private investigator."

"I do."

"And who was Miss Alice?"

"Bloody hell," said he. "I'm not here to explain the birds and the bees to you. The two old girls lived together. You know. Like man and wife."

Well, I confess I was so shocked I slid off the sofa to the floor.

"Welcome to Greenwich Village, Niece. All the laundry hangs on the line down here."

"A Boston marriage," I murmured, for I had read about this. Two women. Lesbians. But if Mr. Melville thought I'd be repelled, he was wrong.

Such was my introduction to Greenwich Village, my new life, and Harry Melville. But more of that later.

I think Harry was quite surprised to find me when he opened the door. "Well, Oliver," he said. "Long time no see." He'd taken to calling me Oliver because he liked the shock on his clients' faces when he referred to his associate Oliver and then introduced me. And I'd taken my new name to heart, as it had been my grandfather's, and cast Olivia to the wind, except professionally, of course. "What do you have there?"

He was looking at my feet. He reached down and picked up the package, standing back so that I could enter. "You've brought me a present," he said.

He knew it wasn't a present, but he did enjoy ragging me. "No, I haven't. It came for me and I quite forgot and carried it out with me. Put it down. I want you to see something."

So saying, I removed the drawing of the dead woman from the envelope and handed it to him. He set my package on his desk, gave the frivolous bow a careless snap, then took the drawing. He looked from the drawing to me, back to the drawing. "A decent likeness," he said.

"That is not a drawing of me," I said, impatiently. I took one of the cigarettes from the case he offered me.

"Who then?" He lit us both up.

"The woman murdered in Chumley's courtyard."

His face showed no emotion. "Where did you get this?"

"Detective Brophy brought it round this afternoon. The police haven't been able to identify her. Everyone has remarked on her resemblance to me. In fact, they think we're one and the same."

"Your long-lost twin?"

"Don't joke, Harry. It frightens me."

"Coincidence." He handed me the drawing.

"I don't think there is such a thing. Have you ever seen her before?"

He jerked his thumb at me. I didn't think it was funny. "What's in the box?" he asked.

"I don't know. It came earlier today and because of the drawing, Mattie and I forgot all about it."

He picked it up. "There's no address."

"It was delivered."

"Something you ordered?"

I shook my head. "Oh, give it here, and I'll open it. I came to talk with you about the likeness between me and the murdered woman and you're curious about a package." I stubbed out my cigarette and untied the bounteous bow.

"I heard she had her throat cut," Harry said.

"Yes." I unwrapped the William Morris–style paper and opened the box. It was filled with tissue. I moved the tissue aside and a chill came over me. I threw the box down. I felt ill.

"What is it?" Harry crouched and emptied the contents of the box on the floor. "What's gotten into you, Oliver?" he said. "It's only a pair of high-heeled shoes."

Chapter Five

*A*re they your size?" Harry held up the shoes.

"I don't know and I don't care." I tried to slip the drawing back in the envelope, couldn't because my hands were shaking. Gave it up.

"What are you so upset about?"

"Upset? Upset?" I was sputtering. "Good God, Harry, the dead woman had shoes like these. Look at the height of that heel. Have you ever known me to wear shoes like that?"

Harry leered at me. "There's a lot I don't know about you, Oliver."

"Damn you, Harry." Furious, I stamped my foot, forgetting I wore no shoes.

"Don't do it, Oliver," Harry said, seeing what was coming before I did. He took the drawing and the envelope from my hand and held me.

To my mortification, I burst into tears.

"Shucks, I thought I told you not to do that," he said.

I pushed him away. "I'm frightened and you're not helping me."

"What do you want me to do? If I were you I'd be careful who I was running around with at all hours."

"Oh, shut up, Harry, you're no one to talk. Besides, you know everybody I run around with. I met most of them through you."

Which was true. After all, he had taken me up, a charity case, he'd said, and introduced me to Chumley's, where I met Jig Cook, the inspiration behind the Provincetown Players, and the novelist and playwright, Susan Glaspell, his wife. They'd invited me to audition for the next play.

The writer, Floyd Dell, had said, "Not another redhead," as he shook my hand, explaining that not only I, but Edna Millay and Louise Bryant and at least two other of the Village girls all had red hair and that the Village must indeed have a special attraction for red-haired girls.

Charity case, indeed.

Harry held up the shoes again. "Definitely not your style, I can see that. Try them on."

"Why?"

"I want to see if your admirer knows enough about you to send you the right size shoe."

He was serious. So I moved some of his papers to the floor and sat on his broken-down couch and slipped on the shoes. They were a perfect fit. The insides were lined with silk. "They're well made." Gathering up the skirts of my dressing gown, I stood, wobbling. I felt ten miles tall. "What do you think?"

"Not bad," he said. He knelt and sifted through the contents of the box that I'd spilled on the floor.

"Thanks." I sat down and tore the shoes from my feet. Enough was enough. That's when I saw the impression in the unblemished leather sole near the instep. It looked like a bent sword. In the curve of the sword was a little diamond. "Harry, look at this." I handed him one shoe and picked up the other. The same impression was on both soles.

Harry stared at the sole and rubbed his hand over the impression. "Why would someone send you an expensive pair of hand-made shoes?"

"I'm not sure I care for your implication," I said.

"And why not enclose a card or a note?" he continued, choosing to ignore my comment.

"All right, advise me. What shall I do?"

"About the dead woman? I'll look into it. About the shoes, this is some sort of trademark. You can ask your girlfriends and see if anyone recognizes it."

"I'm not going to walk around showing these shoes to anyone."

"You don't have to." He rummaged around the top of his desk and came up with a pencil stub and a sheet of writing paper, the top of which held some numbers, the bottom, almost clean. Holding the clean part against the sole of the shoe over the trademark, he rubbed the pencil gently over the paper. When he set the shoe down and held up the paper, I saw he had transferred the design to the writing paper.

I took the paper with the trademark and put it into the envelope along with the drawing. "Harry, there's something I haven't told you . . . something I haven't told anyone."

He leaned against his desk, crossed one leg over the other, and folded his arms. "Shoot," he said.

"While we were waiting for the police to finish whatever police do, a very attractive man bought me a drink."

"Of course."

"No. Please don't comment, Harry. He's a writer, and quite a good one. Andrew Goren is his name."

"Another groove in your bow, Oliver?"

I colored nicely, I hope. "Not yet. Maybe never."

His eyebrow shot up. "What?"

"Please, Harry, I'm being very serious. Andrew Goren told me the dead woman was his wife. He left me in Chumley's, saying he was going to talk to the police."

"Then the police have identified the woman."

"No, they haven't. Detective Brophy didn't mention Andrew Goren."

"And I take it you didn't either?"

"Well, he seemed so nice. And he's such a good writer. I didn't want to get him into trouble."

"For maybe killing his wife? If he killed his wife, and I'm not saying he did, what the hell do you think he'd do with you?"

"Send me shoes?" I said flippantly, though Harry had a point.

I am a trusting soul, not very savvy about men, though I don't think anyone but Harry realizes it. I love them as they pass through my life making only a ripple here and there. And now, I was thinking maybe I'd dramatized—as I am wont to do—all of this.

But Harry had a very stern look on his face. "I'm serious, Oliver. Stay away from Chumley's. And no romantic trysts for a while. I'll check this Andrew Goren out, but you—" He pointed his finger at me. "You take better care of yourself."

Chapter Six

*N*o *romantic trysts.* I dumped the shoes into their box, took the envelope, and bid Harry a wounded good night.

My house was still. In my bedroom, I set the box of shoes on the floor and gave it a savage kick under the bed. The envelope went on my desk. The room was cold, and clutching my shawl around me, I shifted the curtains aside to close the window. Below, the only sign of life came from the street lamp, which cast a fuzzy sphere into wavering whorls of fog. Abandoning the window I lay down on my bed and lit a cigarette, inhaled slowly, exhaled slowly, and watched the glow of the ash as it accommodated to the movement of my hand.

No romantic trysts, Harry had said. He didn't understand. Or maybe he understood too well. I need the romance; I need to feel that every day is new and exciting. Dangerous. The Village, having brought me back to life, keeps me alive with injections of adventure.

The very geography of the Village is stimulating. Narrow crooked streets cross over other narrow crooked streets and disappear, only to turn up again, twisted in a slightly altered direction. It is an oasis amid the bustle and commerce that is New York City.

I am surrounded by free spirits and dreamers, eccentrics, writers and actors, artists, social activists, all drawn here by the mystique of the Village. Everyone is young and gay and daring; money is scarce, but ideas are plentiful and wine is cheap. We eat together, drink together, play together. I learn from them and they from me. I can do as I like, dress as I please, live as I like, and love freely. I can never give that up, which is why I will never marry.

I left the last of the cigarette in the dish to burn itself out with tendrils of lazy smoke. I was wide awake; I could sense the shoes pulsating in their box under my bed. I knew I was avoiding thinking about Andrew Goren and his dead wife. I felt his hand again on my shoulder, his warm gin breath on my lips. I wanted him. But Harry was right. What if he was a murderer? And, if he was, why would he have done such a dreadful thing? I pushed him out of my thoughts.

The shoes throbbed their way back into my consciousness. I had a secret admirer. Who said that was bad? Maybe he was an incredibly wealthy Arabian prince who had read my poems and wanted to shower me with presents. Because he came from another culture he didn't realize that this was a bizarre gift for an American girl living in Greenwich Village in 1920.

Oh, hell. I was not going to sleep this night.

Under my desk, tucked away in a dark corner behind some manuscripts, was a bottle of gin. I crouched in the dark, and groping, found it. I could tell by the weight, there wasn't much to it. Leaning against the leg of my desk, I sat on the floor, knees under my chin. I uncapped the bottle and lifted it to my lips. It would do, it would do.

I finished what was left in the bottle and fell asleep with my head on my knees. When I awoke, I had a crick in my neck and my feet had gone to sleep along with the rest of me.

I rose, staggered over to the window and parted the curtains. It was darker than before. The street lamp had gone out. Bedford Street was quiet, abandoned by both automobile and pedestrian. I was not afraid, because Harry was here in the house, because Harry made me feel safe.

I stood staring down at the darkness, remembering my second meeting with Harry Melville.

When I awoke that first morning in my new home, I did not remember my encounter with my exotic tenant. I lay back feeling blessed and listened to the pale sounds of the Village awakening around me.

I am free, I thought. My own person at last. In my own home. Just Mattie and me. And then, as if I had summoned her, there came a soft rap on the door and Mattie appeared with a cup of coffee, her eyes shining with laughter and two bright spots on her cheeks.

"I've drawn your bath," she said. "We have a visitor. He's waiting downstairs."

Our visitor was H. Melville, Private Investigations.

He made a halfhearted attempt to stand, but he was really more interested in the fat omelet with the thick slab of bacon and fried potatoes that Mattie had just placed before him. I noted that a small plaster covered the bruise on his forehead and that his eyes were bloodshot. The ashtray was filled with cigarette stubs.

I sat down opposite Mr. Melville, and Mattie filled my bowl with uninspiring oatmeal and poured coffee into three cups.

"Harry tells me you met last night," Mattie said.

"Harry?"

"Harry, it is," he said. He was wiping up his plate with a soft roll.

In the light that streamed through our kitchen window, I saw that his hair was the color of sand, that he wore it long and tied back with what appeared to be a shoelace. His eyes were truly black with sheer lashes that gave him the odd aspect of having no lashes at all. Harry pushed back his plate and offered Mattie a cigarette, which to my everlasting astonishment, she accepted. When he offered me one, I declined, although I must admit I was not even then a stranger to cigarettes. He waited until he lit his and Mattie's, then he fixed me with his eyes and said, "I would like you to come with me."

"Where?"

"To see my client. Explanations are in order, and I think perhaps that you hold in your mind a piece of vital evidence."

*   *   *

Which is how I came to be Harry's sometime associate in his private investigations. Harry says that my inquisitiveness is inherited, just as my house was, from my great-aunt Evangeline, or Vangie, as he called her.

I let the curtain drop and moved away from the window. Tomorrow I would try to find the artisan who had made the shoes. Bennett Newman, one of the Players, supported himself by doing the fashion sketches for department-store ads in newspapers. If he didn't recognize the trademark, he might know who would.

As for Harry, I was confident that he would come up with the reason for my likeness to this murdered woman and perhaps find her murderer at the same time.

I lit my lamp and sat down at my desk. I reread my unfinished poem in the type-writer. I was confused.

The sonnet was complete. But the words were not mine.

Someone had written the last couplet for me.

Chapter Seven

Faster, faster, see you fly—
High-heeled shoes will make you die.

I felt violated. A stranger had come into my home uninvited. Probably when I went to see Harry. Whoever it was had brazenly gone to my room, had sat at my desk where I sat now, and read my work. Put his hands on the keys of my type-writer. It was an unwelcome intimacy, not unlike rape. By setting his words to it—badly, I might add—he'd marked it, as a male dog does with one lift of his leg.

My unease grew with each succeeding thought, until, I must admit, I was terrified. A thousand different emotions surged through me. Yes. I sat down again and rolled a clean sheet of paper into my type-writer. Poised fingers on keys. Typed. No words appeared on the paper. There was no ribbon. It was gone. He'd taken it. My words were on that ribbon. Why had he taken it? A souvenir? I closed my eyes. My thoughts were birds in cages flying against the bars. I needed to write. In the back of my desk drawer I found an old ribbon. I rarely throw anything away. I threaded it into the type-writer—I was good at this—and began to type.

Curiosity he calls it: there is no harm.
The pillow she lies her head upon, it cedes
Her smell. Shoes kicked carelessly disarm
Him. He takes one with him when he leaves.

He will return for the rest of her when
It suits him. He has given her fair notice,
Has he not? Left his calling card as men
Will

It was barely dawn when I heard Mattie on the stairs. I stopped working and opened my door.

"Good morning," she said, calling to me over her shoulder. "Have you been working through the night again?"

"I paid Harry a visit," I said, following her downstairs and into the kitchen. "To talk about the drawing."

"I'm glad you did." She filled the kettle with water and lit the stove. "See what the milkman has left us."

I walked through the small foyer, down the stairs, and opened the door to the common vestibule. Two bottles of milk were waiting for us, none for Harry. I carried them by their long, cream-filled necks into the kitchen and set them on the table.

"Harry said he would look into the woman's death." I was wondering how to tell Mattie about our uninvited guest, when she began to mumble under her breath.

"Crumbs everywhere. Crumbs. Raid the larder. What a mess. It's a wonder we don't have a colony of ants this morning."

The perfect opening. Our night visitor had been hungry. "I didn't raid the larder. While I was talking to Harry, someone came into our house. He was in my room, too."

"Dear God." Mattie sat down hard. "How can you know that?"

"He finished my poem—the last couplet—for me. And—may I say—badly."

"First that poor girl's murder, then the drawing, now this. What are we going to do?"

"We'll keep the door locked, for one thing." I liked the strength I heard in my voice. And I rather liked the delicious little frisson of fear that flowed through me. If only I could harness this. My fingers itched to get back to the keys.

"I'm going to telephone Detective Brophy and tell him," Mattie said. She got up and put the milk in the icebox.

"Of course," I said, making to leave the room.

"Are you going to sleep?"

"No. I have an appointment at *Vanity Fair* and an errand to run."

I bathed, then put on my nicest day clothes, a green blouse and a long black skirt with the little matching jacket. My mirror told me I looked smart, but not too stylish, which was the impression I wanted to make on my first visit to *Vanity Fair*, to meet the editor who had just begun to buy my poems.

With some regret, I'd stopped selling my poems to *Ainslee's* now because *Vanity Fair* paid so much more. It was a matter of economics. I think poor Edward Hall, who'd been my editor at *Ainslee's*, took it very personally. He felt I'd abandoned him for money. But it wasn't that at all. He then, as Whit now, had started to demand more of me. More than I was willing to commit.

"Hold that still, Oliver, goddammit." Bleary-eyed, Harry stared at the writing paper I held up for him.

I'd rung his bell and pounded on his door until he yelled, "Bloody hell!" So I knew I'd awakened him. I kept on pounding and ringing until he dragged himself to the door. When he opened it he was still buttoning his trousers. He looked like a derelict, unshaven, hair straggly, smelled of cigarettes and booze. He did not invite me in. "What are you dressed up for?"

"He was in my room, Harry. He dared to finish my poem." I shook the paper at him.

"Automatic typing," Harry said, rubbing his bloodshot eyes. "Not that I believe that spiritualist garbage, but you could have forgotten—"

"I do not write bad poetry, and I would never forget what I wrote, Harry. Besides, this is not my typing. And don't ask me how I would know. I know. The *a* and the *n* don't stick for me because I have a different touch. They stuck for him. And furthermore, he stole my ribbon."

"A ribbon. You woke me out of a sound sleep because you misplaced a piece of silk?"

"My type-writer ribbon, Harry. Dammit, he took my type-writer ribbon. My words are on that ribbon." He stared at me as if I was speaking Greek, and I wondered, was I making any sense at all?

Finally he said, "Okay, okay. Has Mattie made coffee?"

"Yes."

"Give me ten minutes to get my heart pumping." He closed his door abruptly.

I went back to the kitchen. Mattie had fixed me a boiled egg and French toast. I wanted coffee.

"I left a message for Detective Brophy," she said. "You look very nice. Be sure to wear your hat."

"Harry will be here in a few minutes," I said. "We must keep our doors, front and back, locked." I stared out the kitchen window at our garden, which, in spite of a low fence, was open to the gardens of the other houses along Bedford Street, as well as the gardens of those houses behind us. Anyone could have come over the fence and just walked into our house and up the back stairs.

"Where are you going?" Mattie called. "Your egg will get cold."

"I'll only be a minute." I lit a cigarette and went down the back stairs. The back door was ajar. It was slightly warped and didn't close properly. I stepped outside. A chilly fog spread out over the backs of houses and across the yards, isolating our world in grayish light.

Our garden was small, with a tiny stone birdbath and a flag-stoned walk. The birdbath itself was rather unique, not in the usual well and sculpture on the center rise, but in the choice of sculpture: two women voluptuously entwined forever in stone.

A sparrow perched atop looked at me accusingly; the birdbath was dry. The pail that was usually near the back door was already under the spigot. Mattie must have started to replenish the bird-bath and been interrupted. I turned on the spigot. Something moved in the pail. Quickly, I shut off the spigot and peered into the pail.

Floating in the shallow water was a rag doll, the type every child had. But this one had hair of red wool and a penknife through the small red heart in the center of her chest.

Chapter Eight

A squeaky sound escaped my lips, but I didn't scream. I refused to be intimidated, if that's what he intended, although I confess to a moment of sheer panic. I dropped my cigarette on the damp earth, picked up the pail and took the stairs two at a time.

Harry was just coming down the hall. Deprived of speech, I held the pail up for him to see its contents.

"Bloody hell," Harry said. He reached in and rescued the rag doll, holding it over the pail to catch the drip. The knife slipped from the sodden mess and landed point to the floor, stuck and quivering.

Mattie's color was gray as the outdoors and she slumped into a chair, hands over her eyes. I lit a cigarette and handed it to her.

"At least we know now how he got in," I said, finding my voice again. "We have to see to the back door."

"I'll call Mr. Jenner," Mattie said. "He'll know of someone who can fix it."

"We can block his return, at least by the back stairs. But he knew that perfectly well." I pointed to the doll. "He left me another calling card."

Crouching, Harry laid the doll on his knee. "Give me a towel, will you?" He plucked the penknife from the floor and studied it. I saw at once that it had a wooden handle. It wasn't a penknife, but a sharp carving tool of some sort. Harry folded half of the towel around it and then wrapped the body of the doll in the other half.

"What do you intend doing with that?" I asked. I went out into our foyer and lifted my cape from the rack.

"Take it to the precinct. Going somewhere, Oliver?"

"I'm going to trace the trademark on the shoes."

"What shoes?" Mattie demanded, coming back to herself. She looked from me to Harry and back to me. "What trademark?"

"Remember that gift package that was delivered yesterday?" I said. "Did you see who brought it?"

Mattie frowned. "The doorbell rang and when I went down, no one was there, but the package was sitting neat as you please right at our door. I thought it must be something you ordered. I forgot about it when Detective Brophy brought the drawing."

"It was a pair of expensive high-heeled shoes."

"A mistake, then," Mattie said. "Wasn't there a card?"

"No. Mattie, the woman who was murdered wore a similar pair of shoes."

"God save us. Olivia, you must not leave the house until they catch this monster."

"I second that," Harry said.

"In broad daylight, who will bother me?"

"It'll keep."

But I wasn't to be dissuaded. "I have an appointment with Mr. Crowninshield at *Vanity Fair*," I said. "Uptown. On the way home I'll stop by Bennett Newman's studio. He may recognize the trademark."

I rode the subway to the offices of *Vanity Fair* and Condé Nast in the Graybar Building at Forty-fourth and Lexington. It was very important for me to be seen by Mr. Crowninshield as clever and sophisticated, if somewhat bohemian. I wanted him to publish more of my work, as I'd quite outgrown *Ainslee's*.

Frank Crowninshield proved to be a lean, ascetic-looking gentleman with silver hair and eyes almost a match. His office was the height of elegance, the walls covered with glistening

Chinese wallpaper. Miss Mayor, his secretary, brought me coffee in a Wedgwood cup and saucer—he already had the same in front of him on his lacquered desk—and while I sipped, he told me how much he liked the two sonnets I'd sent him the week before.

So thrilled was I by our meeting and the sale of two of my poems, that when I rose to leave, of course, I forgot I was holding the cup and saucer and spilled coffee all over my last decent outfit. "Oh, dear," I exclaimed. "I'm so sorry." I felt the clumsy fool. Just when I was trying hard to make a good impression.

"Nothing to fret about, Miss Brown," Mr. Crowninshield said, in a kindly if Edwardian manner. He summoned his secretary. "Miss Mayor always knows exactly what to do on these occasions."

Meekly, I followed Miss Mayor out of the room. She took me to a large dressing room, where four very tall, really beautiful girls were having absolutely ravishing hats arranged on their heads by a severe-faced woman with a thick Hungarian accent.

Miss Mayor handed me a towel, and I began to blot the coffee from my poor blouse, which clung to me. And I with nothing on underneath, having let my laundry pile up while Mattie was away.

"The fashion section will feature hats in the spring," Miss Mayor said. "We don't usually do the layouts here, but today . . ." She paused as she looked through a huge closet of clothing in muslin garment bags, then back at me, measuring me with her eyes. "Ah, this should do." She pulled a tailored gray suit from the closet. "There's lingerie in the drawer."

I shook my head. "You've been more than kind. I'll have everything cleaned and returned to you."

"Oh, no need to do that. These are what remain from different sessions. Just help yourself."

She left me then, and I helped myself to silk lingerie (I had all but given up corsets), and while the woman with the Hungarian accent fussed over her models, I became for a short time a different girl. I shoved my stained clothing in a paper bag and prepared to leave.

"No, no! You cannot go anywhere like that, Mademoiselle."

The Hungarian woman had flattened herself in front of the door and wouldn't let me past.

"What are you talking about?" I asked. She looked rather like Gertrude Stein in size and shape, and therefore quite intimidating. "You have to let me pass." Intimidating or not, I was growing more and more irritated.

"Those dreadful things you're wearing." She pointed to my feet, then took me by the shoulders and set me in front of a mirror.

I was wearing my best, though quite out of fashion, sandals, of course without stockings.

"Try these. We look to be about the same size." She actually took off her own shoes and thrust them at me. I felt her warmth in my hands. The shoes had a little curved heel and were very seductive.

"I couldn't really, but thank you. It's not often a total stranger would give me her shoes."

"I always carry a second pair," the woman said. She snapped her fingers and a girl I hadn't seen before ran over with another pair of shoes. "You have very fine feet. You should display them in quality footwear. With stockings."

I snatched a pair of stockings and two elastic bands from the lingerie drawer, leaned against a column and pulled them up to my thighs, then rolled them back over the bands. When I tried on her shoes, I found them singularly comfortable.

"There now," she said. "Take a look at yourself."

She was right. It was undeniable. "Thank you," I said, meaning it. I really have to take more care in how I dress, especially if I am to begin giving readings of my poems. I pay very little attention to current fashion and do not read *Vogue* magazine.

It was then I realized that this very person might recognize the rubbing of the diamond and sword trademark I carried with me. I pulled it from my handbag a bit crumpled and smoothed it. "Madame, I wonder, do you recognize this?"

Madame slitted her eyes, an amused smile flitted across her face. "But of course," she said. "How could one not?"

Chapter Nine

I'm afraid, Madame, that I've had a very poor education."

She looked at me with regal pity. "It is obvious you were born yesterday, as they say. Observe the soles of the shoes you are wearing."

I took one off, balancing myself like a stork on one leg. I knew now what I would find. And there it was: the diamond and sword trademark I was trying to identify.

"Can you tell me what it means?"

"They are Eppie Diamonds, only the best-designed shoes in the world."

I left *Vanity Fair* on a mission. The receptionist had let me use her telephone directory and I found an address for Eppie Diamond listed as 418 West 17th Street, in Chelsea, a neighborhood north of the Village, filled with wide, privately owned brownstone houses.

Since I knew where the company was located, it seemed to me the logical thing would be to have the actual shoes with me when I visited the designer. I decided instead to drop in on my fellow Player, Bennett Newman, on the way home and ask him what he knew, if indeed he knew anything, about Eppie Dia-

mond. So it was back to the Seventh Avenue subway for me, in
my hand-me-down Eppie Diamonds.

Madame Ilona Gabori, the hat designer, had presented me
with her card and directed me to call on her for a new hat. I
think she had little admiration for my serviceable black straw to
which I had pinned a small cluster of yellow rosebuds.

Hats . . . caps, bonnets . . . sonnets, straws . . . paws . . . All
kinds of frivolous rhymes went through my head as I got off
the train at Fourteenth Street and climbed the stairs. I had
never been to Bennett's flat, although I knew he lived and
worked in a studio over a printing shop off Eighth Avenue. He
didn't have a telephone so there was no point in calling ahead.
I'd just drop in.

His studio turned out to be an illegal living space on the second floor of a warehouse. The printing company's name and em-
blem, a group painting of printers around a press, in the Dutch
manner, was emblazoned on the front of the otherwise forbidding building. Glaser Family Printers. Our magical city could be
difficult about someone residing in a commercial building, although it happened all the time in the Village and below Hous-
ton Street.

I truly love the smell of printer's ink. It is a deeply acid wine
that, upon inhaling, makes me heady with words. When I
walked in the front door, what I saw first were reams and reams
of paper. I could hear the presses going. A woman sat at a desk,
typing slowly. She had to be of the family Glaser because even I
type much faster. She looked up with something like relief. "May
I help you?"

"I'm looking for Bennett Newman," I said, hoping she
wouldn't take me for a city inspector. She didn't.

"Outside and around the corner. Where it says Exit. He's the
first door on the right when you come up the stairs." She went
back to her typing.

I had thought I might get a job as a secretary when Mattie and
I first arrived in New York, but thank God, I started selling my
poems. I would have made a dreadful secretary, as I'm so easily
distracted and keep none of my opinions to myself.

Bennett was a dear boy. Handsome, dark-eyed, big as a bear.

He'd come out of the Navy an ensign and had turned up at the Playhouse in his uniform, looking dashing beyond belief. I'd grown very fond of him and he, me. He was always begging me to run off with him, but it was a lark. He was a dear romantic boy and he did love me. But I think he liked talking about it more. There are men like that. Still, we had some good times together.

I knocked on his door.

"Come on the hell in," was his response.

"Am I interrupting?" I stepped in and closed the door.

"Oliver! What a delightful surprise!" He was sitting on a high stool at a drafting table. He set down his pen and came to greet me with a big wet kiss on the lips. "You look smashing," he said.

While he opened two beers, I kicked off my new shoes and curled up on his sofa. His flat really was a studio. He had two drafting tables and high stools and shelves of pots holding pens and pencils, brushes, inks. A lovely Coromandel screen half hid a made-up mattress on the floor.

The room was spotless. I got up and walked around, my beer in hand, taking a good swallow. I was parched.

"Look at you," he said, offering me a cigarette from his case. "Rolled stockings. Oliver Brown, the height of style."

I lifted my skirt and wobbled my knees. I have really nice knees, or so I've been told. "I've just come from *Vanity Fair*, where, since I'm about to become a famous poet, I left more fashionably dressed than when I arrived. What do you think of the new Oliver?" I put a cigarette into my holder and tilted for a light.

"Old or new, to me you are always beautiful. Why not run away with me? We can get married and buy a cottage in the country with a white picket fence and live out our days, me painting and you writing."

"Oh, you're a sweet old thing, Bennett Newman, but I have to say no. I'm a bachelor girl and always will be."

"Alas, Oliver, you think nothing of breaking my heart."

I stood on tiptoe and patted his broad cheek. "I will always love you. But I need your help with something."

"Anything, m'lady. I am yours to command."

I scooped up one of my shoes and pointed to the trademark on the sole. "Eppie Diamond."

"So it is."

"You know him?"

"Her."

"Oh, Eppie Diamond is a her."

"Everyone inside fashion knows Eppie. She makes shoes to order, charges mint prices."

"You must tell me everything you know about her," I said, settling back on the sofa.

"She's not what you'd expect," he said. "You should talk to Mackey. He works with her."

"Mackey?"

"You know him. Theo McGrath. We were in the Navy together. I introduced you two myself at Chumley's months ago."

Theo McGrath. I tried to put a face to the name. A face materialized. A beautiful boy-man, slim, tender-lipped, sensual lashes. "I remember him. I called him Little Mackey."

He nodded. "Eppie runs him ragged. She designs, he handles the business, she demands, he fulfills." He grinned. "It's a great relationship. Sort of like a marriage, don't you think, Oliver? Why don't we finish our drinks and run off together?"

"Today is not a good day for that, Bennett." I finished my beer and took a last drag of my cigarette. "I'd love to talk with Mackey. Why doesn't he come out to the Players?"

"Eppie is very possessive. She thought he was having too much fun away from the business, without her."

"Oh?"

"Not what you're thinking, Oliver. Mackey moved in here with me last month, although I haven't seen much of him lately. Why the sudden interest in Eppie Diamond?"

"Someone sent me a pair of her shoes but there was no card enclosed. I thought I might call on her and find out who sent them." I got up and slipped into my shoes.

"Mackey will—" That was as far as he got because we could hear running footsteps, then the door was flung open, revealing a skinny apparition with pink hair in accordion folds, chalk-white face powder, eyes outlined in black. She looked as I'd imagined Frank Baum's Wicked Witch of the West. Through a ruby slash the apparition demanded, "Where is he?"

Bennett shrugged languidly, though I discerned a bit of green in his color. "Well, he's certainly not here."

"You're hiding him."

"Don't be ridiculous. Why would I hide him? He's a big boy. He doesn't have to hide."

"I will not tolerate this!" The door closed, and the apparition was gone. We heard the footsteps receding, and finally, silence.

I stared at the door. I felt as if I'd walked into the middle of a melodrama and didn't know my lines. "What on earth—?"

"I'm sorry I wasn't able to introduce you," Bennett said. "I just couldn't seem to find the proper moment."

"There will never be the proper moment as far as I'm concerned," I said. "That's not anyone I'd like to know."

Bennett began to laugh. "That's funny, Oliver, I thought you told me you wanted to meet Eppie Diamond."

Chapter Ten

After that scene I wasn't sure I wanted to meet Eppie Diamond at all, but then I thought of the shoes in the box under my bed. And there was also the murdered girl. I would persevere. But not today. I was suddenly weary, with the kind of bone-dissolving weariness that warns me I am near breakdown. I went home to a quiet house; Mattie was out. Ignoring the stack of mail she had left on my desk, I divested myself of my costume, and crawled into bed. Sleep came at once, but with it a most disturbing dream.

I tend to agree with Siggie, that dreams have some meaning, though for me, psychoanalysis, which Whit always harps on, is out of the question. Any analysis of my soul is certain to ruin me as a poet.

In my dream I was in Grand Central Terminal, in the waiting room, with others whom I didn't recognize. There was a strong element of fear. We were having our heads transferred to other bodies. I saw thin red lines on the necks of people who'd already had the surgery. Transfer my head to another body? It was most certainly not going to happen to me. Not to me and my lovely neck, its slim length my pride. But there was no way out; I was trapped.

The doorbell woke me. I was in a sweat, tangled in the bedclothes. Where was Mattie? My kimono was lying across the foot of my bed. Had I put it there? I didn't remember. The doorbell rang again. I wrapped myself in the kimono and went downstairs. And downstairs again. Through the etched glass of our door I could see the shadow of a man, his back toward me. He turned and saw me. Damn. It was Whit.

"Open the door, Oliver." He shook the doorknob. He was holding a newspaper.

I unlocked the door and opened it. "You woke me from a sound sleep." I turned and walked back up the stairs. "Close the door behind you." I was uncivil, I know.

He followed me into the kitchen, which smelled of sugar and butter. The fragrance emanated from what was under the linen towel on the table. I filled the kettle with fresh water and lit the fire. "Have you seen this?" Whit held the *News* in front of my face.

It was there. The drawing of the dead woman. In the newspaper, the resemblance was particularly chilling. "I'm hardly dead," I said.

"I can see that. I'm worried about you. Why wouldn't you see me yesterday?"

"I was tired. I wanted to sleep." I poured a few drops of boiling water in the teapot, sloshed it around, poured it out, then measured in the tea leaves, poured the water again and covered the pot with a cosy. "The detective brought the drawing by yesterday."

"Everyone thinks it's you."

"Who's everyone? You certainly don't. Mattie doesn't. Harry Melville is trying to find out who she is—was."

"You don't seem disturbed. Aren't you upset about the likeness? I hope Mother and Dad don't see the papers. They'll be very unhappy."

"Sit down, Whit." I took two teacups from the cupboard and poured the tea. Mattie had left a pitcher of milk on the table and the bowl of sugar cubes. I removed the linen towel from a plate of fresh-baked butter cookies. "I've never met your parents, so why would they be upset?"

He pulled out a chair and sat down. "Our names are mentioned because we found her. It also says she resembles a local poet."

"Well, I like that," I said. "It doesn't even mention the poet by name."

My little jest went right by Whit. "Mother will be mortified that my girl—"

"Whit, dear, I am very fond of you, but I am not your girl."

"How can you say that, Oliver, when we've been together these last two months? I've asked you to marry me."

"I don't want to marry you, Whit. I don't want to marry anyone. I want to write my poems, act with the Players, and have fun. We can continue being friends, but our relationship is over." I offered him milk, then sugar, and thought, with a little smile, a poor surrogate for the substance of Oliver.

"Please don't say that, Oliver." He reached for my hand and pressed it to his chest. "This is cruel. I'm deeply in love with you."

"I'm sorry." Very gently, I took my hand from his. "I don't mean to hurt you."

"I think you should see Dr. Lesser so you can work out your difficulty in committing yourself to our relationship."

"Listen to me carefully, Whit. I'm not having any difficulty. I don't want to marry you. We no longer have a relationship. It's as simple as that. I don't need to discuss how I feel with a psychoanalyst." I pushed the plate of cookies to him. "Have a cookie."

"Is there someone else?"

"No." I sighed. I never learn. I should keep relationships with men platonic. I always plan to and it never works out that way. "Did you, by any chance, send me a pair of Eppie Diamond shoes as a gift?"

"Eppie Diamond? The crazy woman Mackey works for?"

"The very same."

"Her shoes cost a fortune. I'm just a poor editor. I thought you said there wasn't anyone else." He helped himself to a cookie. He seemed to be taking my rejection fairly well.

"I must have a secret admirer. There was no card. And they fit perfectly."

"It was probably Mackey then. Why don't you ask him?"

"I intend to." I had a thought, but knew at once it was on the wrong track. Still, I said, "Whit, you didn't come by to see me very late last night, did you?"

"No. I got drunk and passed out. It's not every day one literally stumbles across a dead body." He poured himself more tea. Was he fixing to stay for a while? "Mattie told me you were exhausted."

"I was and am. Finish your tea. I'm going back to bed."

"Why did you ask about last night?"

"I went down to talk to Harry about how much the murdered girl looks like me and someone came into the house while I was gone."

"How do you know?"

I looked at him suspiciously. Even Harry had been more upset than Whit with this information. "Whoever it was wrote the final couplet on the sonnet I was working on. I'd left it in my type-writer."

"Too much wine, Oliver. You really should think about seeing Dr. Lesser."

"Go away, Whit." I gathered my kimono around me and went upstairs in a huff, leaving him alone in the kitchen.

"I'll see you later at rehearsal," he called up to me. "Why don't you wear your new shoes?" I heard his laughter and his footsteps, then a door opening and closing. He was gone.

I went downstairs and locked the door. Was I crazy? I didn't think so. Had Whit's reactions always been slightly off? Maybe that's what had attracted me to him in the first place. That and *l'esprit d'aventure*. A nice phrase, don't you think, for the lust I can never quite own up to. My brain was tempest-tossed. I just wanted to put my head down and sleep for a few hours.

Rehearsal tonight was a must, for we were doing Gene's new play for an audience on Friday night. I caught up the pile of mail and took it with me to bed. Letters about my work. Another particularly nice letter from the poet Stephen Lowell, full of praise for my last poem in *Ainslee's*. He and I had been exchanging admiring notes for a year now, and I greatly admired his poetry. In fact, though we'd never met, I'd grown quite fond of him and looked forward to his letters. I set this one aside to read again later.

The last was a letter telling me that my poem, "Careless the Living," had won a contest, prize enclosed. A check for a hundred dollars. Now that was nice. I would go shopping and buy some nice clothes and lingerie and call Madame Gabori and let her fit me with a stylish hat.

I went right off to sleep and the next thing I was aware of was a soft hand on my cheek and Mattie's sweet voice. "Olivia?"

"Ummm," I said. I rolled over on my back. "What a lovely sleep I've had." I opened my eyes. She was wearing her hat and her coat. "Are you going out?"

"No, I've just come in. I was with Detective Brophy this afternoon."

"Delicious. Am I going to lose you to him and have to live in this great old house all by myself?"

She made a clucking noise. "Olivia, Harry telephoned just as I came in the door. He's on his way home. He wants to talk with you."

"Then I must talk with him." I ran my fingers through my tousled hair and stood, undecided about how I should dress. Oh, to hell with it. Harry's seen me in worse shape. "What does he want to talk about? Did he tell you?"

Mattie took off her hat. "It's the dead girl. They know who she was."

Chapter Eleven

The hat is gone, my head is bare
My spirit soars, emancipated.
Society is over-rated.
I've cut my waist-length hair.

My shoes are lost, my feet are bare
On wings I fly, elated.
My joy is unabated
I blow convention to thin air.

Do fabricate for me, my friend,
And I will do for you.
Let's sup on love, and bread and wine.

Let sorrow bend
What is not true,
Until at last, it's spent its time.

I could smell the gin as I came downstairs.
Harry was fixing martinis.

My sonnet was Italian in form, not a form I write in normally, and had come full of strange symbols, an inner code. But I accept the eccentricity of my muse; she has a mind of her own. And she'd worked me in her enigmatic way.

Now I deserved my reward. I could feel my nose twitching.

"Um, yes, please, a very dry martini," I said. "Just what the girl needs."

"I'm making enough for you too, Mattie." Harry kept his back to us, fussing with the fixings.

"I don't know, Harry." Mattie stopped in the foyer to hang up her coat and hat.

"You're going to need it, girls," Harry said. He poured gin into the cocktail shaker and stirred, added olives to three glasses, then poured.

"Lovely," I said after my first sip. There's nothing quite like a good martini to restore one's sense of well-being.

"Drink up, Mattie," Harry said.

"Oh, do, Mattie, otherwise Harry will never let us in on what he's discovered."

"First tell me about the shoes, Oliver," Harry said. By this time we were all sitting, more or less relaxed. The smoke from our cigarettes was making the room hazy, or maybe it was because I'd put gin on my empty stomach again. "Did you trace them?"

"The trademark belongs to a woman named Eppie Diamond who designs and cobbles them to order out of her shop in Chelsea."

"Aaaah," Harry said.

"What is the *aaaah* for?" I asked, a trifle more peevish than I meant it. Or maybe exactly as peevish as I meant it.

"What you've already deduced was on the shoes found with the body."

I nodded. "The wide strap across the arch. Very smart."

"Then Eppie Diamond was able to tell you who sent them to you?"

I held out my glass. "I need another, Harry, please."

Mattie got up. I knew she was annoyed with me. "You will be home for supper, Olivia?"

"No, Mattie, dear. I have rehearsal. I'll get something to eat at Christine's." Christine's is a nice, really cheap little place conveniently above the Provincetown Playhouse.

"You will fade away to nothing," Mattie said. But she didn't leave. She remained in the doorway, listening.

"You haven't answered me, Oliver." Harry poured me half a glass and what was left went into his.

"About what, Harry?"

"Eppie Diamond."

"I didn't go."

"Why not?"

"I want to bring the shoes to show her and the shoes are still at home in their box under my bed. I was on my way there when I thought that Bennett Newman—you know him, Harry—Harry knows him, too, Mattie. He's one of the Players. And he's a graphic artist. He does the drawings for the department-store fashion ads. I thought Bennett would be able to tell me a little about Eppie Diamond so when I went to see her, I'd know how to talk to her."

"I'll take it from here tomorrow."

"No, you won't, Harry. I know what I'm doing. Bennett told me his friend Mackey works for her—"

"Mackey?" Harry frowned. His eyes lost their focus. Then he looked surprised, as if he'd discovered something. "Came around with Bennett once or twice? That one?"

"Yes. He's moved in with Bennett. From what Bennett told me, this Eppie Diamond started taking over his life. Then while he's telling me, La Diamond barges right into Bennett's place looking for Mackey. She is truly the most bizarre woman, and her behavior is rude, to say the least."

"Was Mackey there?"

"No. Bennett said he hadn't seen him in a couple of days. Why?"

Harry took my empty glass from my hand. "Because they've discovered one thing for sure about the dead woman you stumbled on outside of Chumley's."

"What is that?"

"She wasn't a woman."

Chapter Twelve

Mattie's gasp was an explosion.

Recovering, I said, "What do you mean, she's not a woman?"

"He was a transvestite, Oliver. A man dressed as a woman."

"But she—he—looked so real . . ." My voice trailed off. I was remembering the streaked makeup, the vague sense of the familiar, as I sat waiting for Whit to return with the police. "He was made up to look like me."

"Dear God," Mattie said. She came back into the room and sat down beside me on the sofa, taking my hand.

"Yes."

"But what about Andrew Goren, Harry? He said she was his wife."

"We'll have to find Andrew Goren and ask him. Of course, there's always the chance that you didn't hear right—you were pretty upset—"

"No chance at all," I said firmly. "I know what I heard. And I'll find him."

"Please let Harry do it, Olivia," Mattie said. "What if he's the murderer and he gets you alone with him?"

"Mattie's right." Harry gave me a really stern look. "I'd rather you didn't go wandering off by yourself. Either we'll do it together, or better still, I'll do it and then give you a yell. Besides, you're going to see a lady about some shoes."

The Provincetown Playhouse, on the street floor of 133 Mac-Dougal Street, is a small auditorium with wooden benches for the audience. Backstage are dressing rooms, a business office, and places to store scenery. Although our subscription audience is now well over a thousand, we still insist that there are to be no free tickets, not even for critics. It's a matter of honor. Also a matter of honor is our choice of the plays we perform. These must be experimental. They must try to break new ground. With the steady growth of our subscription we had recently agreed to salary two people who are part of the troupe. One is Lewis Ell, who does general carpentry, takes care of props, and designs the sets. The other is Nina Moise, otherwise known as General Coach.

It was hard not to feel the excitement as we all gathered in Christine's. Charles Gilpin, the first Negro actor we had worked with, had taken to the part immediately. He is older than most of us, very muscular, handsome with his milky-coffee skin, and has the saddest eyes I've ever seen.

Harry and I were the last to arrive. Jig Cook, who was directing, had brought a bottle of whiskey and we all solemnly passed it around as the thumping of the drums came from the theatre below. Real food was an afterthought.

"Where's Gene?" Harry asked. He was flushed and it wasn't from the booze. We were all drunk without having drunk much. The sound of the drums from below made our hearts race and our blood hot.

"Provincetown," Jimmy Light said. "He was here a couple of days, fretting over the drums, saw a couple of rehearsals, seemed to be pleased, and ran back to the Cape."

The company was in the last intense hours, preparing for the opening on the first of November, of Gene O'Neill's *The Emperor Jones*. The set had had to be redesigned because Jig had insisted on building a dome, and he'd done it all himself with plaster, cement, netting and steel bars.

The Cockney trader is the only other big part. The rest of us, poor peasants, filled a variety of tiny roles of natives, ghost-prisoners, and spirits. We blacked up, faces and bodies.

It is an astonishing play, mostly monologues, but just the kind of daring thing on which we'd built our reputation. We had high hopes for both Gene and ourselves.

I'd missed only one rehearsal, but it didn't matter anyway since the weight of the play fell on Charles Gilpin. I did have a small part in *Matinata*, our curtain-raiser, since *The Emperor Jones* is a short play, only eight scenes.

After rehearsal, since none of us wanted to go back to Chumley's that early, we repaired to the saloon known officially as Columbia Gardens, but dubbed by us, The Working Girls' Home, on Eighth Street and Sixth Avenue. We ordered beers and I looked for Harry, who'd struck up a conversation with Bennett Newman as we left the Playhouse.

It was not Harry, but Edward Hall, who caught my attention. My smile brought him right over with a kind of puppy-dog eagerness that made me uncomfortable.

"Oliver," he said. "I've missed you."

I gave him my cheek to kiss. Edward was accessible, not one of those tall boys I had to crane my neck up to. His fawn-colored eyes were moist and doe shaped, his hair, wavy brown. He had a sensitive mouth.

Actually, he was a sweet old thing. "I miss you, too," I said. And I did. No one I knew read poetry quite as Edward did. We'd been soul mates in our love for literature. But constancy is not my nature. This is the issue on which we had foundered. Now I gave him my hand. "Why can't we just be friends?"

"We'll always be friends, Oliver. I swear," he said fervently. He kissed my hand. "I—" A whole contingent more of our friends arrived and Edward and I became separated.

I found myself sitting with Whit, who seemed gracious and charming, as if we'd never had our altercation. But I was wrong.

"So where are the shoes your new lover gave you, Oliver?" he said suddenly. "I thought you were going to wear them tonight."

"Whit—" I had the strongest feeling that Whit had sent the shoes, for some purpose which was not obvious to me for the moment.

"Hello, everyone." Whit raised his voice. "Oliver has a new lover."

"You mean that mere slip of a girl has tossed you over, Whit?" Charlie Ellis said.

"Actually," I said, "I did toss him over and I have no new lover, but anyone who would like to apply, may get on line."

Everyone laughed. Well, almost everyone. Edward, whom I could scarcely see among the others, did not laugh.

Rae Dunbar, who was sitting on my other side, leaned over and whispered, "If you and Whit are finis . . ."

I placed my hand on her shoulder, my cheek to hers, inhaling a musky scent from her dark hair. I murmured, "Green light."

"Then, Oliver, now you're free to run off with me," Bennett called. "Just say the word. I'm ready."

Harry signaled from behind Bennett, pointing to me, then to Bennett. I had no idea what he meant. And was never meant to know, for Edward stopped him and they shook hands, leaning toward each other in order to hear themselves converse.

"I'm ready to discuss it, Bennett," I said, straight-faced. "Why don't you walk me home?"

"You don't scare me, Oliver," Bennett said, jumping up.

I took out a dollar to pay for my beer, but Whit waved me off. "Have a good life, Oliver," he said. He seemed a little hangdog, so I gave him a pat on the head.

Rae winked at me and slid into my chair.

I looked for Bennett and didn't see him. Where had he gone? Oh, there he was. He paid the tab and came back for me.

"Good night, you beautiful people," I called, locking arms with Bennett.

It had grown cold and the wind came in sharp little gusts. I shivered and wished I'd worn my cloak. Overhead, an icy disk of a moon threaded through wisps of scudding purple clouds.

"I'm going over to Eppie Diamond's tomorrow to talk to Mackey," I said.

"I'm worried about him." Bennett seemed to have quite forgotten he wanted to run off with me. "I haven't seen him in two days and obviously neither has Eppie. One day, maybe, but two days is not at all like him."

"Has he done this before?" We were strolling westward toward Bedford Street.

"On occasion. He likes to play."

I had the most unpleasant thought, and I had the distinct feeling that Harry had also had the same thought. What I remembered of Mackey was his slim body and feminine features. Not unlike mine. "Does Mackey like to dress up as a woman, Bennett?"

As soon as I said it, I knew. Bennett's arm became rigid under my hand. "Oliver—he's obsessed with you."

"He seems such a dear, though I hardly know him. I guess he caught it from you."

I meant it as a joke, but Bennett didn't laugh. He stopped and took me by the shoulders. I could feel the rough strength in his hands, but I wasn't frightened. Out of the corner of my eye I saw someone duck into a store entrance. Harry was following us. I felt an enormous sense of relief.

"No, Oliver, you don't understand. Mackey doesn't want to make love to you. He wants to get into your skin. He wants to be you."

Chapter Thirteen

Certain that Harry would pop out of a doorway any minute, I bussed Bennett on the cheek and packed him off. But there was no sign of Harry, just a few late-night revelers on their way home or elsewhere, and I was cold. And so to bed, I thought. Harry would keep. It was just as well. Bennett's words about Mackey were spinning in my head.

I fumbled for my key among the ribbons of my corselet. Mattie had sewn a tiny mad-money pocket into the fabric, as I was always leaving my purse somewhere. And now that we were locking our door, this too is where my key rested, wrapped in a two-dollar bill.

The backwash of the evening's euphoria had begun to settle on me and my lids were heavy. My mind had dulled. I unlocked the door and dragged myself up the stairs in the pale glow from the dangling ceiling lamp. At the top of the stairs I turned it off and followed the soft trail of light Mattie had left for me up to my room.

My bed was turned down, waiting for me, the pillows soft and plump. I tore off my clothes, dropping them on the floor where I stood. My nightie was nowhere in evidence. Well, to hell with it, I thought. I burrowed under the covers and fell asleep at once.

Siggie is of the opinion, and I know for a fact he is right in this one respect, that the mind—the brain—continues to function during sleep. There have been times when I've awakened with lines of poetry bursting forth whole from my supposedly sleeping brain.

It was the backfire of an automobile that woke me. I didn't know it at first. I shot up from my bed like Jack-in-the-box; fragile fingers of light were stealing through my draperies.

My missing nightie was on the floor at the foot of my bed. I pulled it over my head and sat at my desk. Rolled paper into my type-writer, typed. A mess. I'd forgotten, my ribbon was worn through. I tore the paper from the machine, dug in my drawer and found a pencil. Words raced from my fingers to the blank page.

> My skin is holy cover for my soul
> That suffers me but won't allow
> Another entry to its place.
> We, my soul and I, give no permit;
> Ungodly he, who dares infringe,
> Must die in the attempt.

My hand, still clutching the pencil, stabbed at the paper, at the poem I'd just written, the poem that had come to me full blown when I awakened. "No Trespass." The point of the pencil left ragged tears in my poem. What was I doing? I dropped the pencil and watched it shiver, then roll off my desk.

Whit would say I was not dealing with my anger. He'd said it often enough. What hath Sigmund wrought, say I.

It was unavoidable. The dead body in the alley was Mackey. It had to be. And he'd been murdered because he was wearing my skin, or trying to. And what had he been doing in my skin, I'd like to know.

Had he passed himself off as me and angered someone?

Or had I angered someone and had the murderer thought he was killing me?

And what about Andrew Goren's now grotesque statement, "She was my wife"?

I went back to bed and lay on my back, smoking, thinking, until Mattie arrived with coffee early in the morning.

"You look like a tar baby, Olivia," she said, eyeing my brown makeup, which I swear, I'd washed off my face before we left the theatre the night before. "I'm running your bath." She drew back the draperies, inviting the lemony sunlight into my room.

I grinned at her. "Wait till you see me tomorrow. We're doing full-body makeup. I'm going to be *weally doity, darlink*." I was beginning to feel better.

"Ummm." She was standing in the doorway as if she had something else to say.

"Yes?"

"If you can get another ticket, I'll invite Mr. Brophy to come as our guest."

"I think Harry has a spare. We'll get one. Go right ahead and ask Mr. Brophy." I put out my cigarette and sat up to sip my coffee. "Have you seen Harry?"

"It's a little early for Harry."

"Well, I'll go down and bang on his door after my bath."

I dressed with more care than usual because I was going to Chelsea to see Eppie Diamond. I put on the very costume I'd been given at *Vanity Fair* the day before, gray down to Madame Gabori's former shoes. The shoes. That reminded me I was going to take the gift from my unknown admirer with me. I got down on my knees and reached under the bed for the box, pulled it out, then sat back on my heels.

Should I take the shoes without the box, I wondered. No. She might recognize the box, although it had no markings on it. I had just gotten to my feet, the box in my arms, when Mattie screamed, not once but again and again.

I dropped the box on the bed and ran downstairs and into the kitchen. It was empty, though I could smell toast and butter.

As I called, "Mattie, where are you?", she screamed again. It was coming from the vestibule we shared with Harry. My heart battered against my chest. Something had happened to Harry. The door to our staircase stood open. I plunged down the stairs. Mattie had stopped screaming, but I could hear her breathing heavily and saw her standing at the foot of the stairs. The door was open. She looked up at me and cried, "Oh, Olivia."

"What's happened? Is it Harry?"

She was pointing to something on the floor. I stepped around her. I saw at once what had frightened her and for a moment it frightened me, too, but then I got angry, even more, furious. Mattie had obviously come down to collect our milk. The bottle was there all right, but it wasn't filled with milk.

Whatever the filling, it was the color of blood.

Chapter Fourteen

I sent Mattie upstairs to telephone Mr. Brophy, while I pounded on Harry's door loud enough to wake the dead. Harry was either more than dead or not there. I preferred to think he was not there. He must have gone off on something personal after seeing I was home and safe.

Harry Melville is, in fact, particularly secretive about his private life, though I'd seen him once with an attractive, older woman, the type that wears the best clothes, is a supporter of the arts, but is disappointed in the monotony of life, and love, with her banker or broker or lawyer husband. And then, for all I know, he could have had a wife hidden away somewhere.

Regardless, it was Mr. Brophy and another, slightly older, detective, a Mr. Walz, along with an oversized man in uniform, Officer Delaney, who came by a very short time later and inspected the evidence. Officer Delaney collected the milk bottle of blood and took it away with him in one of Mattie's shopping baskets.

Mattie had recovered somewhat, though she told Officer Delaney, "Don't bother to return it," meaning the shopping basket. "I'll have nothing more to do with it."

We repaired to my kitchen, we two and the two detectives, where Mattie almost feverishly proceeded to cook up a mountain of pancakes and coffee for all of us.

"I want you to tell us everything again, Miss Brown, from the beginning. Start with what you did that evening prior to the time you found the body," Detective Walz said. He'd been staring at me openly since his arrival, and I resented his vulgarity. To Brophy, he said, as if I were not present in the room, "The resemblance is uncanny." He produced a small pad and a blunt pencil from his pocket. Touching the point to his tongue, he looked expectantly at me.

I was boiling mad. I paced back and forth in the crowded space, unwilling to sit. "I've been over this a million times." I admit to hyperbole here. I am, after all, a poet.

"Olivia." Mattie shook her head at me. She set down a plate of pancakes oozing with syrup and butter in my place at the table.

"I'm not hungry, Mattie."

"You may not be hungry, but your brain needs nourishment, Olivia," she retorted.

Surprised at the sting in her tone, I sat down at the table like a good girl, and went to work on the pancakes.

Detective Brophy said, "I brought Detective Walz along because he's working the murder with me and I think that these things that are happening to you are connected."

"You think I was supposed to be at Chumley's, supposed to stumble over the dead . . . person?"

"No," Brophy said. "That was obviously a coincidence, although I understand you do frequent Chumley's late in the evenings."

I watched Detective Walz taking notes and speeded up my speech. "I and at least fifteen or twenty of my friends and acquaintances. We often stop by after rehearsals, or performances, along with actors from all the other theatre groups, and painters and writers." I noted with some satisfaction that Detective Walz was having trouble keeping up.

"That evening you were with Mr. Whitney Sawyer?" Brophy asked, although he knew this already.

"Rehearsals had been cancelled because of the rainstorm and the flooding. Whit and I had dinner at the Waverly and didn't see anyone there, so we went over to Chumley's. The courtyard in front of Chumley's is always dimly lighted, but that night it was not lit at all and a pond of water had formed in the depression where the cement walk had settled."

"Who found the body?" Detective Walz said, readjusting his eyes from his pad to my face.

"While we were fording the pond, I tripped over a shoe and fell. Then Whit fell in when he tried to help me up. He found her . . . him, I guess."

"You know it was a man, not a woman?" Walz said, his voice heavy with suspicion.

"Harry told me." I winked at Mattie, who was pouring coffee all around. She then piled more pancakes on everyone's plates.

Brophy said, "Harry Melville, the gumshoe who tipped us on the East Side strangler—"

Walz interrupted. "You notice his name always comes up lately?" The question was obviously rhetorical because Brophy didn't answer and Walz didn't seem to expect an answer.

"Detective Brophy brought the drawing of the person we thought was a dead woman around the next morning. You've seen the drawing, Mr. Walz. You know it looks like me. That's why you've been staring at me so rudely for the past hour." I was delighted to see the quick flash of anger. "Unless of course, I've misjudged you and you've fallen in love with me."

"Olivia!"

Walz cleared his throat. "I'm a married man, Miss Brown."

"Since when has that made a difference, Detective?" I said it sweetly, but no one was fooled. "More coffee for everyone, Mattie, dear."

"Let's get back to the subject," Brophy said. "You dragged the body out of the water . . ."

"Yes. We could see she—he was dead. I'd lost my shoes in the pond, so Whit went off to find a cop."

"And you saw no one in the area while this was happening?" Walz asked.

"There were people in Chumley's . . . playing chess."

"Drinking gin is more like it," Walz said. "Continue."

"Playing chess," I asserted. "Someone—Max, or Edward Hall,

I think—went inside and told them we'd found a body and that Whit had gone for the police."

"Did anyone leave before the police got there?"

"No. Everyone was damned curious about it all. I swear I saw no one leave. Do you think the murderer was sitting in Chumley's waiting for someone to find . . . the poor thing?"

"It's possible," Brophy said. "We know everyone who was there, so your telling us that no one left is a help."

"The next evening you had a break-in?" Walz asked, not ready to concede that my observation was helpful.

"I'd spent the evening writing, then as the drawing so resembled me, I brought it downstairs to show to Harry. Because I was frightened by the likeness, he offered to see you about it in the morning. I went upstairs and found someone had finished the last couplet of the poem I'd been writing."

Walz's reaction was just what I'd already heard from Harry and from Whit: "You're sure you didn't do it yourself and forgot?" Although it was phrased as a question, I knew his intent.

"I'm a writer," I said, with ice in my voice. "I know what I've written. And I know what someone else has written. And furthermore, I don't write bad poetry. He wrote: 'Faster, faster, see you fly—High-heeled shoes will make you die.' I can show it to you."

"A child's rhyme," Walz said. "It's of no value."

No value, I thought. We'll just see about that. "And furthermore, whoever it was stole my ribbon."

"Your ribbon?" Walz set down his pencil and looked at Brophy as if it was undoubtedly Brophy's fault that he was wasting his time here about a hair ribbon.

"Type-writer ribbon, Mr. Walz. The intruder wrote the last two lines of my poem and went off with my type-writer ribbon."

"And the doll comes in where?"

"Melville brought in the doll and the knife," Brophy offered.

"I'm asking Miss Brown," Walz said.

Oliver, my dear, I said to myself, you are really thick. Detective Walz is leading the questioning and is, therefore, Mr. Brophy's superior. "I realized in the morning that not only did we not lock our front door, but the back door leading to the garden couldn't be locked because the door had warped and we'd never bothered to repair it."

"It's been replaced now and we keep it locked," Mattie said. She put the last of the pancakes on a plate, poured herself coffee, then stood leaning against the warm stove, for there was no room for her to sit.

"I went down the back stairs and out into the garden. There was no sign at first that anyone had been there, but of course, if anyone wants to get into the garden, it's easy enough as the fencing is low and our neighbors are all friendly." I smiled my most charming smile at Detective Walz. "It is Greenwich Village, after all."

He didn't return my smile. "Where'd you find the doll?"

"The birdbath was dry. I turned on the faucet and saw something floating in the bottom of the water pail. It was a rag doll made out of a lisle stocking, with glass button eyes, red wool hair, and a big red heart sewn on its chest." I heard Mattie's quick intake of breath and looked over at her. "I carried it upstairs and gave it to Harry. You saw the knife? Was that the knife that killed the person in front of Chumley's?"

"Not likely," Brophy said. "It wasn't sharp enough."

"You have to do something," Mattie said. "Olivia is in danger. He couldn't get back in now that we're locking the doors so this morning he pours out our milk and replaces it with blood."

"It could all be a practical joke." Walz put his pad and pencil back in his pocket. "We don't even know yet if it's real blood or colored water."

"Oh, yes," I snapped, "the murdered person in front of Chumley's, whom you have yet to identify, is only a practical joke."

"That could be a coincidence."

"Mattie," I said, standing abruptly. "Show these gentlemen out, please."

I went upstairs in a rage, speechless with frustration, took up my purse and the box of Eppie Diamond shoes. When I came downstairs again, Mattie was stacking the dishes in the sink. The detectives were gone. "Apparently, I'll just have to be murdered for someone to take me seriously," I said.

"Please don't make jokes, Olivia." Then, to my dismay, Mattie burst into tears again.

I took her in my arms to comfort her. "Oh, dear, oh, dear, now don't cry, Mattie, please. It'll pass. And that horrible Detective Walz could be right. Everything other than the dead person could be someone's sick idea of a joke."

Mattie sat down and dried her eyes with the ends of her apron. "I don't know, Olivia. I just feel as if someone evil, someone we can't see, is watching us. Can you imagine, he was outside early this morning waiting for the milkman . . ."

I patted her hand and murmured reassuringly, but if truth be told, I had the same feelings. Then I remembered her reaction when I told the detectives about finding the doll. "What was it that surprised you about the doll, Mattie? You'd seen it. Didn't you remember?"

"I did, Olivia, but it was wet and I was frightened. I didn't take a clear look at it. When you described it just now, I recognized it."

Chapter Fifteen

*Y*ou've seen a doll like it before?" I felt the tingle of excitement.

Mattie nodded. Her eyes were red-rimmed and I realized, looking at her, that the events of the last few days had taken their toll. Before this, she had always looked after me. Now I was the stronger one and would have to care for us both.

She said, "There's a blind Polish woman who sells them sometimes in Washington Square Park. I bought one from her myself last week and gave it to Mr. Santelli for his little girl's birthday. I always thought they were very sweet and plain enough for a child not to be afraid to touch."

I barely listened to what Mattie was saying. The word *blind* kept repeating itself in my head. My hopes were dashed. But what did it matter anyway? Even if the woman could see, how would she possibly remember everyone who bought a doll?

Putting it out of my mind, I told Mattie to listen for Harry and tell him about the milk bottle of blood and the visit from the detectives. I was going to call on Eppie Diamond in Chelsea and learn what I could about the shoes.

I threw my cape over my shoulders and took my poor black straw from the hat stand and pinned it to my hair. On the way

out, I pounded on Harry's door again, but there was no acknowledgment from within.

November had crept in overnight as the harbinger of winter,
for it was cold and blustery. In spite of the hatpin, I had to hold
tight to my hat, while also accommodating the box, against the
rush of wind. I stopped at the stationer's for a new type-writer
ribbon, which I tucked into my pocket with the nickels for the
subway.

I took the subway to Eighteenth Street, rehearsing for my
meeting with Eppie Diamond, the magnificent harpy. From here
I walked to Seventeenth Street, then west. I passed a series of
commodious brownstone houses, at least double the width of my
little house on Bedford Street. These all had impressive stone
steps leading to stately front doors. Chelsea has a very staid at-
mosphere, being inhabited mostly by solid middle-class families
with children. Automobiles—most of them Fords—were nu-
merous.

Eppie Diamond's atelier was near Ninth Avenue, in another
spacious brownstone, with majestic stone stairs leading to the parlor floor and stone lions on opposite balustrades guarding the entrance. Behind a leafless dogwood tree, a discreet sign in the
lace-curtained ground-floor window said: EPPIE DIAMOND, BY
APPOINTMENT ONLY.

I opened the low gate and stepped into the small flagstoned
square that led to a door under the stone steps. I rang the bell.
There was no response. How does one get an appointment, I
wondered, if there is no telephone number to call? Of course,
there had been a telephone number in the book at *Vanity Fair*, but
I'd neglected to copy it down.

Slowly, there came to me a very familiar sound: the unmistakable clack, clack, clack of a type-writer. I rang the bell again
and waited a minute or two, then knocked on the window. I'd
quite lost my good manners. The sound of the type-writer
stopped for a few moments, then resumed. No one came to the
door. Finally, I gave it up and climbed the stairs. The front door
had a grand brass door knocker in the shape of a woman's shoe.
Quaint, I thought. I knocked firmly, and now sensed a flurry of
activity from within the house.

A Negro maid in a black dress with white collar and cuffs came to the door. Music surged around her.

"I would like to see Miss Diamond," I said. "My name is Olivia Brown." I set the box down and took one of my cards out of my pocket. It was a little creased but it said: MISS OLIVIA BROWN. The maid looked at me and at the box I was carrying. Although she took my card, I could see it was doubtful that Miss Diamond was going to make herself available.

"It's the Sabbath," the maid said.

Mr. Sherlock Holmes would have been proud of me. As Jews keep a Saturday Sabbath, I deduced that Eppie Diamond was Jewish.

"I won't keep her long. I received a pair of her shoes as a gift, but the card was missing. Such an elegant gift deserves an acknowledgment, don't you think?"

Although she didn't so much as blink, the maid held the door open for me. I picked up the box and stepped in. That was as far as the invitation went. "Please wait here," she said. She didn't offer to take my coat.

I lingered in the front hall, feeling the poor supplicant at the door of a wealthy benefactor. Before me was a broad, Persian-carpeted hallway decorated in the French style, with gold leaf and ormolu on every surface except the walls, which were covered to the chair rail with the palest of blue-striped silk. Two closed doors faced each other on either side of the hall. An elaborate staircase with carved banisters led to the second floor. Surrounding me was a pleasant, spicy presence and the rich sound of a skillfully played piano.

The chandelier was a burst of crystal dewdrops reflecting me, the little match girl, in its facets. I set the box down and tilted my head back and from side to side, playing with the different reflected images of myself.

"I'll take your cloak, Miss Brown." The maid had reappeared so suddenly, I hadn't heard her. She brushed her hand against the chair rail and, abracadabra, a cavernous closet appeared to my immediate left. All my exclamations of delight fell on dead air.

My cloak suitably provided for, the maid hid the closet again and led me up the carpeted staircase. We walked but a short distance down another hallway and stopped in front of a door. Someone was playing Chopin at a grand piano. It was lovely.

The maid opened the door, announced, "Miss Brown," and left. The music didn't stop.

Still holding the box of shoes, I came into the room. Eppie Diamond, in a scarlet silk caftan, her strange pink hair in a crocheted snood, played beautifully. I chose a proper bergère and sat quite happily till she came to the end of the étude.

After the final notes, she rested her hands on the keys and sighed, then turned to me. "You are the poet Olivia Brown?"

Immediately disarmed, I said, "Yes." I was mesmerized by her triangular-shaped face, the single point being her chin. Her eyes, small dark slits in a white, white field, were wide spaced, making the other two points. Her mouth was an open gash.

"You are very good." Her hands were restless, her fingers clustered with rings and gemstones, catching the light.

This was not what I'd rehearsed. "Thank you. You play beautifully."

"I see you are wearing my shoes."

I looked down at my feet. Of course I was. "They were a gift."

"I made them for Ilona Gabori," she said, sternly.

"Yes, I met her at *Vanity Fair*. She insisted on my having them because she thought what I was wearing was ghastly. Do you recognize every pair of shoes you make?"

"Yes. Each one is made for someone in particular. It is my signature."

"Then I am glad I came to you today, although I'm sorry to interrupt your Sabbath," I said.

"It is a privilege to meet so fine a poet," she said. "How can I help you?"

"I received this package, a pair of your beautiful shoes, and there was no card."

"That would never happen," she said. "Let me see them." She rose, like a wraith, and came toward me. I lifted the box to my lap and raised the lid.

Her head snapped back. "No," she said, "It's a mistake." If it was possible, her face blanched even whiter.

"Excuse me?"

She turned away from me. "My secretary has been ill. If you'll leave the shoes with me, I'll have him check who they were made for as soon as he gets back."

I thought to mention I knew Mackey and that he probably wasn't coming back, but held my tongue, not wanting her to think I was too familiar with her business. Sometimes playing dumb produces interesting data. So all I said was, "I'd rather hoped to get the information now, as the more time that elapses the ruder it is of me."

"You must leave them with me," she said. "I have your card."

Very likely she had a bell hidden in the floor somewhere under the rug, for the maid came to show me out, and one-two-three, I was back in the hall without the box of shoes, being helped on with my cape. The bum's rush. What had happened, I wondered. Who had the shoes been made for? Certainly not me, for the shock on her face when she saw them would not easily be forgotten. I suppose I could have insisted on keeping the shoes, but the information I wanted was more important than a pair of shoes.

The doorbell rang as I prepared to leave. The maid opened the door and ushered me out. Standing on the steps were two well-dressed ladies. "Ah, Camille, good afternoon," one woman said.

"I'm afraid Mrs. Goren is not receiving anyone today," Camille said.

I could hear the women clucking as I went down the stairs to the sidewalk. It wasn't until I was almost to Eighth Avenue that I realized Camille had said *Mrs. Goren*, not Miss Diamond. Goren, I thought, as in Andrew Goren, my phantom lover? My murderer?

Chapter Sixteen

A blast of cold air surged up Seventeenth Street and tore my hat from my head, playing it as a child plays a kite. I ran after it, shouting, "Stop, thief," which was quite ridiculous, but not really. Near Eighth Avenue, with an impudent spin, the wind dropped my poor boater in front of a passing automobile, which promptly ran it over. I was left with a clump of raggedy black straw.

Holding it to my breast, I sat on the curb close to tears. It had been my first grown-up hat, my only hat for these last years. I'd clung to it though it was quite out of fashion because it was the last vestige of a life I'd led before I came to Greenwich Village. Now it was gone. It felt like the end of something and at the same time, a beginning.

I am a fatalist at heart. I feel that everything in life, mine in particular, happens for a purpose. Would it be the loss of my beloved hat that altered the path of my life and swerved me in the direction of Madame Gabori?

But not yet. Tonight was opening night. I picked myself up, tucked the straw remains under my arm, and using my last nickel, headed home. I could nap for a few hours . . . if my busy brain would allow it.

My thoughts returned to Andrew Goren. Was he the person I

heard on the type-writer in Eppie Diamond's studio? And what was he to Eppie Diamond? He could be her son. He could even be her husband, a May and December marriage.

Yet I swear I heard him say as we sat in Chumley's that awful night Whit and I found the body, *She was my wife.* Could I have been mistaken? And *she* turned out to be *he*. It was all too perplexing.

Then there was little Mackey. Was it he lying in the morgue pretending to be me? Or was he just ill, as Eppie Diamond indicated, if that's whom she meant when she mentioned her secretary.

I got off the subway at Sheridan Square and walked toward Bedford Street. Maybe it was wrong of me not to tell Brophy and Walz my suspicion about Mackey. On the other hand, why had no one reported Mackey missing? Bennett, his best friend, had spoken of Mackey in the present tense last night when he walked me home, yet Mackey still had not returned.

Detective Walz with his scornful attitude was thoroughly detestable to me. I would wait till the analysis of the blood in the milk bottle, then I'd mention the possibility of Mackey to Detective Brophy.

When I banged on Harry's door, there was still no response, so I unlocked mine and climbed the stairs, calling, "Mattie, I'm home."

"Oh, thank God, Olivia." Mattie's answer came in a thin and fragile voice that so frightened me I took the rest of the stairs on the run.

"What is it?" I burst into the kitchen. Mattie was sitting at the table staring at a glass of gin, next to the bottle of Booth's. Its piquant aroma made the inside of my nose tingle.

"It's Harry." She was all choked up. "He's in the Ward Building at St. Vincent's, in a coma. Mr. Brophy telephoned only a few minutes ago." She drank the gin in a great gulp and began to cough.

I took a glass from the cupboard and poured myself a drink. My hands shook. "What happened?"

"They don't know. Someone named Luke O'Connor brought him in early this morning."

"That's the owner of Columbia Gardens, where we were last night." I set my glass down, empty. "I'm going to St. Vincent's."

"I'll go with you."

The Ward Building, at Eleventh Street and Seventh Avenue, is within walking distance. We rushed up Seventh Avenue and presented ourselves to the Shaker-bonneted Sister of Charity at the front desk, where the odor of antiseptic loitered discreetly.

"Are you family?" she asked. Her face was dry and papery and faintly lined.

"I am his daughter, and this is his niece," I said, giving Mattie, who was nothing but honest, a warning look. "The police just notified us that Papa had an accident."

We were allowed to go upstairs, but were told we could only stay a few minutes as he was very badly hurt. By the time we arrived at the door to Harry's room, we were both in tears and holding on to one another.

I opened the door carefully. It was dark, the shades drawn. Four beds, three of them unoccupied. A Sister of Charity rose from her chair near her patient's bed and came toward me. Her white aproned gown covered an ample torso.

"I'm his daughter," I whispered. "The police just notified me." I motioned to Mattie. "This is my cousin."

"He has not recovered consciousness. You may come in for a few minutes only. We don't want to tire him."

Tire him, I thought. How can I tire him if he's unconscious? I didn't inquire aloud.

The nun took another chair in the corner of the room. So, anything I said to Harry would be overheard. Mattie followed me into the room. The primary smell, again, was antiseptic. I was sorry I hadn't brought the bottle of Booth's with me. Harry was more likely to come out of it if the primary smell was gin. An urgent laugh lodged in my throat.

A crucifix was mounted on the wall over the bed. Jesus in agony. Harry would see the irony.

As for Harry, I would never have recognized him. The figure on the bed was absolutely still except for the miniscule rise and fall of his chest under the blanket. Even in the semidarkness, I could see the swelling that obliterated his features. His head was swathed in bandages. His eyes were closed.

Mattie's hand found mine. I sat down in the chair the nun had vacated and put my lips next to where I imagined Harry's ear to be.

"Harry Melville, don't you dare die," I intoned. "Don't you dare, do you hear?" I took his limp hand between my two. His was cold as ice. "Don't you dare die, Harry," I said again. "I won't let you."

The sister stood up. "I don't think—"

"Please, Sister," I said, then what should happen but Harry's hand moved just a fraction. "Harry, you hear me." His hand moved again. "Sister, his hand is moving."

She bent over Harry and took his pulse. "Yes," she said.

"Harry." I put my lips next to his ear. "You've been in an accident. Your face is swollen, so even if you try to open your eyes, you won't be able to. They've got your head wrapped up like some Indian potentate."

"I must tell the doctor Mr. Melville is responding," the sister said. "It's better that you leave now. You may return tomorrow." She went off in a flurry of white skirts.

"Should we wait outside?" Mattie asked, but I shook my head at her.

I said, "Stand at the door and watch for them. They'll throw us out as soon as they get here." Harry squeezed my hand again. "Oh, good, you're going to be all right. What happened? Did your lady friend's husband catch you out?"

For a moment I thought he was going to speak. I almost missed the tiny groan that came from his swollen lips. "Ol . . ." I moved my head so my ear was near his lips. "Ol . . ." Nothing else.

"Harry, try again. What is it?" I could feel the pressure of his hand in mine. I was practically lying on the bed with him. "You're not worried about missing the opening tonight?"

Mattie, standing at the door, said, "They're coming."

"They're going to throw me out in another second, Harry. I've got to get to the theatre anyway."

"Ol . . . no . . ." Then with a supreme effort, he pushed the words up from his throat through distended lips. His hand slipped from mine. "Shwonem," he said.

Chapter Seventeen

*D*ye," Brophy said, "the kind used to color textiles. Or ink. And the bottle was wiped down. Not one print on it. Charley Walz swears it's a joke."

"Well, it's so funny it's scaring us to death," Mattie said.

"It's meant to," I said. "I feel as if someone wants to hurt me. What happened to Harry?"

"The owner of Columbia Gardens brought him in. Found him in the alley under the bathroom window with his head bashed in. Must have been a fight."

"We were all there last night after rehearsals. There was no fight unless it happened after Bennett and I left . . . Well, if it was a fight, I'll bet Harry gave the other chap what-for, and he might turn up as badly damaged."

"I don't know about that, Miss Brown. The crack on Harry's head was in the back. Someone hit him good and hard with a brick or a pipe."

An awful thought came to me. "Mr. Brophy, do you think this has anything to do with the murder and what has been happening to me?"

"Right now there's nothing that points in that direction, Miss Brown. My advice to you is to stay close to home, and if you're going out, stay with a group. Don't be alone with anyone."

"This is good advice, Olivia," Mattie said.

Poor Mattie. She knew well enough I wouldn't take the advice. I said, "I hope you'll be able to come to the theatre tonight, Mr. Brophy."

"I will, and thank you and Miss Mattie for the invitation."

Leaving Mattie and her admirer, I went upstairs to lie down for the short time I had before my call at the theatre. I was worn out. And somehow, between the confusion of my costume change at *Vanity Fair*, my visit to Eppie Diamond, and the assault on Harry, I'd misplaced my little gold locket, a gift from Franklin, my fiancé who had died in the War. I must have taken it off and left it somewhere. I did that sometimes when I'd had too much gin. I gave the bathroom a cursory look, but it wasn't there. Well, Mattie would find it. I lay down on my bed and closed my eyes.

Harry would have a long recuperation, the doctor had told us. There might have been some damage to his brain, and if so, it was too early to tell. Dr. Olivia Brown's medical diagnosis is that Harry's brain would heal but Harry's pride would take longer.

Shwonem, he had said. And *no*. What had he said no to? What had I just said to him? Something about the opening tonight.

Whoever had filled our milk bottle had access to dye. That meant someone at Eppie Diamond's . . . or a hat maker . . . an artist . . . Bennett was an artist . . . or . . . the Provincetown Players. Our costumes were often dyed. Emma worked on costumes. So did Rae. I let my mind wander through the Players. More than one was a practical joker. It was the kind of semi-intellectual pursuit nurtured in the fraternal life of the Ivy League.

I didn't sleep. Instead, I put the new ribbon in my type-writer, then a clean sheet of paper. A rhyme was rolling around in my head.

> *Red as rust, as Reed,*
> *As robin's breast,*
> *As blood, as mead.*
> *A soldier's crest*
> *Of courage. The Square.*

The dye, the dead,
My heart. My hair.
I swear,
I fear the color red.

Fear was the wrong word. Wrong. My fingers played the keys. No. I didn't have it yet. It would come. I changed my clothes and headed for the theatre. The word came to me then. *Dread.* The doll had red hair. *I dread the color red.*

A pulsating excitement permeated both backstage and the theatre when I went on in *Matinata,* the curtain-raiser. Though it was a very lovely little light comedy, I could feel the restlessness in the audience, as if they were politely telling us to get on with it so they could see what they had come to see. *The Emperor Jones.* We, competent performers that we are, were able to squeeze a rustle of laughter from the audience here and there, and at last the curtain came down with a swoosh. Two polite curtain calls, then intermission. In the narrow wings some of the other actors were already in blackface. I ran back in the girls' dressing room.

The small space was crowded. The girls had stripped down and were browning up for *The Emperor.* Pots of greasepaint stood open on the makeup table. A voluptuous scene. I stepped in and closed the door. I could hardly breathe. Arabian nights. Frankincense and musk. A cigarette burned to ash in the metal tray.

Emma, her skin a rich brown, was already a blue-eyed native, her breasts like nippled melons. "Oliver," she said, tilting her head to me. And all the while she was massaging the brown greasepaint into Rae's back with long strokes, downward, downward, flank and buttock. Rae turned slowly, dipping her fingers into the pot, as did Emma. Limbs long and sleek, breasts in lazy roll. Light glazed my eyes.

I took off my costume, the rest.

They opened their arms to me. I dipped my fingers into the waxy greasepaint, soft flesh to soft flesh, undulating, fragrant.

Rae's whisper was husky. "Sweet Oliver."

"Time." The knock broke the spell.

We parted gently, hands lingering, moving with little motion, smiling, drunk with desire.

The applause was thunderous. I'd never heard the like for any play the Players had done before. Afterward, people poured onto the stage, into the tiny dressing rooms, congratulating all of us, though it was Gene's triumph and Charles Gilpin's. And Jig Cook's as well, since he had put it all together.

We were all heading over to Columbia Gardens, where Luke O'Connor was giving us a mostly booze party, and I was late. Still in blackface, I'd been waylaid by a sweet couple, subscribers, who knew my work. By the time I got to the dressing room, everyone else had gone. I cleaned myself as best I could with the cold cream and then soap and, by that time, cold water. But I was brown in every crease.

I dressed and tied my hair back in a scarf. On my way out I heard voices onstage. I came back and stood in the wings for a moment. The rehearsal light arced over the stage, making the darkness beyond even darker. Jig was talking to someone, his arm over the chap's shoulder, pointing up at the lights.

He must have caught a glimpse of me out of the corner of his eye, for he turned. "Oliver! This is great. Come on out here. I want you to meet someone. You're to have one of the leading roles in his new play."

Thrilled, I swept forward like the great stage star I would be. The playwright turned. My hand was already out and I was saying, "I'm de—"

My heart stopped. It was Andrew Goren.

Chapter Eighteen

Well, I mean, swell . . . really . . . swell . . ." I kept talking on like a damned fool, while Andrew Goren unclothed me, figuratively speaking of course. I felt his hands as surely as if he touched me, and there was more. He'd penetrated my mind, and while I denied him, he waited for me. It's not often that I'm at a loss for words, but I was now.

"Andy wants to read the play to you before rehearsal," Jig said. His eyes moved from Andrew to me, and back to Andrew, then his laugh boomed. "You two work it out."

"How is tomorrow around five? My room on Mercer Street," Andrew said.

"No. My place," I said hastily, remembering Harry's exhortation. "Five is fine. I'm at—"

"I know," Andrew said.

Tiring of the interplay, Jig tugged at his white forelock. "The Working Girls' home then?"

I nodded and tore myself away, as bee from honey. I needed the sharp bite of nicotine to clear my mind. On the street, with shaking hands, I inserted the cigarette into my holder and lit up.

The cold stung my cheeks, but the night was so clear every constellation was visible in the sky. I drew the chill into my lungs along with the soothing fumes of my cigarette.

Passion as a threat, I thought. Did love have anything to do with passion? Doth not passion wane? And what is it that is left in its wake? The cessation of . . .

Two lovers, arms twined, lips absorbed, absorbing, came down the street. They passed so close to me, I felt their need with a pang of envy. I leaned against the bricks and smoked my cigarette, then stepped to the gutter and dumped the remains.

The party was in full swing in the smoky room. Most of us paid little heed to Prohibition. There was always wine and gin and plenty more to fill the punch bowl.

"Oliver!"

Whit made his way toward me. I have to admit I was glad to see him. He thrust a teacup in my hand. Gin, I thought, oh, lovely gin. Gratefully, I lifted the cup to my lips. Punch with a gin undertone. It had a slightly bitter taste, but oh how good it felt going down.

He was saying something, but I could hardly hear him over the din. All I caught was "Harry."

"What?" Fear is an errant emotion. It strikes when one leasts expects it. The punch sloshed, responding to the quick jerk of my hand. I took another quick swallow.

"Someone attacked him. He's in St. Vincent's." He looked down at me, his eyes cooler than they would normally be. "Didn't you know?"

I was relieved to see Rae Dunbar approaching and raised my cup to her. "I went to see him before the show."

My attention was on Rae, so when Whit grabbed my shoulders and shook me, I was startled and dropped the teacup. "You saw him?" he said. "What'd he say?" The teacup hit the floor with a plunk, bottom down, and broke neatly into two almost equal pieces; the gin very politely seeped out and rapidly disappeared into the floor that had, I do believe, imbibed much worse.

We stared down at the split teacup and the spilt gin for a moment. Then I said, "Really, Whit."

"I'm sorry, Oliver. I was concerned about Harry."

"I didn't know you and Harry were that close. I think perhaps you may be concerned about something Harry might have said to me?"

"What could he have said to you that would concern me?"

Rae bent down between us and picked up the two pieces of the teacup, then straightened. "Have I interrupted something?" she asked.

"Not at all," I said. "I was just telling Whit that Harry is recovering nicely when my hand was jostled."

"Oh, there's Jig," Rae said.

Taking up both length and width of the doorway, Jig in his flowing black cape paused, waiting for the applause. It came in a great roar of appreciation. Since Gene had gone back to Provincetown, it was Jig we celebrated. He'd spotted O'Neill's genius early and we continued to present his work, though Gene had given *Beyond the Horizon* to Broadway.

The presentation of *The Emperor Jones* on our small stage was the apex of Jig's dream, and we were all there to partake of it.

When Jig stepped into the room, Andrew Goren became visible behind him. I saw Andrew's eyes slowly survey the room. I knew whom he was looking for and made myself a farthing behind Whit and Rae.

"There you are, Oliver," Bennett Newman said. His jolly voice was loud enough to be heard over the din. "And with empty hands. Tsk. Tsk. We'll fix that soon enough." The cigarette parked in the corner of his mouth bobbed as he spoke. He took my elbow and steered me to the refreshment table, where a huge punch bowl sat, and all the keg of ale needed was a spin of the spigot.

I lit a cigarette while Bennett filled my cup. "Is Mackey here?"

"No, he hasn't come back. But I'm not worried. I told you he does this."

I studied Bennett's dear face. "Where does he go when he disappears?"

"I don't know." Bennett shrugged. "It's his life."

"But what about his friends? He must have friends."

"I've never met them. But why are we talking about Mackey? We should be talking about us."

"Us?" The question was raised by none other than Andrew Goren.

"Oliver and me," Bennett said without skipping a beat. "We're going to run off together, aren't we, Oliver?"

"No, we're not, Bennett. Do you know Andrew Goren?"

"We've met," Bennett said.

I watched the men shake hands, as if they were about to begin a prizefight. Wary. They were dressed in a similar fashion, flannel shirts, dark trousers. Andrew, much taller, dark, ascetic; Bennett, the picture of Wisconsin.

"We were talking about Mackey," I said.

Bennett frowned. "No, we weren't."

"What about Mackey?" Andrew said.

"He appears to be missing," I offered.

"No, he doesn't," Bennett insisted.

"He's my mother's assistant, and he hasn't been to work for a few days."

Bennett's manner changed. "You're Eppie Diamond's son?"

"Yes."

"When did you see Mackey last, Andrew?" I, the picture of innocence, asked.

"This afternoon."

"Well, there, Oliver, you see. He's back and he's fine. Am I right, Goren?"

Andrew's face was expressionless. "Only insofar as you think lying on a cold slab in the morgue is fine."

Chapter Nineteen

So there it was, out in the open.

"You *are* joking, Goren." Even in the awful light, I could see Bennett's usually ruddy skin had turned pasty. The rest of his drink went down in one long swallow; his eyes filled. Holding the back of his hand to his face, he turned and walked away from us, threading his way through the crowd with some kind of purpose.

It was an astonishing performance. I watched Andrew watching Bennett as he moved among the other revelers.

"Well," I said.

He touched the nape of my neck, and my skin quivered. "Let's get out of here, Olivia."

I found my cape on a hook, and he his long scarf, and we trooped out to the street, squeezing by others who, knowing there was a party here after every opening, were coming in. We stood on the sidewalk breathing the fresh air. The night was lovely.

"Come home with me," he said.

Under ordinary circumstances, I would have. But I had a lot of questions that remained unanswered. So I said, with more determination than I felt, "No."

"Shall I take you home, then?"

I was beguiled and not at all afraid, and I didn't want to go home. I shook my head.

We started walking. Away from Mercer Street, away from Bedford Street, toward Washington Square Park. I thought, God help me, tomorrow morning the real Olivia Brown will be found in the park with her throat cut.

The park had an ethereal glow, fuzzy light from street lamps. The benches were not all empty. Lovers and transients. The ardent strum of a guitar. As we sat, a fragment of Baudelaire—*Be beautiful! and be sad!*—wavered for a moment over us, forgotten by a previous pair of lovers, then distilled in the air.

"You want to know about Mackey," Andrew said, after we had passed his flask of gin back and forth at least four times, with not a word exchanged. He slipped his arm around my shoulders.

"Yes."

"I didn't really know him."

"But you said he was your wife."

"I said, 'She was my wife.'"

"Yes."

"You'll think me very naive."

"I think we're all naive." His shoulder was not soft, was not a safe haven for my head. I sat up under his arm.

"I met a girl in a bar in Chatham, on the Cape, last spring. She told me she was a poet."

I looked up at him; his face was shadowed in the hazy light. His eyes were staring at something I could not see. "She told you her name was Olivia Brown," I said.

"You knew?" He was astonished. I had his full attention now.

"I guessed, from the drawing of the dead girl . . . from things Bennett told me about Mackey. You fell in love with her."

"I fell in love with you."

"Did you? You married this girl you met in a bar?"

His arm tightened around me. "I married you."

I pulled away from him. "You married someone who told you she was Olivia Brown. You married Mackey. Didn't you make love?"

"You wanted to wait."

"Pshaw," said I, louder than I intended. I got to my feet.

"After we were married, you told me. We were married by a justice of the peace in Hyannis." He gave me a smile that wrenched my heart.

Darn, I thought. I wanted to hold him, make things right. I leaned over him, pulled his head to my breast, stroked his hair. "You found out he was a boy."

"It was humiliating. I ran away. I've been in Paris for the last six months. When I got back, he was here, working for my mother, and so much a part of her life, I couldn't say anything against him."

"No more," I said, stepping back. "It's too much for me to contemplate. I'll see you tomorrow." Now it was I who ran away.

I heard him call, "Wait!"

When I neared Bedford Street, I changed my course. I wanted to be with Harry this night.

St. Vincent's was shrouded in darkness, as was the street, but I could see flickering candlelight and bobbing kerosene lanterns amid a lot of activity surrounding the hospital. I stopped a uniformed officer to ask what had happened.

"The electrical power went off," he said. "There'll be no trolley service for a while. Stand back, Miss."

I stood back, then skirted the hospital and crossed the street. A gaggle of nurses were talking to another officer and a man in a business suit. Two workmen carrying a stepladder squeezed by them. Well, there was no point in my groping my way up to Harry's room in the dark. I'd wait awhile; if the lights were not back soon, I'd go home. I lit a cigarette and sat down on the curb under the darkened bishop's-crook street lamp. I was tired and had had too much to drink and too much excitement for one night.

Words and phrases danced in my head. If only I had a pencil and a scrap of paper . . . A slight movement from across the street, from a street-level window of the hospital, caught my attention. Stealth, I thought, not moving. Someone was climbing out as if he didn't want to be seen. He walked to the corner, then light came blazing, everywhere, and for a second, he stood in the

frame of a street lamp like a deer caught in an automobile's head-
lights, before he bolted.

I was on my feet, rushing toward the hospital. All I could
think was Harry. Was he all right?

For in that tiny moment I'd recognized the man who crept
from the window, determined not to be seen, as my old lover,
Whit Sawyer.

Chapter Twenty

*W*ell, there was no sense in wasting an observation. I used Whit's egress window and became part of the general turmoil: patients crying, sisters rushing back and forth, heads peering from doorways.

Not a soul questioned me as I walked up the stairs with a sense of purpose. In fact, one particularly harried-looking sister nodded at me as though I belonged.

When I opened the door to Harry's room, I had an unpleasant surprise. It was empty. No Harry. No sister. No patient whatever. The bed was made up and waiting for a new arrival.

Harry, I thought, oh, Harry. The shock induced tears, and then I couldn't stop.

"Miss Brown," a soft voice murmured.

I turned, drying my eyes with my fingertips, only to have more tears take their place. It was the sister who'd been with Harry yesterday. "Sister . . . Harry—"

"We've moved Mr. Melville down the hall to a private room. Come along."

"I thought—"

"I know."

"I came over to be with him when I heard about the electricity." I've become such an accomplished liar. The lie just slipped right out before I could even think about it.

> *To be honest with you, lover,*
> *Yesterday I loved you well*
> *But today I love another*
> *And tomorrow, who can tell?*
> *My credo is, as you must see,*
> *Truly serious inconstancy.*

I'd been sitting in the chair next to Harry's bed for an hour, working my poem over and over in my head while Harry lay like the dead, his chest barely rising and falling. When I'd finished it, I spoke aloud.

I knew he heard me, though he hadn't moved since Sister left me in the half-light, because he wiggled his fingers. Taking his hand, I leaned close and blew at him. He smelled of antiseptic and plaster. My breath was gin and cigarettes.

He groaned and the swollen skin around his lips twitched.

"I know there's nothing you'd like better than a martini and a cigarette right now," I said.

His fingers danced in my hand. I lit a cigarette, then put the mouth of my holder to his mouth and held it for him while he took a tortured inhale.

"Ahhh," he muttered, then started coughing.

Alarmed, I reclaimed the cigarette quickly. Tears flecked his eyes, and I could do nothing for him.

Finally, the agonized coughing stopped and he lay quiet. I could see him trying to muster his strength.

I said, "Shall I tell you about the opening?" I bent and stubbed out my cigarette against the metal foot of his bed.

He didn't respond, so I took his hand and just began. "Harry, I can't begin to tell you what a sensual experience it was."

"Ha," he said, or something very like it, and his fingers danced again against my palm.

"When I left the theatre, Andrew Goren was on stage talking to Jig."

The door opened. A sister with a plaster on her forehead poked her head into the room. "Everything all right here?" I stepped away from the bed. She came in and looked down at Harry, took his pulse. It would be racing right now, I was sure. Sniffing the air like a bird dog, she said, "No more smoking."

"Yes, certainly, Sister. Right, Harry?" Harry didn't move. "I think he's sleeping, Sister."

"With this pulse? I shouldn't think so. Playing possum, are we, Mr. Melville?" She chuckled and left us.

Harry made a snorting sound as soon as the door closed.

"Where was I?" I moved back to the bed and took Harry's hand in both of mine. "I can't say this isn't an interesting situation, Harry, with you mute and me center stage." His hiss put an end to my trifling levity.

"Okay, okay. Jig's going to do Andrew Goren's play and I'm to play the lead. Actually, my phantom lover wrote it for me, so I'm to have my stage career after all."

Harry groaned. His movement increased and I had the unpleasant sensation that he was about to get up out of bed and give me what-for.

"Harry, believe me, there's nothing to worry about. He told me he'd identified Mackey's body today. Would you believe Mackey was passing himself off as me last summer in Chatham? Andrew met him in a saloon and fell in love and married him."

I swear I heard someone say, "Sheeshus Cwisht!"

Perhaps it was I, because in telling it to Harry, the whole thing sounded preposterous. "I know what you think, Harry, but I'm going to tell you the rest." He was growling under his breath. I waited for a moment. "When Andrew discovered the person he married was a man, and certainly not Olivia Brown, the poet, he ran off to Paris. He came back a few weeks ago and there was Mackey ensconced with Andrew's own mother, Eppie Diamond, as her assistant."

This time I heard Harry loud and clear. He said, "Clap!"

"Clap? As in applause?"

"Clap as in shit," Harry said.

"Oh, well," I said. "I guess you're feeling better." I got up and raised the window shade. It was getting light. "By the way, did Whit come to see you tonight?"

Harry was silent.

"I saw him sneaking out of here while I was waiting for the lights to come on." I poured a small amount of water into a glass and, putting my arm about his shoulders, held the glass to his lips. He drank some and I took the glass and my arm away. "Florence Nightingale, I'm not, my dear, and I miss my partner—my sleuthing partner—so I insist you get your derriere out of this bed as quickly as possible."

A faint snore alerted me that I'd bored Harry to sleep.

Ah, well. It was home for me with the milkman in the sweet soft hours of dawn in the Village.

On the way downstairs, with the hospital awaking around me, I encountered the sister with the plaster on her forehead. "I'm home to my bed," I said.

"Thanks for coming to help," she said.

As we passed on the stairs, she pressed her hand to her forehead and winced.

"How did you get that wound?" I asked politely.

"We had an intruder, a thief, who took advantage of the darkness," she said. "I caught him in Mr. Melville's old room and he knocked me down."

Chapter Twenty-one

I dreamed of an isle of women, breasts
Unfettered, moving languidly, lucid
In gold sunlight. A wave crests,
Sends water streaming over yellow sand. Did
I tell you, water the color of eyes,
Gray to green, as mine. No surprise,
Sense you all, my doctored dreams
Where nothing is the way it seems.

I roused myself late in the morning, bathed and dressed, and came downstairs carrying the poem I'd left in my typewriter several hours earlier. There was coffee and a note from Mattie saying she'd gone to see Harry. Also, a plate of fresh biscuits under a tea towel.

My poems come from a kind of inner self who seldom lets me know directly what is on her mind. I was thinking I might call my new poem "Sense You All," wondering what that meant, and whether that was too self-conscious, when the doorbell rang.

The kitchen clock said eleven forty-five. I didn't move. I was not ready for visitors.

It rang again.

But perhaps it was a delivery. I moved into the hallway and opened the door to the staircase.

The bell rang once more, demandingly, I thought. No deliveryman's ring. I plodded down the stairs and saw the two coppers, Brophy and Walz, standing at my door. Worse, they saw me. I let them in.

"Gentlemen," I said, without the slightest pretense that they were.

"Miss Brown," Brophy said.

"Do come in. If I'd known you were coming I would have put on my glad rags."

They followed me up the stairs. The parlor was for truth above all else. I took them into the kitchen and sat down. Walz lit my cigarette for me.

"I wouldn't mind a cup of coffee," Walz said, eyeing the biscuits.

"Help yourself. The cups are in the cabinet behind you." I made no move to either welcome them or play host.

Brophy took down the cups and poured the coffee. They both sat across from me. Distinct feelings of claustrophobia made me uneasy.

Walz made no pretense of reading Mattie's note, which I'd left on the table with my poem. "Mattie's gone to see Harry Melville," I said, needlessly.

"He'll live," Walz said. "He's got a hard head."

Oh, dear, I thought, the man does speak in clichés.

He took up the typed sheet of my poem, "Sense You All," and as he read, his face became an unattractive blotch of reds. Yet he didn't put the poem down. I felt he was going to assault me. And he did.

"Pornography, Miss Brown?" Walz said.

"Poetry, Mr. Walz."

"Bohemian pornography, Miss Brown."

"What makes you a judge, Mr. Walz? I presume you've heard of Dr. Freud?"

He didn't respond. He dropped my poem back on the table.

Brophy said, with some discomfort, "The body you found has been identified as Theodore McGrath."

"Theodore. Well, what a great big name for such a slip of a boy."

Walz watched me. "I'm very curious to know why you're not surprised, Miss Brown."

"I knew Mackey was missing, Mr. Walz. I put two and two together." I did not see fit to mention either Mackey's obsession with me, or Andrew. Why? I don't know. I should have, and perhaps things might have been different if I had.

"How well did you know him?" Walz asked.

"Only in passing. I met him a few times through a mutual friend."

"Mr. Bennett Newman," Brophy supplied.

"Yes. Have you spoken to Bennett? He will be very upset."

"We've just come from Mr. Newman's . . . studio," Walz said. "He told us that Mr. McGrath was obsessed with you. Were you aware of this?"

"No." At least not while he was alive, I thought.

"He was identified yesterday by Mr. Andrew Goren," Walz said. "It's very odd, isn't it, Miss Brown, that every thread we unravel leads back to you?"

I agreed. "Very odd indeed, Mr. Walz."

After they left, having had no satisfaction from me, I believe, I took my pornographic poem and raced upstairs. I rolled a clean sheet of paper into my type-writer and typed one word: *obsession.*

Whose?

I left everything and went down to the foyer, took my cape from the hall stand and tied a scarf about my head. I intended to go to Washington Square Park to see if I could find the blind Polish woman who made the rag dolls.

The one thing I knew for certain was that Mackey was not responsible for the break-in or the fake blood in the milk bottle. Or the doll, for that matter. But what could the dollmaker, a blind woman, possibly be able to tell me? We would soon see.

It was cold, much colder than it had been earlier that morning, and the sharp wind whispered beguilingly of snow. At midday, the Village I knew was just starting to awaken. I love the small shops on West Fourth Street, but I was steadfast.

The park benches were sparsely occupied. It was far too cold for anyone to sit still for any length of time. Romance was making love in front of a fire, not on a frigid bench in the park on a wintery day.

I walked past the fountain, circled the Arch, and back toward MacDougal Street, before I saw her. She sat alone on a folding chair, her lap covered by a tatty wool blanket. A small coal heater crackled at her feet. The dolls were lined up in the lid of a cardboard box, set on the box.

As I approached, I saw the dog—a mixed breed but heavily weighted toward golden retriever—peering out from under the blanket. The dog kept his eyes on me, wary, but not threatening.

The woman wore layers of clothing, coat, shawl, long skirt, rough wool gloves with the fingertips cut out. Her face was powdery pale, her eyes covered by a white film. The babushka shrouded her head. She looked as if she would blow away in a strong wind.

"Excuse me," I said.

She cocked her head and confusion brushed her face for a moment; her smile, timid, revealed a gold front tooth. When she spoke, her speech was sibilant with broken English. "Did your friend like the doll, Miss Olivia?" she said.

Chapter Twenty-two

I was literally beside myself. I stifled a cry of pure frustration. How was this possible? I said, "You are mistaken."

Her features folded in on each other. "Oh, I'm sorry. I thought you were someone else."

"But how—?"

"Because I don't have sight?" She tilted her head to the side. Wispy strands of white hair crept from under the babushka. "It was the perfume . . . the scent of roses."

"You also called me by name."

"I don't know your name, Miss."

"My name is Olivia."

The woman focused her milky eyes on me. "You are playing a cruel joke on a blind old lady."

"No, please, I'm not. I think someone is playing a joke on me. My name is Olivia Brown, and someone gave me one of your dolls, but with a knife in its heart."

Hand over her mouth, the old lady shuddered. "That is not a joke."

"No, it's not. I think someone has also been pretending to be me—this very person you mistook me for."

"She told me her name was Olivia. Like you, she wore the

scent of the rose. You and she have the same height, but you are not the same."

I sighed. Mackey. I looked down at the dolls lined up in rows. Every one had yellow yarn hair. "All your dolls have yellow hair. The doll I received had red hair."

"She wanted a special doll," the old lady said, "for a special friend with red hair. My daughter found me red yarn . . ."

"I have red hair," I said. "Did she tell you how to find her when the doll was ready?"

"She said she would find me. And she did, last week."

I pressed a dollar into the old woman's gloved palm and thanked her. Deep in thought, I meandered out of the park on Washington Square South.

Obviously Mackey had ordered the doll and collected it. But Mackey was quite dead by the time the doll was delivered to me. So who had done it? And was this the person who had killed Mackey?

"Oliver!"

I looked up. I was standing about a foot away from Rae Dunbar. She locked arms with me.

"I saw you in the park and I've been calling to you and you haven't heard a thing." With her grin, the skin rippled along her small hooked nose, and two deep dimples appeared in her cheeks.

"I'm sorry," I said. "I was thinking about . . . a poem." I felt the cold deep in my bones and pulled my cape tighter around me.

"Look where we are." We were standing in front of Romany Marie's Gypsy Tea Room. With a mischievous glint in her eye, Rae gave my arm a tug and said, "Come on. Let's go in."

The door had a little bell attached and Romany Marie looked up from her anarchist newspaper. "Girrrrls," she said. Her English was heavily accented with Rumanian. She sat on a stool behind the counter, resting her enormous bosom near her ubiquitous cup of Turkish coffee. Tearoom it may have been called, but the tea was not the draw. Yet she didn't serve any hooch.

Once, the Hudson Dusters, the notorious Irish street gang whose clubhouse was on Hudson Street just below Horatio, invaded the tearoom and demanded she serve them her strongest drink. Her strongest drink was coffee, she told them. Okay, coffee, they said, as the rest of her customers made for the door. After three rounds of coffee, Romany Marie said they'd had enough, folded her arms over her heavy bosom and presented her bill. They paid and left and never returned, supposedly because they respected Romany Marie's lack of fear and because Gene O'Neill, whom they called the Kid, and who was their favorite bohemian, asked them not to.

There was always good conversation and food at Romany Marie's. She let chits pile up for hungry artists who couldn't pay the fare. And gypsy she never was, though she wore the attire: the skirts, the shawls, a fringed turban, gold hoop earrings and beads. On occasion, she even read a palm.

It came to me that everyone in the Village was playing a part. Even I. It was what had drawn us here. This brought to mind the story our grocer, Mr. Santelli, had told us—about a young girl named Dorothy who wanted desperately to be a writer and live in Greenwich Village. Her parents had been horrified and threatened to lock her up. She left home one day and was never seen again. But then, she could be right here in Romany Marie's, playing her part.

I looked at Rae. She'd stuck her head into the kitchen to say hello to Romany Marie's husband Damon Marchand, who did the cooking.

Who was Rae, really?

We ordered the Turkish coffee and had our choice of tables, as the café didn't begin to fill up until much later in the day. By evening, it would be jammed, and would stay so till dawn.

A ruddy warmth came from the wood fire, and we sat close to it; our knees met under the table. Rae's eyes were intense, hazel, protruding slightly under heavy lids. A smooth cap of dark hair was cut to follow the shape of her head. She studied me as I did her, our shells melting. Our fingers wandered across the table and touched.

"I moved in with Whit," Rae said.

I nodded. "One does what one must."

"Coffee!" Romany Marie set the mugs down in the center of

the table. "Vud more?" The coffee was thick and black. The scent, sensual. Sense you all, I thought. That's what it means.

We shook our heads. We wanted to be alone. Romany Marie knew the signs. She went back to the counter to rest her breasts.

I asked Rae, "Do you write?"

"I write, but not like you," Rae said. "I teach school."

"You're playing hooky."

"I'm subbing. I become permanent next term."

"Where are you from?"

"Brooklyn."

"I'm from Albany."

"I know."

"We're all drawn here for the same reasons. Free exchange of ideas . . . love . . ."

"All love must be free," she said.

How could I not agree?

We sat back and sipped our coffee, bittersweet. Romany Marie brought over a plate of strudel. "Eat, girrrrls. Too thin not good. Nudding to hold on to, no, Damon?" she called to her husband.

He came and stood in the doorway and smiled at her, a smile so full of love, the overflow was intoxicating.

"Do our fortunes, Romany Marie," Rae said. "Oliver?"

I looked down at the little face of the wristwatch I'd won last year, first prize in a poetry contest. I'd forgotten to wind it. "I'm late for an appointment." I knew Andrew would be waiting for me, yet I stayed on.

Rae was clearly disappointed. "A short one," she said.

"Cannot do short," Marie said. She took Rae's hand, turned it palm up and stared into it. "Ahh, love," she said. "Much love. Too much."

The little bell on the front door rang. We all looked up. Bennett Newman came in. Behind him, a tall man in the uniform of a naval officer.

"Well, look who's here," Bennett said. The man in uniform favored a cane and walked with a decided limp.

Romany Marie folded Rae's fingers over her palm. "Vee start again later." She turned to the newcomers. "Vud you have?"

I stood up and wrapped myself in my cape. "I have to go."

"But your fortune," Rae said.

"It can wait," I said. Bennett's friend was staring at me, then he smiled. "Have we met?" I asked him.

"If you are Olivia Brown," he said, "we have been corresponding for some time."

"You are Stephen Lowell," I said, delighted. "Home from the wars." Stephen Lowell and I had had a correspondence, filled with mutual admiration, for some time. He'd achieved recognition for his poetry of love and war, life and death. His ship had been torpedoed, and he, along with a few other survivors, had almost perished on a life raft during the three weeks before they were rescued by a British cruiser.

"We were at Harvard together," Bennett said. "He was the brave one."

"I'd love to stay and talk, but I'm late for an appointment," I said. "Come for a drink later. Bennett?"

"Sevenish, Oliver?"

"Fine." I went back to Rae, bent, grazed her soft cheek with mine. "You come, too, and bring Whit."

"Maybe," she said, touching my lips with her fingers. Then she repeated Romany Marie's warning. "Too much love."

"Never too much love," I whispered for her ear only.

Chapter Twenty-three

Of course, I was tardy, but I needn't have worried. My little house was redolent of butter and sugar. Mattie's dope. Better than muggles.

I found Mattie and Andrew entertaining each other like old friends over tea and sweet cakes. I could see she liked him because she was smoking with him. Mattie finds smoking an intimacy to be indulged in only with friends.

"I'm sorry I'm late," I called. When I hung up my cape I saw a black canvas bookbag, the kind carried by students, on the floor, leaning against the hall rack. "How did you find Harry, Mattie?" Andrew was standing when I came into the kitchen.

"Grumpy and difficult."

"Good. He's getting better." I smiled at Andrew.

"Will you have tea?" Mattie set a cup on the table.

"No. Wine, I think. Andrew?"

"Wine. I've a bottle of red in my bag."

"Perfect. Mattie, would you like to hear Andrew read his play?"

"Mr. Brophy is expected." Her eyes didn't meet mine.

"Oh," I said, "You're a sly one, you are. Come, Andrew." I took two glasses from the shelf and led the way to the parlor. A play, written for me, that I was to star in, what more could a girl want?

The afternoon was cloudy and overcast, and although Mattie had drawn the draperies, and had lit the fire, the parlor was full of conflicting moods. Andrew stood behind me, close enough for me to feel his heartbeat meld with mine.

"You'll need more light," I said.

"No, this is fine." He sat cross-legged on the carpeted floor, so that the firelight lit the pages of his manuscript.

I closed the door. When I turned back, he was opening the wine. A small drum rested between his knees. I set the glasses down in front of him. I was curious about the drum, but I held my curiosity in check.

"Sit here." He indicated the closest chair, a grand, broad-seated armchair that had probably been Great-Aunt Evangeline's favorite, since it showed more wear than any other in the room.

I shook off my shoes and curled up in the chair, and as always, I had the not unpleasant sensation of the chair putting its arms around me. We lit cigarettes and smoking, watched each other. His eyes were blue fire, feverish.

He poured the wine and handed me a glass. "To the poets and their muses," he said.

"To the muses and their poets," I said.

We touched glasses and drank. He leaned back against my chair, his dark, shaggy head near my lap, and opened his manuscript. "*The Choice*," he said. "Act One, Scene One . . ."

It was the story in free verse of a great love spread over hundreds of years, two lovers separated by fate, sometimes for good and sometimes for evil; they live and die and are reborn and meet and love and . . . A Greek chorus commentary ran through it, the part to be played by a boy who accompanied his observations banging on a drum, which Andrew did to great effect.

When Andrew finished reading, I sat in my chair, hardly aware of the tears running down my cheeks. I was overwhelmed, impossibly aroused. I held his head and kissed his hair. He'd devoured me. I wanted to do the same for him. He set the manuscript aside, gave the drum a final thump, then on his knees, he took me—already more than willing—in his arms.

We made love the first time on the rug in front of the fire, and then, when Brophy rang for Mattie, we collected the wine bottle and the glasses and I took Andrew to my bed. If I gave any thought to Harry's warnings, it was fleeting, for Andrew Goren was the consummate lover. We paused for wine and smokes, and lips breathed kisses and merged with caresses and caresses became kisses . . .

Of course, I'd forgotten entirely that I'd invited people for drinks. Rae and Whit were the first to arrive. I threw on my dress, ran a comb through my hair. Leaving Andrew with an abashed apology, I hurried downstairs to make sure we'd left nothing overt in the parlor. The doorbell rang again. Mattie didn't answer, so she must have gone out with Brophy.

I gathered up Andrew's manuscript and the drum and hid them away in his canvas bag. The parlor kept its secrets.

Whit had brought a bottle of gin, and I opened the olives and took down the glasses, while Whit made martinis. And then Bennett and Stephen Lowell came with Mary Voise, carrying wine. We were all laughing and talking and I was bustling about, setting out apples and cheese. I drank martinis and Stephen and I began reciting poems at each other, I his and he mine.

The world was gin and poems, laughter and—I had my back to the door, and when I finished my dramatic recitation of a sonnet of Stephen's I particularly liked, no one spoke.

"What? No applause?" Their eyes went beyond me. I spun round and saw Andrew in the doorway, a strange light in his eyes, or maybe it was a spark caught from the fire. I'll never know for sure.

"Andrew," I said, "Come in. I think you know everyone—"

He ignored me, moving into the room only to pick up his canvas bag.

"Andrew just read me his wonderful new play—" I caught his arm.

He stared down at me as if I were some loathsome creature and slapped my hand away.

Chapter Twenty-four

On the bandstand the harlequin poses,
Arms aloft, he directs the tune,
And everywhere, the sense of roses
Obviates the dead, too soon.
Which is husband, wife, the boy, the girl?
And still the dancers dip and swirl,
As scent and revelers blend and merge,
The tune's exposed: it is a dirge.

In truth, I'd been put off by the ridiculous tale
Andrew had told me about Mackey. The very lushness of Andrew's aura had faded rapidly. Then he'd read his play and quite
seduced me with his brilliance.

When I awoke in midmorning of the next day, I felt weak
from too many martinis, too little food, and a night spent talking, talking, talking, and finally, after everyone left, writing.

Andrew was gone from me. Only the sense of him on the
bedclothes remained. I rolled over on my stomach and breathed
him in, and with each breath the little shocks echoed deep
within me. What had made him turn on me as he had?

Afterward, everyone had been moderately well mannered
about Andrew's presence and his rude departure, except for
Whit, who said with utter smugness, "Eat and run now, do they,
Oliver?"

To which, Stephen Lowell responded, "I'll have you on the
street right now, man, if you don't apologize."

I said, "Whit's just a poor sport, Stephen."

"I apologize to one and all," Whit said, bowing to me and to the rest.

"Come away with me, Oliver," Bennett said, taking me in his arms. "Now you see you must."

And I had rejected him, but I have to admit that had the offer come from Stephen Lowell, I might have accepted.

In a short while, Mattie came with coffee and we sat together on my bed with our cigarettes, not talking. I thought, Time must stop here. This is the girl I'll always be. *Je ne regrette rien.*

I bathed and dressed and let Mattie ply me with soft-boiled eggs and bread and butter, though I had no appetite and was feeling somewhat frail.

Pushing the almost empty plate away, I lit a cigarette. "So where did you go off to with Mr. Brophy?" I offered her my case.

Mattie filled our cups with coffee and took a cigarette. She fussed over lighting it, picked crumbs off the tablecloth, and cleaned a speck only she could see on the cover of the sugar bowl, until I suspected she had something difficult to say.

"Out with it," I said. "Did Mr. Brophy make love to you last night?"

Mattie broke into embarrassed giggles. "Oh, heavens, no, Olivia. He took me to meet his mother."

I laughed, too, though I understood the ramifications of this all too well. Mattie is an essential part of my life. I didn't want to lose her. If she were to marry, she would have children, and she would be lost to me. "When a man takes you to meet his mother, it's serious."

She agreed. "It is that."

"Has he swept you off your feet? Am I going to lose you to convention?"

"Oh, Olivia, I am not headstrong and I do not rush into things as you do."

"Quite right. Well, what was the mother like? I can almost guess. She's a widow. He's the only son so he supports her. She is Irish to the core and wanted her son to become a priest—"

"Joan Brophy may be all of that, but it did not come up in the conversation."

"Joan is it? Well! What did you talk about then? Corned beef and cabbage and our Savior?" I asked.

"You are a wicked girl, Olivia Brown. Actually—" Mattie was certainly enjoying herself at my expense. She laughed so, she could hardly get her words out. "We talked about the Vote. She wanted to meet me to make sure her son was not interested in the wrong kind of girl. Joan Brophy's a radical suffragist."

"God is good," I said. "And full of wonderful surprises." I patted her hand. "I suppose Brophy was pleased and asked for your hand in marriage on the way home." I was joking, of course, but imagine my conflicted feelings when Mattie nodded. I made a show of clutching my breast. "What did you tell him?"

"I told him I would give him my answer once he's found the person who's been threatening you."

Mattie packed a tin of cookies for Harry while I put on one of the sweaters, all green—we Browns are green-eyed beauties— I'd discovered packed away carefully in Great-Aunt Evangeline's cedar closet. I looked quite like a street urchin in the sweater, which came to my thighs, but I have never been one with my finger on the pulse of the latest fashion. In the Village, among my friends, it is the intellect that matters.

The light was thin and brittle, the cold compelling. It demanded I breathe deeply, that the skin of my cheeks stiffen and sting. My senses stirred to life. Crisp, burnished leaves, gold and red, flecked the sidewalk, eddied in the gutter. As I strode along, I was feeling mighty snug with my cape wrapped over the sweater. I was Olivia Brown, the poet.

And then, Olivia Brown, the poet, stepped off the curb, popped the strap of her sandal, tripped, and sat down in the gutter on her poetic derriere. A gentleman came to my aid, as did the nice Italian grocer whose store was nearby. The gentleman reached a hand down to me.

"Are you all right, Miss?" he asked.

My rescuer had hardly got the words out, when he dropped

his hand and left me. The grocer scurried into his shop and peered out from behind cans of tomatoes in his front window.

The cause of all that energy was the charge, "Beat it, pal." The voice alone would have scared the devil himself. The face that thrust itself in mine had a flattened nose; red hair sprouted from under a wool cap. The mouth was a thin, vicious line. A scar ran down the left side of his face from brow to scruffy goatee. He clamped his grubby hands on my arms and lifted me out of the gutter. "Youse oughta watch where youse goin'," he said, squinting down at me.

"Thank you," I said. "Good-bye." My feet walked, but the creature wouldn't let go of me.

"No, ya don't," he muttered. "I got me orders."

Chapter Twenty-five

*W*hat orders?" I protested. "You can't take me anywhere I don't want to go."

A lot of good that did me. With one hand holding the tin of cookies and the other clamped to my elbow, he propelled me with certain dispatch along the street. And I couldn't fail to notice that everyone was giving us a wide berth. Only when I stumbled over the torn strap on my shoe and almost went down again, did he stop.

"So what's da problem here?" He had the breath of a dragon, and the pupils of his pale blue eyes were tiny black dots. Although not much taller than I, he was brawny and mean and his hands were like a vise on my elbow.

Reaching down, I pulled off my shoe and shook it in his face. "See this. The strap tore. That's why I tripped in the first place."

He took my shoe and fingered the torn strap. "Tony'll fix it." So saying, he picked me up like a sack of potatoes and carried me half a block, then set me down in front of a shade of a shop set between two buildings.

Tony turned out to be the Italian shoemaker on the corner of Seventh Avenue and Tenth Street. His swarthy skin actually paled when he saw who his next customer was. In fact, the customer before us, a man in a broad-brimmed black hat, backed away and waved us ahead of him the instant he saw us. My captor smacked my shoe down on the small counter and commanded, "Sew dis."

My shoe was quickly mended and back on my foot.

He shoved the tin of cookies at me. "Let's go."

"Wait." I fumbled in my pockets for a dime and set it on the counter.

"Put dat away," my captor growled.

Tony held up his hands; his mustache trembled. "Oh, no, Miss," he said, "I don't take no money from a friend of Mr. Farrell." His eyes were so pleading I took my dime back.

"So where are you taking me, Mr. Farrell?" I said, mildly amused and no longer fearful, though I should have been, because being fearful makes one wary. Being wary makes one very aware of what is going on around one. Good advice for the Village, good advice for a poet.

"Youse can call me Red, Miss," he said, with what I think was meant to be a smile.

He didn't offer me anything further, but he didn't need to. I was pretty good at arithmetic. His name was Red Farrell, and by the way everyone behaved in his presence, I knew he was one of the notorious Hudson Dusters, whose territory was everything south of Thirteenth Street and west of Broadway. That meant the Village proper.

Though they were nocturnal, as was I, I'd seen very little of them. They tended to stick to the houses they occupied, rent-free of course, below Horatio and around Bethune, and on Hudson. They terrorized a neighborhood with atrociously loud parties, with music and dancing, hooch and cocaine, with food supplied for free by frightened local merchants. Every so often they'd be raided by the police and closed down. They'd move into another house in the area and start all over again.

But what did they want of me?

I found out soon enough when Red Farrell fast-walked me into St. Vincent's. The sisters expressed no fear of him, treating him instead as an incorrigible who might yet be saved. And Red's behavior with them was courtly and almost charming. He removed his wool cap; his hair was an inferno. One of his ears had been bitten and chewed. He was a sight to behold.

Up the stairs we went, past the stained-glass depictions of St. Lawrence and the Sacred Heart, and down the hall toward Harry's room, where one of Red's cohorts was sitting in a chair tilted back on two legs against the wall. I left curiosity and be-musement, jolted back to unease. What had Harry done to them? Had they been responsible for his beating? If so, had they returned to finish him off?

I decided this was a foolish thought. If they were a threat to Harry, why would the sisters not have been nervous with them around?

On closer inspection, the man in the chair was not a total stranger. His unlikely moniker was Goo Goo Knox, and I'd seen him with Harry, leaving Harry's flat one night, shortly after I arrived in New York.

When Goo Goo Knox saw us, the front legs of the chair hit the floor and he jumped to his feet. He whipped off his wilted derby and bowed to me. "Nice to see ya, Miss." He didn't wait for me to respond, but said to my escort, who had finally dropped his hold of me, "What's up, Red?"

"She fell in da road and I done me duty."

"Whacha got in da box, Miss?"

"Cookies, Mr. Knox. I was on my way here, and while I don't want to seem ungrateful, I could have done without the keeper, thank you very much."

"We was watchin' you dint get into trouble, Miss," Goo Goo Knox said.

That did it. The ancestor who gave me my green eyes and red hair also bequeathed me my Irish temper. I pointed a furious fin-ger, first at Red Farrell and then Goo Goo Knox, and yelled, "You have no right to interfere in my life."

Would you believe, they flinched? "Now, Miss—" Red Farrell said, "it was a service we done."

"Service? I don't want your service!" My voice rose and I feared I'd do something banal, like stamp my little foot.

Goo Goo jerked his thumb toward Harry's closed door. "We dint do it for youse, we done it for Sherlock."

Chapter Twenty-six

*H*ey—"

When I'm determined, there's no stopping me, as you've no doubt already noticed. I flung open the door, shot into a gin-sodden room adrift in smoke, and slammed the door behind me.

They were sitting on Harry's bed, three of them, one more disreputable than the other. One of them held a bottle in his hand in midmovement. Harry was propped up in a chair, wearing a ghoulish grin, his leg in its plaster resting on the bed. Four pairs of eyes flattened me against the door.

"Olwer," Harry mushmouthed.

One ruffian got up off the bed and sauntered over to me. He wore a long, dark green velvet jacket, baggy trousers, and an aviator type once-white silk around his neck. With his long dark hair, and bushy brows that hung in wiry threads over his black eyes, and his smashed nose, he was no one you would want to encounter on a lonely street at night, or even, for that matter, in broad daylight. He gave me the once-over, as if I were a piece of meat at the Washington Market.

"You can look but you can't touch," I said.

Harry gave the equivalent of a guffaw. "Whad I tell you?"

"Sherlock sez youse okay." He offered me his hand, which was encased in a leather glove. "I'm Ding Dong," he said.

"Olwer," I said, while my hand was being pumped.

"Dat dere's Rubber Shaw, and dat, wit his hat on—where's yer manners—is Kid Yorke."

Kid Yorke bobbed his head; his derby bounced once onto his shoulder, and then dropped into his waiting hand.

It was a performance. I applauded.

His eyes were blue, but bloodshot, his face a freckled meadow. Reddish lips broke into an almost childlike grin at my reaction. One front tooth was missing. I understood why he was called Kid. Rubber Shaw offered me a swig of what was in the bottle, but I shook my head. I was already woozy from the fumes, and I'm a little discerning about with whom I drink. He shrugged and passed it over to Harry, tilting it to his lips. Harry took a hefty swallow. He was definitely feeling better.

I stepped away from the door and the boys offered me the bed, which I took, and on which they quickly joined me. All rather chummy.

Harry listed in his chair. "I think we'd better get him back in bed," I said, getting up. The boys must have agreed with me, because they jumped up and moved a mildly protesting Harry back to the bed, then returned to it themselves. I sat in the newly vacated chair.

"All right, then. What's going on, Harry? Why were you having me followed?"

He squinted at me and said, "Shuh—shuh—Ding Dong—"

I couldn't figure out whether he was trying to shush me or tell me something important. However, his scurrilous chums seemed to know what he meant.

Ding Dong, who was clearly the man in charge, said, "He's tryin' to say youse in danger, Miss. Right, Sherlock?"

Harry nodded. The strength was back in his hands, for he gave mine a squeeze and pointed to Ding Dong.

"He asked us to watch dat nuttin' happened to youse."

"Oh, Harry, really. This is crazy. You're set upon by a jealous husband and you think *I'm* in danger."

Ding Dong's eyes disappeared under his brow. "Jeeze, Sherlock, she's sure got a mout on her."

I was about to give Mr. Dong a little more lip when there

was a knock on the door and my friend, Red Farrell, let Sister Agnes in.

She took in the scene and snapped, "Off the bed. And put out those cigarettes right now, boys, or you'll have to leave. And no hooch." She took Harry's blood pressure and sighed. "Doctor says we can send you home tomorrow, though I rather wonder how fast you'll heal with all these . . . distractions."

Harry chortled and the boys danced around, punching and pommeling each other, as if they'd robbed a bank and gotten away with it.

Sister Agnes took it all in with an air of skepticism.

I said, somewhat apprehensively, "But who will take care of him?" I ignored the growl that Harry was emitting.

"We've arranged for a visiting nurse."

"A noice!" the Duster called Rubber said. "She better be good, because Sherlock is our friend."

"She'll be fine, I'm sure," I said, relieved, although I was certain Mattie would keep Harry well fed and I would look in on him often.

"You have five minutes, boys, and then it's out with you so my patient can rest," Sister Agnes said.

"Tra la," I said under my breath. She didn't hear me, but Ding Dong did, and elbowed his chums, nodding at me with approval.

"Olwer's okay," Ding Dong told Harry.

"All well and good." I opened the cookie tin and offered it around. The boys helped themselves, more daintily than I would have thought, to the delicate sugar cookies. I broke off bits and fed them to Harry. "But before we were interrupted, you were telling me why I needed protection."

"Shwon em," Harry said. The sweat of pure frustration appeared on his upper lip. "Shwon em!"

It was what he'd said that first day I'd seen him after he was attacked. I still couldn't make hide nor hair of it. "I'm sorry," I said. *Shwonem?* "Shwonem." The Dusters were looking at me as if I should know what Harry meant. I didn't.

"Shwon," Harry said, painstakingly.

I repeated, "Shwon." Wait, Harry was having trouble with esses. I eliminated the sh. I had swon. "Swon?" I said.

"Yesh. Sh won."

"Yeah," Ding Dong said. "See? She's gettin' it."

"Sh won," I said. "It's one?"

He was nodding his head like crazy. "Sh won em."

Then I knew what he was trying to tell me and why he'd put the Hudson Dusters on my trail.

He hadn't wanted me to go to the theatre that night. He'd kept saying, "Shwonem." What Harry had been trying to tell me was that whoever had smashed him was one of our group.

It's one of them.

Chapter Twenty-seven

I didn't know how to deal with any of it.

"Sherlock sez one'a youse mutual friends smacked him wit a pipe in da toilet," Ding Dong said conversationally. He licked the sugar residue from his fingers and took the tin box from me and offered it to the others.

"I can't believe that. They're our friends."

"Shtay way fwom them!"

What really frightened me was not the sudden volume in Harry's voice, but I was beginning to understand his butchered speech. "Harry," I said, "You know very well I can't stay away from them. We're doing *The Emperor Jones* again tonight. The critics are coming."

Ding Dong looked to Rubber and Kid. They all nodded in unison. "Weeze gonna watch out for Olwer, Sherlock, so doncha worry none. Right, boys?"

I stopped on Bleecker Street for a bottle of red wine, some Roquefort and a crusty loaf of Italian bread, and went home.

Mattie was standing at the kitchen window looking down at our backyard, where Lizzie, our laundress, was struggling against the wind to bring in the dry linen for ironing. I could see Mattie's attention was somewhere else. On Mr. Gerald Brophy, perhaps.

"Harry's coming home tomorrow," I said. "He's to have a visiting nurse."

Mattie smiled. "Oh, I can just see that." She focused on my bundles. "What have you there?"

"Brain food. A little wine, a little cheese, and a small crusty loaf. I'm sharing."

She shook her head. "I've eaten and I want to do some marketing before the day disappears on me."

"Harry thinks one of our friends hit him with a pipe."

"Dear God." Mattie sat down.

"I don't want you to be frightened, but he's got the Hudson Dusters watching over me. Us." I uncorked the bottle and sniffed. Nice.

"The Hudson Dusters? They're hoodlums, Olivia. Even the police are afraid of them."

"They love Harry, they trust him. I think he uses them in his investigations." I loaded up a tray with my repast, glass, knife for the cheese, and adjourned to my room.

I put a fresh sheet of paper into my type-writer and typed a clean version of my last poem, thinking I would work on something new afterward. I sat and stared at the blank sheet, but it was no use. I couldn't concentrate. I kept thinking: friend.

I pushed back my chair and took a sip of wine. The tray was on my right, perched somewhat precariously on a book of Elinor Wylie's lovely poems. I carried the tray to my bed where it was safe to think I wouldn't get crumbs in my type-writer and so be forced to write paeans to bread and cheese. The type-writer anthropomorphic.

I lay on my bed, tore off a chunk of bread and spread the lumpy Roquefort over it. Crumbs scattered over the spread, but I knew I was safe. The bedspread wouldn't demand a sonnet.

The wine did not work its usual magic, did not take the edge off my anxiety. I could feel myself growing more and more agitated. If Harry was right, someone I knew was trying to hurt me, and I had no idea why. And although I'd hoped that the attack on Harry had nothing to do with me, I couldn't kid myself, or him, anymore. Everything had started with Mackey's death. No, I was wrong. Everything had come out in the open with Mackey's death. The evil had been present, but concealed well, before Mackey.

Whit had been furious with me, but he hadn't killed Mackey. I knew that because we'd been together. But the others: Rae, Bennett, not Jig surely, but even Edward Hall. And Andrew Goren. His behavior was exceeding strange. My cheeks began to burn; I could still feel the sting of his slap on my hand.

In spite of Harry's warnings, I'd invited Andrew into my bed. He could have cut my throat. But he would never have gotten away with it. Mattie had seen him. But what good would that have done? I'd be dead. And they'd have to bury me without my locket.

I sat up and pushed the tray aside. Swallowing had become difficult. Hands shaking, I took a sip of wine. What was I to do?

Wash my face. I got up and did just that. I stared at my face in the mirror. It was a good face, with a saucy nose. Very elegant neck and nice shoulders. Bobbed red, almost copper, hair.

And cold feet. Bare feet. The cold was seeping its way up from the tile of the bathroom floor. I went back to look for my shoes. Shoes. I stopped in my tracks. I hadn't followed up on one lead. The Eppie Diamond shoes. Eppie Diamond had never gotten back to me. Who had ordered them?

I picked up my watch from my desk. There was time for me to swing by Eppie Diamond's house before I was due at the theatre.

This time I dressed with more care, with stockings, put on my green jersey dress with the long sleeves. I was going to be cold in my cape, which was unlined.

I knocked on Mattie's door.

"Come in, Olivia."

She was sitting, sleepy-eyed, in front of the radiator, darning stockings. "I've let them go too long, and here winter's upon us." We both went bare-legged and sandaled until the cold forced us otherwise.

"I've lost my locket," I said, trying to keep my voice steady.

Her needle paused. "It must be in the house somewhere, Olivia. Don't worry now, we'll find it."

"I know." I kissed the top of her head. "I'm off to the theatre."

She took notice of my dress and stockings, but said, "You're earlier than usual."

"I'm going to stop by Eppie Diamond's house to see if she's discovered who sent me those shoes." Actually, I knew she knew who sent them but was holding back. It was time she told.

I took the subway from Sheridan Square to Eighteenth Street, then walked to Eppie Diamond's house, girded to confront her and demand the information. When I turned down Seventeenth Street, I saw that it was partially blocked to traffic and that a small, silent group of people had gathered, appeared to be waiting.

Then an ambulance crept down the street, and passing me, pulled up in front of Eppie Diamond's house.

"What's happened?" I asked a sturdy woman holding a market basket full of parcels.

"It's the lady that lives there. Someone broke in and killed her."

Chapter Twenty-eight

*T*he obituary was not in the evening paper.

I walked through my performance; my concentration was off. The audience couldn't have cared less, because everyone was waiting for *The Emperor Jones*. And when it was over, they stood up on their benches and cheered us. It was thrilling.

Afterward, I had a few beers with Bennett, who was feeling pretty bleak about Mackey, and Stephen Lowell, and the others, at the Working Girls' Home. Edward was hanging around, looking for an opening to talk to me. I didn't give him one. After a while, I didn't see him anymore. Rae and Whit left early. I kept trying to find a moment to talk to Jig about Andrew Goren, but he was surrounded by friends and people who are drawn to success, even so fleeting. For we all knew that Gene was moving uptown, so to speak: that he was taking his plays away from us. The lure of Broadway is compelling.

I didn't feel like going home.

"What's the matter with you, Oliver?" Bennett said, his eyes full of concern. He was waiting for me outside the bathroom door, after my fifth trip.

"Girl stuff." I was afraid to meet his eyes because he'd see at once I was lying. I obfuscated. "Harry's coming home in the morning."

"Well, that's good news, little one." He gave me a loving pat on the head.

Bennett was a dear soul. I felt guilty I couldn't confide in him . . . I shook myself out of the temptation. No one except Harry, I told myself. What I said instead was, "You didn't find my little gold locket at your place, did you?"

"No," he said. "Come have another drink. Stephen is going back to Chicago."

He sat me on the stool between them and signaled for refills. Stephen's arm came round my waist. I loved his touch, the prickle it stirred deep inside me.

"You're leaving," I said. I didn't want him to go, but I knew he had a wife and child in Chicago.

"In the morning."

"I'm sorry."

"I have every reason to be back."

"Stephen, old sport, hands off my girl," Bennett said. The drinks were set before us and the empty glasses removed. He put his arm around my waist also, so that he and Stephen were holding onto each other as well as me. It was sweet, I thought.

When they walked me home, I gave each a kiss good night, and as they went off I could hear them arguing pleasantly about whom I'd kissed with more fervor.

> *Certain kisses demonstrate*
> *Fondness, though don't relate*
> *To lusty thoughts and deep desires*
> *That serious love in truth inspires.*
> *But darlings, you, and you, and you,*
> *Dearest friends, so tried and true,*
> *I would not lead you on to dream*
> *There's more to us than it may seem.*

The words had spilled recklessly from my fingertips to the keys onto the paper. I was writing avoidance poetry. I pulled the poem from the type-writer, sent it spinning to the floor, and rolled in a fresh sheet.

The soul dies slowly, withering away
Without constant care. It hungers for
The clean, fresh air, the sunny day
For thoughts so pure they can restore
Diminished center, balance, intuition,
The intricate asymmetry. Fruition.

I slept not at all that night. The wind rattled my windows and leaked through the walls. I shivered under the blankets, unable psychically to keep warm. Sat up, and smoked another cigarette. My throat was raw and I had a gigantic headache. Finally, around five o'clock I pulled on Great-Aunt Evangeline's sweater over my nightdress, went downstairs, and brewed myself a pot of tea. I was too queasy for coffee.

My house spoke to me, muted whispers in door frames . . . Take care . . . tread softly . . . Murmurs rose from floorboards . . . Listen . . . listen . . .

Mattie caught me nodding over a cup of tepid tea and an early proof of Elinor Wylie's "Nets to Catch the Wind," which her publisher had sent me for comment. The nodding, I hasten to say, had nothing to do with Miss Wylie's lovely poems.

I felt I was having a kind of nervous breakdown. My work was suffering. I was ill. It was time for Harry to come home. I missed my anchor.

"You look dreadful, Olivia," Mattie said, her face suffused with worry. She filled the kettle and lit the stove, planting the kettle right on the heat. The heat thawed me slightly, but I shivered without cease. She put her hand to my forehead. "You have a fever. Go on up to bed. I'll bring a hot-water bottle."

"Hangover," I said. "Nothing more."

"You will put yourself in the hospital, for sure."

I got up, a trifle unsteady on my feet, I have to admit. "Eppie Diamond's been murdered," I said.

"Eppie Diamond? The shoe lady?" Four little cubes of sugar went into a cup, then tea leaves into the teapot. "How do you know that?"

"I went to see her yesterday. There were police going in and out of her house, and an ambulance. Someone said she'd been killed."

"Well, you don't know that for sure, Olivia, and this has nothing to do with you. I worry about you. You get so involved in other people's lives."

"Oh, Mattie, it's connected to us, don't you see? She's—she was—Andrew Goren's mother. Mackey worked for her. And Mackey's dead. I think she knew who sent me those shoes. And now she's dead."

"Up to bed with you," Mattie said firmly.

"If you promise you'll get me the morning papers."

"Olivia!" But she promised because she saw I was adamant, and that it would get me up to bed.

I had a vague memory of the hot-water bottle and the toasty feeling, but I was already more than half asleep.

Sometime later, the doorbell woke me, setting off a chain reaction. My heart and my head took antiphonal turns pounding. A wave of soaking perspiration wet my nightdress and the bedclothes.

I pulled the covers up to my chin and waited. Mattie's soft timbre came to me, then others, not so soft, more demanding. Men. Then quiet. The pounding in my head began to subside. I was safe. I slept.

When next I woke, I felt more myself. And I was hungry. I lay still, listening to my world. I could hear traffic on the street below. A dog barked. I became aware that the wind had stopped. Sunlight glimmered through the draperies.

I was trying to sit up when Mattie opened the door to check on me. "I'm awake," I said.

She smiled at me. "So I see. Stay right where you are, Olivia. I'll bring up a tray."

"And the newspapers?"

"And the newspapers." She left me. Had there been a hesitation in her voice? Something she was keeping from me?

"Is Harry okay?" I asked when she returned, tray in hand, newspapers under her arm.

"I have two patients," she said. "I want both of you to behave, do you hear?" She set the tray on my desk, with the newspapers, and plumped up my pillows. I sat up, watching her for some hint of what she was up to. Because she definitely was keeping something from me.

She slid the tray over my legs. Buttered toast, marmalade, hot tea and a glass of orange juice. I started with the orange juice, which was thick with pulp. "Oranges in November?" I said. "Spendthrift."

"Eat and don't talk," Mattie said. She pulled over my desk chair and sat down. I noticed she left the newspapers where they were.

"What's in the papers about Eppie Diamond?"

"That she's dead."

"Mattie! How did she die?" I finished the last bit of toast, drained my tea, and moved the tray so I could slide my legs out onto the floor.

"Back in your bed, Olivia Brown." Mattie shook her finger at me. "I'll not have you getting sick, too. I'll be busy enough with him downstairs."

"Okay, then, tell me how she died."

"It was cruel," she said, shuddering. "Same as the other but worse."

"How can anything be worse?"

She brought me the newspapers. "It's not in the papers, how it was done."

"Then how do you know?"

"Gerry Brophy and Mr. Walz were here earlier to talk to you. They told me she was cut from ear to ear—I can't even talk about it without my stomach pitching and rolling."

I leaned over and patted her hand. "Don't say anything more. I don't see how I can help them. Did they say why they want to talk to me?"

"Olivia, where were you yesterday afternoon?"

"Mattie, you don't think—"

"No, I don't, although you did say you were going to see Eppie Diamond before you went to the theatre."

"But I told you, by the time I arrived, the police were there and she was dead. Her maid can verify that, I'm sure."

"She'd sent her maid out on an errand. The police think you were there at three o'clock."

This was truly exasperating. "Mattie, dear, that's ridiculous. How could they? I didn't even leave here until four."

"I know that, Olivia, and I told them it was impossible, but your name was in Eppie Diamond's appointment book for three o'clock."

Chapter Twenty-nine

$\mathcal{H}$arry's door was ajar.

"Moicer?"

I recognized Ding Dong's unmistakable tones.

"Yeah," Harry said, "See what you come up with."

Pressing the toe of my sandal against the door, I nudged, but the squeak, which I had forgotten about, gave me away.

Ding Dong jerked the door open full, his face a terrifying scowl. "Olwer!" he exclaimed, putting two fingers to his derby. Rubber Shaw actually took his cap off for a moment, then back it went on his hairless dome.

"Good day to you, Mr. Ding Dong, Mr. Shaw. Harry. I hope I'm not interrupting," I said, knowing I was. *Moicer.*

Harry was on his feet—well, not quite. He leaned in a lop-sided way on a crutch. He flicked his eyes from me to his disreputable pals, who were pawing the ground, like high-strung stallions, anxious to get going.

"See ya, Sherlock." Ding Dong gave Rubber a poke and the two of them ducked out the door.

Harry set his crutch on his desk, which was remarkably clean, and sat down in the only chair, now shockingly devoid of stacks of papers.

"I'll never find anything ever again," he grumbled. His pronunciation was sharper and his face, though a kaleidoscope of colors, was starting to look almost human.

I took out my case and offered him a cigarette, then fit one into my holder. Bending to catch a light from his match, I smelled less antiseptic, more gin. And orange juice. "Mattie's been plying you with orange juice?"

"It's not bad with a little gin."

"I see she's also cleaned up. God, I've never seen the place so neat."

"I'm ruined." Morose, he bobbed his head toward the scarred oak filing cabinet. "It's all in there now, alphabetically." Since I'd known him, I'd never seen him open it.

"I suppose that was Great-Aunt Evangeline's."

"She parked everything we worked on in there, very organized, case by case. I never looked at it."

"Were you in the middle of a case? I can finish it up for you."

"Only yours."

I waited for him to continue, ask a question, or something. I began to pace the small room, which I could now do because there were no obstacles except for a sack on the floor near the door. Since Harry didn't seem inclined to say anything further, I felt the compulsion to fill the void.

I said, "So it seems." And still he said nothing, inhaling and exhaling with conspicuous pleasure. "Eppie Diamond's been murdered. Same modus operandi as Mackey. Did you know?" When I passed the sack again, I took a look at its contents. Apples. A donation no doubt from one of the Dusters' neighbors. I helped myself to one, rubbed it on my dress to make the skin shine, then took a bite. "The boys are thoughtful, but how're you going to manage to eat an apple?"

"I guess they figured you'd cut it up in small pieces for me, Olwer." He gave me that ghoulish grin.

"You know me, Harry. I'm not handy with a knife."

"Someone is."

"Yes." I sat on his broken-down sofa and we both pondered the situation.

"Before she died, she didn't by any chance tell you who ordered those shoes, did she?"

"What do you mean, 'before she died'? I didn't see her yesterday."

"Yesterday, the day before, the day before that. Who cares? Besides, Goo Goo Knox followed you over there."

"Then he knows I never went inside, that I never saw her. He can tell that to the police."

"Don't count on it, Oliver. They don't have much love for the cops or the cops for them. You need an alibi?"

"My name was in her appointment book for three o'clock. I got there around four forty-five."

"Why were you late?"

"I wasn't late. I don't know why my name was in her appointment book."

"Ah . . ."

"Yes."

"Merde," Harry said. He looked at the charred stub in his hand. I offered him a new one, and he lit it from the other.

I agreed. "I did find the old lady who makes those rag dolls. She's blind, but when I approached her in Washington Square Park, before I even spoke she called me Miss Brown."

"How could she—"

"My perfume. Roses. She asked me how my friend liked the doll. As soon as I spoke she knew I wasn't the person who called herself Olivia Brown. It was eerie, Harry. All her dolls have yellow wool hair. This person had special-ordered one with red hair. Mackey was pretending to be me when he ordered the doll. He told her it was a gift for a friend."

"With red hair."

I nodded. "And someone else delivered the goods to me in the water bucket. What is symbolic about the water bucket, Harry?"

"He was in the house, Oliver. He finished your poem. Something scared him off and he left the way he'd come—out the back door and through the gardens. I think he intended to leave the doll in your room."

"So you're saying the water pail might have been an afterthought?"

"Yes. He wanted to get rid of it. He had no way of knowing

you'd find it yourself, but he could be certain that whoever found it would let you know."

We sat in amicable silence again, until I said, "What do we do now?"

"We see what my boys come up with."

"You sent them to find Andrew? Is that why they were going to Mercer Street?"

He looked at me a long time, his expression unchanged. I began to squirm. "Oliver, you—" He took a long drag on his cigarette and managed to look disappointed in me.

So he knew. The Dusters must have been watching the house. "Aw, Harry," I said, "I didn't intend it, it just happened. He came and read me his play—"

"And you fell in love with him," Harry said, with exaggerated irony.

I was contrite. "I did. And, Harry, it was so beautiful . . . until—"

"Until?"

"I'd forgotten I'd invited Rae and Whit over for drinks. And Bennett brought Stephen Lowell. Andrew was furious. I couldn't very well tell them to go away and come back another time, could I? Andrew left in a rage, and I haven't seen him since. Nor do I want to. I'm going to tell Jig I can't do the play." I smiled. "So I'm all yours. Put me to work."

"Until you fall in love again."

"Pshaw, Harry. Why should it be different for me than for a man?"

"All right, Oliver. See what you can find out about Eppie Diamond. But be subtle."

"I'm always subtle, Harry. What do I do about those two detectives, Brophy and Walz? Mattie didn't wake me when they were here earlier. They'll be back."

"Tell them the truth. I mean, that she was tracking down who ordered the shoes. That's all. Do not offer any further information."

"Okay." It was a struggle to get out of Harry's sofa since it was so low to the ground. When I was on my feet, I remembered my locket. "Harry, my little gold locket . . . I seem to have lost it. Did you find it here?"

"You're asking me? Ask Mattie."

"I did. She hasn't seen it."

"It'll probably turn up."

"It has." We heard Walz's voice before we saw the detective. I'd left Harry's door open and who knows how long Walz and Brophy had stood there before Walz spoke.

"Don't you guys believe in knocking?" Harry said.

"The door was open," Walz said.

"We heard you asking about your locket when we came in," Brophy offered.

Walz glared at him, which meant they probably hadn't heard anything previous to that.

"Did you find my locket, Mr. Walz?" I asked.

"We most certainly did, Miss Brown. Show her the locket, Brophy."

Brophy took a locket from a small envelope and held it up. The chain was broken, but it was mine. Tears came to my eyes. I was so glad to see it again. "Oh, thank you." I held out my hand. "Wherever did you find it?"

"Put it away, Brophy," Walz said.

"I don't understand." I looked at Harry, bewildered. Leaning heavily on his desk, Harry raised himself to his feet. What was he thinking? I turned back to Walz and Brophy. "Why can't I have my locket?"

"It's evidence, Miss Brown," Walz said. "We found it clenched in Miss Eppie Diamond's hand."

Chapter Thirty

*W*alz didn't arrest me, though I could see ego was fighting it out with logic.

"I lost my locket sometime during the past week," I said in an embarrassingly tiny voice.

"You don't have anything, Walz," Harry said.

"I have the locket—"

Harry made a rude noise. "Someone could have planted it. What time was Eppie Diamond killed?"

"Her maid found her at four o'clock," Brophy said.

Walz added, "And I have the appointment book with Miss Brown's name written very clearly at three o'clock."

My voice came back with my outrage. "Aside from the fact that I was still here when she was killed, how could I have cut Eppie Diamond's throat and not have been covered with blood when I got to the theatre at five?"

"You could have come home and washed up."

"Let me get this straight, Walz," Harry said. "She could have come home on the street, covered with blood, and not be seen by anyone?"

Walz clung stubbornly to his hypothesis. "Someone of your description was seen in front of Miss Diamond's house after the murder."

I sighed. "I went to see her last week about a pair of shoes that were sent to me without a card. She promised to check on who had ordered them and get back to me. But Mackey was her assistant, as you are well aware, and so I didn't hear from her. I stopped by to remind her, but the police were in front of the house and someone told me she was dead. That someone could have told you I was not covered with blood." From his slight eye movement, I knew I was right. "I went directly from there to the theatre."

"What did she tell you that made you kill her?" Walz demanded, sticking his ugly mug right in my face. I stood my ground, a difficult task, for he had the breath of a gorilla in heat.

"Jesus Christ, Walz!" Harry smacked his desk with his crutch. "Look at her. She's a little bit of a thing. Do you honestly think she could hold someone down and cut a throat at the same time?"

"It's all right, Harry. You see, I don't fit Mr. Walz's concept of a nice girl, so therefore I must be a murderer."

"Miss Br—"

"And he knows I'm not. He knows that someone is trying to hurt me. But he thinks I'm to blame because I live my own life."

Harry laughed out loud. "If you have nothing to add to that, Walz, don't let the door hit you in the ass on your way out."

"We're not finished here, Melville," Walz said, shaking his head vigorously, like a frustrated bulldog unwilling to let go of a bone.

I asked Brophy, "May I have my locket?"

"It's evidence," Walz said.

"The chain must have broken when I was at Eppie Diamond's to ask about the shoes."

"Shoes again? Where are they? I want to see them."

I looked at Harry. He nodded, sat back down in his chair, his face beginning to show the strain. His leg resting on his desk again, he closed his eyes.

"The day after Whit and I found Mackey's body," I said, "a beautifully wrapped package was delivered to me here. When I opened it I saw a pair of new shoes, like the ones Mackey had been wearing when he died. There was no card."

"Sure," Walz said. He lit a cigarette and leaned against the wall, smoking it aggressively.

Brophy put my locket back into the envelope, decidedly uncomfortable. I wondered how much Mattie had told him.

"You should have told us about this, Miss Brown. Let's see them."

"I don't have them. Had I told you about them, you would have made light of it, as you've done with everything else I've told you. I checked with the fashion people at *Vanity Fair* and found they were handmade by a woman named Eppie Diamond." While this was not strictly true, it was close enough.

"I'm taking you very seriously now, Miss Brown." He couldn't have been more sarcastic. "Where are they?"

"At Eppie Diamond's insistence, I left them with her. She said her assistant was ill but he would know for whom they'd been made. Mackey was—"

"We know that," Walz said.

"I think she knew very well who had ordered them."

"Why do you say that?"

"She recognized the shoes I was wearing as the very same shoes she'd made for someone else. That person had given them to me."

"Would you recognize the shoes you left with her if you saw them again?"

"Perhaps. I'm willing to try, though I don't know what good it will do if Eppie Diamond's not here to tell us who—"

"Brophy, set it up, will you? How about later today?"

"Okay." Walz seemed to have softened some, so I said, "Mr. Walz, my locket is of great sentimental value. It was given me by my late fiancé before he left for France. I would dearly love to have it back."

"Give it here, Brophy," he said, holding out his beefy hand.

His fingers on my locket transmigrated to my throat. I had the most uncomfortable smothering sensation. He tried to open it, and failing, with his clumsy fingers, gave it to me. "Open it," he said.

It was a delicate piece, having belonged to Franklin's grandmother. I opened it, eager for the odd comfort I take in seeing his dear face.

Walz's voice intruded on me from far off. "Is that your late fiancé, Miss Brown?"

I had to hold the locket with both hands to keep from dropping it. The face staring back at me was not Franklin's. It was Andrew Goren's.

Chapter Thirty-one

The room began to pitch and keel. I felt as if someone were holding me underwater. And me with no gills. Why was this happening?

Thanks to Gerry Brophy, I was able to get back to the sofa without fainting dead away. Through a haze I saw faces close to mine, enlarged and pulled like saltwater taffy in the making.

Something tickled my nostrils. The piquant juniper fragrance of gin. Harry's voice: "Let's see that locket." He held his flask to my lips and dribbled a few drops into my receptive mouth.

"Where is it, Brophy?" Walz demanded.

"Don't know."

"Find it."

"I have it." I opened my hand. I'd been holding onto it so tightly that it had dug a hole in my palm.

Harry took the locket and put a drop of gin on my wound. The pain burned the haze away. He was staring at the picture in my locket. He knew it wasn't Franklin, else I would never have reacted as I did. "Who is this, Oliver?"

I could hardly get the words out. "An—Andrew Goren."

"Right," Walz said. "The nut who identified Theodore Mackey."

"Why do you call him a nut?" Harry asked with a straight

face. I knew he agreed with Walz but was fishing for information.

"Never you mind, Melville. You keep your nose out of police business."

I couldn't resist saying, "Mr. Walz has no use for bohemians, Harry. He thinks we're all nuts."

Harry laughed. "It's a tough precinct they've got you in, isn't it, Walz?"

Walz seethed. "Maybe they didn't hit you hard enough, Melville."

"Get over it, Walz," Harry said. "This is the way of the world."

"What is Andrew Goren's picture doing in my locket?" I asked, finally pulling myself together. "And where is Franklin's?"

"You tell us, Miss Brown."

"I have nothing to tell you, Mr. Walz."

"Stop badgering her, Walz," Harry said. He patted me on the head and went back to his chair, taking my locket with him.

"I thought I told you to stay out of our business, Melville."

"You are talking to my client, Walz, so back off," Harry growled. With the tip of his penknife, he pried Andrew Goren's photograph from my locket, then shook his head. "Nothing underneath."

It made me sad. With the loss of Franklin's photograph, I was now cut off for good from my past life. "When I last saw my locket, gentlemen," I said, "Franklin's picture was in it. I have no idea how Andrew Goren's got there."

"But you know Andrew Goren?"

"Yes." I caught Harry's look and buttoned my lip. I unwound myself from the sofa and held out my hand for the flask. "May I have more medicine, Harry?"

"How well do you know Andrew Goren, Miss Brown?"

"Miss Brown has nothing more to say in the matter," Harry said amiably. "Take a walk, boys."

"I'll have that locket," Walz said. He motioned for Brophy to take it from Harry. Harry snapped it shut and handed it over.

"Miss Brown," Brophy said, dropping my locket back in the envelope, "Our men should be finished with Miss Diamond's house by early afternoon. If you can meet me there at three o'clock, we can search for those shoes. Is that convenient?"

I nodded, ignoring Walz's snort. Obviously, further research on Eppie Diamond would have to wait. "I'm perfectly willing to do all I can to find Eppie Diamond's murderer, officers, because I think whoever it was is threatening me as well."

Harry lit a cigarette and raised his leg up on his desk again. "It's quite possible, Walz, that this whole affair has nothing to do with my client."

"Let's go, Brophy."

Harry smirked. "Don't you want to stay and hear my theory?"

"Not really, Melville." Walz went out the door. Brophy, left behind, shrugged apologetically.

"Well, I'll tell you my theory, Brophy," Harry said. "You're a better listener anyway."

"Brophy!" Walz stuck his head back in the door.

"This is about Eppie Diamond, not Olivia Brown. Mark my words. The answer will be found in Miss Diamond's life."

"What about the milk bottle, the doll, the intruder, the locket, the similarity between Mr. Mackey and Miss Brown?" Brophy asked, taking what Harry said seriously.

"A whole other thing," Harry said.

I thought, that could be, and I think he said it to reassure me, but I knew and he knew it wasn't true. The answer might lie with Eppie Diamond, but I was caught up in it as surely as a mouse in a maze.

"You mean," I said, "that someone not connected to the murders is tormenting me."

"It's possible."

"It's not," Walz said. "Come on, Brophy."

I stopped him. "Mr. Walz, have you talked with her son yet?"

He came back into the room. "Her son?"

"Yes. The man in my locket. Andrew Goren."

"Miss Brown, are you saying Andrew Goren is Eppie Diamond's son?"

"Yes." Harry and I exchanged glances. What was going on?

Walz chortled. "See, what did I tell you, Brophy? My dear Miss Brown, Eppie Diamond didn't have a son."

Chapter Thirty-two

I am in a maze," I said. "I keep trying to get out, but every way I turn takes me deeper and deeper."

Harry must have heard the desperation in my voice because he said, "But there is a way out, and we'll find it. Let's wait and see what my boys come up with."

When the doorbell rang we both were startled. I opened the door and saw Kid Yorke, a dead stump of a cigar between his teeth, gripping the arm of a terrified woman in nurse's garb. In her other hand she carried a medical bag made of black leather.

"Oh, thank the good Lord," she cried. "I'm Nurse Newberger. I'm here to see a Mr. Harry Melville."

"Mr. Yorke," I said. "I think you're being overzealous in your duties." I could hear Harry laughing behind me, and turned round and said, "It's not funny, Harry. Here's Nurse Newberger being manhandled when she's come to see to your health."

"It's okay, Kid," Harry called, sounding somewhat overwhelmed.

Kid Yorke dropped Nurse Newberger's arm. "Apologies, Missus," he said. "Just doin' me duty."

I stepped aside to let Nurse Newberger in and watched Kid Yorke cross the street and park himself on the stoop of a brownstone. He lit his trace of a cigar and smoked it with aplomb.

When I came back to Harry, Nurse Newberger had helped him move to the Murphy bed and was listening to his heart. I waited until she was finished, then said, "I'm Mr. Melville's friend, Olivia Brown. Do you need anything?"

"What Mr. Melville needs is rest and quiet, and healthy meals," she said. She was a tall, statuesque woman in her middle thirties, Semitic in feature, her black hair rolled up under her visiting-nurse's cap. "Not cigarettes, bad company, and gin."

"She doesn't mean you, Oliver," Harry said. His voice was weak, and I knew I bore the blame.

"Yes, I do, Miss Brown," Nurse Newberger said. She plumped the pillows and made Harry lie back, covering him with a blanket. When she took his pulse she frowned.

"He had a good breakfast this morning, Nurse Newberger," I said, contrite. "Mattie, my housekeeper, is making Harry's meals."

"It might be a good idea for me to talk to her," the nurse said. She took a small container from her bag. Harry's eyes were closed and he wasn't saying anything.

I beat a hasty retreat while Nurse Newberger's back was turned and sent Mattie downstairs.

A fresh pot of coffee sat waiting for me on the kitchen stove. The morning paper lay on a tray along with a plate of buttered toast and a boiled egg in its cup. I poured coffee into a cup and carried everything up to my room. Though I had very little appetite, I knew I couldn't exist on love and gin and cigarettes for much longer.

Moving my papers and books aside, I set the tray on my desk next to my type-writer. With the back of my spoon, I cracked the top of the shell and removed it. Steam curled upward. I dug into the egg. The food disappeared with my hardly noticing. I was trying to understand Andrew Goren. Who was he really and what did he want of me?

I lit a cigarette. With my exhale, perfectly formed rings rose in the air. I picked up the newspaper.

An elegant Eppie Diamond, much younger than the one I'd met, stared out at me from the photograph attached to the article on her death. The headline read: DESIGNER MEETS VIOLENT DEATH.

Legendary shoe designer, Eppie Diamond, 50, was found murdered in her home on 17th Street, in Chelsea late yesterday afternoon. According to a police spokesman, Sgt. Louis Vogel, Miss Diamond's body was discovered by her maid, Camille Chaude, at four-thirty when she returned from an errand. "The victim was in a second-floor sitting room with her throat slashed," Sgt. Vogel said. He said investigators had found no sign of forced entry into the house, had recovered no weapons at the scene, and had not determined a motive.

In an addendum to that article, there followed another:

Members of the fashion community expressed shock and sorrow for the passing of Miss Eppie Diamond, famous for her individually designed shoes. Clients of the world-renowned designer have been sending messages of condolence to her home from all over the world. Madame Ilona Gabori, hat designer, said, "She was the last of a kind. Everything was made to order, so by looking at the shoes she could tell who she'd created them for, even after many years." Funeral arrangements have not been made. There are no survivors.

I set the newspaper aside and rolled a fresh sheet of paper into my type-writer.

> *Friends and lovers, come one and all*
> *I have a tale to tell*
> *Of death defied and life recalled,*
> *Of Orpheus in hell.*
>
> *Speak then, piano, from the grave*
> *Of love and death, those two connivers.*
> *Funeral arrangements have not been made,*
> *For there are truly no survivors.*

I stared at the words I'd written. My eyes lost their focus. I left
the poem in the type-writer and went to bed. It was the
strangest feeling, as if she were talking to me from her grave.
What was she trying to tell me?

Or was there something buried in my own unconscious,
thank you, Siggie. I lay there smoking, watching ashes float from
the tip of my cigarette and flake my bosom with gray, unmelt-
ing snow. Stubbing out the cigarette, I buried my face in my pillow. She was trying to tell me something.

Just as I was drifting off to sleep an errant thought whisked
across my poor brain: *the piano*.

Chapter Thirty-three

A huge, almost grotesque, funeral wreath marked Eppie Diamond's door. Densely perfumed lilies, the color of poor pearls, waxy and cold, the huge black taffeta bow lacquered stiff. In rigor, mortis.

Otherwise, the house looked much as it had when I first saw it. Yet its very melancholia was evident in the drawn curtains and the heavy silence separating it from the other houses around. It was not the cold that made me shiver.

At the top of the grand stairs, a bulging mail sack rested against the lion on the right balustrade. Both lions looked bereft and faintly ridiculous in the black taffeta bows about their stone necks.

The low gate before the small flagstoned square at the entrance to Eppie Diamond's workshop wore a smaller version of the wreath on the front door. No sign of life came from the workshop. The leafless dogwood in front was a grief-sticken gray. I didn't open the gate, but I did wonder where Gerry Brophy was and where I was supposed to be.

I climbed the stairs and used the woman's-shoe brass knocker. On the street below, life continued. People went to market, goods were delivered, nursemaids held the hands of toddling children.

The maid Camille let me in with barely a nod, then reached down and dragged the mail sack after us. Her uniform was wrinkled, the cuffs and collar soiled.

"I am sorry for your loss," I said.

She dismissed me with puffed and swollen eyes. "Detective Brophy is in the upstairs sitting room." Reaching behind me for the sack of mail, she pulled it down the hall and out of sight.

May I take your cloak, Miss Brown? I asked myself. Definitely, I responded, and do have a look into the closet while you're at it. Thank you, I will.

The closet to my left was such that unless one knew it was there, one would not know it was there. I've seen their like once or twice in my limited worldly experience. The door opened if you pressed the right spot on the chair rail. Camille had done it when I was last here. My fingers searched, found the tiny knob, and the door opened. A light went on within. I stepped into the closet, my cloak over my arm.

Coats, shawls, carriage blankets, hats. Walking sticks and umbrellas. I hung my cloak from an empty hook, and slowly turned, letting my eyes explore the cave.

"Miss Brown?"

Brophy's voice.

"Miss Brown." Now he was coming down the stairs to catch me in the act.

I wondered if he knew about the closet. Maybe not. I stepped out of the closet and must have given him a mighty scare, for he jumped. "What—what—?" he sputtered.

"I'm hanging up my coat, Mr. Brophy."

"Is that a closet? We don't know about a closet there. How do you know about it?" The poor man was so agitated he blathered, which was totally foreign to the Gerry Brophy I'd come to know, however slightly. He was a decent man and Mattie liked him, so I took pity on him.

"I saw it when I came here with the shoes and Camille took my coat. This time, she let me fend for myself, which I do fairly well, you must admit." I stepped aside. "Come have a look."

He did just that, muttering, "I'll have to get someone back here to go through it." He stepped out and I closed the door, waiting for his exclamation. It came quickly. "How do you open it?"

Smiling, I took his hand before he could resist and guided his fingers along the chair rail until they touched the knob, when the door opened. "It's wonderful, isn't it?" I asked, forgetting momentarily why I was here.

He smiled back at me and closed the door. "Thank you, Miss Brown."

"You're very welcome, Mr. Brophy. But you may call me Olivia. You and only you, not Mr. Walz. And I shall call you Gerry, as Mattie does, if I may."

Brophy, blushing, ushered me up the stairs.

No Chopin, no music whatever, although the room was the same one I'd been in before. The grand piano remained as it had been, but closed, with a dusting of white powder. A now silent witness to a murder. What was not as it had been was the vast ruby stain on the pale-colored Aubusson and the cloying smell that came with it. I stood in the doorway. I didn't want to be here. When I turned to say as much to Gerry Brophy, I saw he was watching me closely. "Have I passed or failed?" I asked.

"This is the room Miss Diamond saw you in?" Brophy asked.

"Yes. She was playing a Chopin étude. She was quite good."

"Did you touch the piano?"

"No. I sat in that chair." I pointed to the bergère. "And waited until she finished playing."

"And then?"

"She asked me if I was Olivia Brown, the poet. And when I said yes, she told me I was very good. I told her why I'd come and she took the shoes from me, saying her secretary was ill and she would get back to me. I've told you all this."

"It doesn't hurt to hear it again."

I was losing my patience. "Do you want me to look at the shoes?"

"I'm waiting for Carmine Colangelo." He took out his pocket watch. "He should have been here by now."

"Who is Carmine Colangelo?"

"He ran Miss Diamond's workshop. He made every shoe she designed."

The ringing of a telephone came from somewhere below. Brophy went out on the landing. I drifted into the room toward the piano.

"Miss Chaude?"

I heard Camille's voice and Brophy's. The piano said not a word. Had they finished with their fingerprint harvest, I wondered.

"Do you play, Miss—Olivia?" Brophy was back.

"Yes. May I? I don't want to disturb fingerprints or anything like that."

"We have finished with fingerprints," Brophy said.

I sat down at the piano, uncovered the keys. With my fingertips, I dusted the powder from the keys. The piano was beseeching me to play. I did not play Chopin. Instead, I chose Beethoven's Sonata in F Minor, the "Appassionata." About love, not death.

As soon as I began I ran into a problem with the F-minor chord. Something was wrong. The fingerprint powder had gotten into the works. I looked at Brophy, tried again. It was impossible. I opened the lid farther, propping it. It was as if something were holding back the chords.

Suddenly, Brophy, who stood behind me, grunted. He took my shoulders and moved me out of the way. "Mother of God," he said. He removed a handkerchief from his pocket, wrapped it around his hand, and reached into the body of the piano.

With a slight tug, he pulled out what had been obstructing the chords and held it in his hand, a look of horror on his face.

"What is that monstrous thing?" I said. Try as I might, I couldn't keep my voice from trembling. I had never seen anything like it.

"This is a trench knife," Brophy said.

Chapter Thirty-four

"A trench knife?" What I saw was a short knife with a brass guard in the shape of knuckles. I did not doubt that it was a lethal weapon. "It looks like something wielded at the Battle of Hastings."

"Not so ancient," Brophy said, troubled. "We used them in the trenches. They're made for hand-to-hand combat."

We? Now here was an interesting image to contemplate.

This discovery had opened the door to all manner of suppositions. Who would own a trench knife? I said, "Does this mean that the murderer of Mackey and Eppie Diamond was a soldier?"

"I don't know what it means, Miss . . . Olivia. We don't yet know if we have one, or two, murderers. These knives were standard issue in the War, and we brought them home as souvenirs afterward."

"You have one?"

He nodded. He was unable to keep his eyes from the brutal weapon, and I wondered, had our nice Gerry Brophy actually killed with one of these weapons?

"I've got to take this in," he said.

"What about the shoe man?"

Brophy looked at me blankly, then gave himself a visible shake. "Oh, I'm sorry. The shoe man. Colangelo. Someone telephoned.

His son is ill. We're going to have to ask you to come back another time."

"If there's a card file, I could look through the records now
while I'm here." I tried to keep my voice flat and disinterested.
Eppie Diamond was able to recognize every pair of shoes made
in her studio; therefore, she must have detailed records, even
drawings or photographs of each on a filing card.

"I'd just as soon be here with you and Mr. Colangelo when
we do that, Miss . . . Olivia." He sent me a little smile.

Oh, dear, he was onto me.

Instead of going home like a good girl, I walked toward Seventh Avenue, with every intention of taking the subway uptown
to Madame Ilona Gabori's atelier, which, according to the card
she'd given me, was on Madison Avenue. But what can I say
about best intentions? Nothing particularly brilliant.

When I reached Seventh Avenue and Seventeenth Street, battered by the cold wind, I realized I was only two blocks from
Ainslee's. Edward still hadn't paid me for the last two poems they'd
printed. I debated with myself. Did I want to see Edward? The
money would come in handy right now, as we had had to replace
the back door and install the new locks front and back. If I could
pry even twenty-five dollars from Edward, I'd go right over to
Messrs. Lord and Taylor and buy myself a warm winter coat.

The money won. At No. 79 Seventh Avenue, I climbed the
stairs to the second floor. Two years ago, I'd sent three poems to
Ainslee's and Edward Hall had responded with a lovely letter and
a check for all three poems. I was overwhelmed by his warmth
and his praise. So I was probably already a little in love with him
by the time Mattie and I moved to Bedford Street and Edward
came to call.

Ainslee's magazine is published from two tiny, cramped rooms,
overflowing with paper and books. Nothing like the smart elegance of *Vanity Fair*.

"Come in," Edward called, in response to my knock.

I popped my head in, feet outside, ready for flight. Only the
top of Edward's head could be seen over a ponderous stack of
manuscripts. "Am I interrupting?" Oh, God, I sounded like a
trilling ingenue.

"Oliver! Come in, come in." He jumped up, delighted to see me. His open arms made contact with the stack of manuscripts. Tottering somewhat indecisively, they began to slide, then gathering momentum, crashed to the floor.

"Oh, dear." I crouched to help gather them up.

"Never mind," he said, crouching beside me. Our knees touched; his lips trembled close to mine.

How, I wondered, do I get myself into these situations? "Edward." I stood up quickly, took out my cigarette case. "I came by in the hope that you could pay me for the last two poems."

He got to his feet. "You can't blame a guy," he said ruefully. I offered him a cigarette and he took one. "I don't understand how you can give me up for Whitney Sawyer. He has no depth whatever and he's morally dishonest to the core."

"He's not as bad as you've painted him." We were both smoking by this time.

"He'll end up on Wall Street," Edward said, disgusted.

"Besides, I've broken it off with him."

"Come back to me, Oliver. I love you. We'll marry, you'll keep writing, I'll keep editing. We'll never be rich, but we'll have a creative life. Our children would be—"

"Stop, Edward. You know I love you, in my way. But it is I who would be morally dishonest if we stayed together."

"Oh, Oliver." He shook his head, though I knew he understood what I'd said.

"What about the money for my poems?"

"There isn't any money right now. Come have lunch with me. I need some advice."

On Fourteenth Street there is an Irish saloon called lyrically, The Harp, where for the price of a nickel beer, we ate thick slabs of hot corned beef on rye bread, and boiled potatoes. It is frequented by workmen, writers and artists, all of whom know a bargain when they see one.

I'd just taken a bite of my hefty sandwich when Edward said, "What is this business I hear about you and Mackey? Was he pretending to be you when he was killed?"

I set the sandwich down, unable to control a shudder. "Looks like it, though it's all beyond me. Someone is trying to frighten me." The beer was thick and dark and foamy. I took a hearty swallow to calm my nerves.

Edward put his hand over mine. "Or worse?"

"No." I pulled my hand away. "Why do you say that?"

"You need someone to look after you, Oliver."

"There, you see, Edward, you don't understand me at all." I picked up my sandwich again. "What was it you wanted advice about?"

"We may have to close down."

"Oh, Edward. I'm so sorry. What will you do?"

"I've had an offer from *Vogue*. If I take it, will you let me have your poems again?"

"Of course. But I still have a commitment to *Vanity Fair*."

"I'm sure we can match what they pay."

I picked up the crumbs of my sandwich with the tip of my finger. "I guess what this means is that I won't get paid for my last two poems."

"I'd pay you myself, if I could." Edward put a quarter down on the table. "How is Harry?"

"He's home and complaining like crazy—"

We both rose. "Not to you, I hope," he said.

"To Mattie. St. Vincent's arranged for a visiting nurse." When we came out on the street, I kissed his cheek. "Edward, I'm sorry."

"I know that. Let's have only truth between us, Oliver."

I nodded, blew him a kiss, started off. I got about half a block when a thought came to me. Turning, I called, "Edward!" But he was gone. I caught up with him on the stairs to his office. "Edward, did you get to know Mackey when Bennett brought him to the Players?"

He looked down at me and frowned. "The Players. Yes. He stopped coming after a few times. Don't you remember?"

"I do."

"Mackey liked to be the center of attention. That's why he didn't come back. Too many other stars."

"I think maybe you knew him fairly well."

"You get to know people well when you're in close quarters. Mackey played a mean game of bridge. That's all we did on the ship coming home after the Armistice."

Chapter Thirty-five

*E*xcept for Harry and Jig, they'd all been to the War. Even Bennett had, though he'd referred to Stephen Lowell as the brave one. He'd probably meant that Stephen had been wounded.

But they hadn't all been in the trenches. When I first met Bennett, he'd worn a naval officer's uniform.

And afterward, they'd all turned up in Greenwich Village.

I traveled home, intensely cold, knowing that unless a check came in from somewhere, I was going to have to take twenty dollars from the cookie jar, where Mattie and I keep our emergency money, and buy myself a warm coat. Of course, my eccentric great-aunt might have left something of that nature in one of those old steamer trunks in the attic. Mattie had been urging me to go through all that stuff with her so that we could get most of it hauled away. And while I admit to a voyeur's inquisitiveness about my great-aunt's most intimate secrets, I hadn't managed to fit in the time to do it.

As I came toward my house, I noted with some envy Kid Yorke warming his hands over a small fire he'd built in the gutter across the street. He gave me a cursory nod, and looked beyond me. I turned to see Red Farrell come into view a block behind me. Had he been following me since I left the house? If so, I'd been so immersed in my thoughts, I hadn't seen him.

And certainly, I hadn't needed anyone to protect me. In fact, I'd felt no sense of danger whatever. Had the anonymous evil that seemed suspended over me disappeared with the death of Eppie Diamond?

I went into the vestibule and gave Harry's doorbell a quick twist.

"It's open," Harry called.

When I stepped inside, I didn't see him. "Do you think that's wise?"

"What?" He stuck his head out of the bathroom, his face half-lathered, a razor in his hand. His suspenders hung loosely over his trousers. He wore no shirt, only a sleeveless undershirt. Surprisingly pale skin framed nasty bruises.

Where was his lover? I wondered suddenly. Why hadn't his uptown lady come to see him?

"Leaving your door open? And, do you think *that's* wise?" I flopped down on the sofa and lit a cigarette. "Your hand's none too steady. Why didn't you let Nurse Newberger do it?"

"That wouldn't give me any pleasure. I was waiting for you. Ow. Goddammit. How about it, Oliver? Before I kill myself."

"Only if you've got a trench knife." I said this with a certain juicy satisfaction because I knew something Harry didn't.

"What did you say?" The spectre that was Harry clumped into the room, a towel around his neck, and sat down at his desk. He'd wiped off the lather and splashed cold water on his coarsely shaved face.

"The barber on Bleecker, what's his name?"

"Rinaldi."

"I'll ask him to come give you a shave."

"Bloody hell." Harry lit a cigarette, steadying one hand with the other. "What were you saying about a trench knife?"

"A trench knife turned up wedged into the strings of Eppie Diamond's piano."

"The murder weapon. Yeah. Ugly piece. Could have been what cut Mackey, too."

"Brophy took it away with him."

"So . . ." He didn't finish what he began, but tilted his chair back, closed his eyes and smoked.

"So I never got to meet the shoe man."

He opened his eyes. "What shoe man?"

"Eppie Diamond's man. One Carmine Colangelo. He actually made all of her shoes in the ground-floor workshop. He was going to see if he could find the shoes I brought her last week."

"Let me guess. He's been slain by our vile villain."

"Oh, pshaw, Harry. His child was ill, so he couldn't come by today. Brophy's going to set up another time. Do you think Eppie Diamond was killed because she would have told who sent me the shoes? And this was all somehow connected to Mackey's murder? Therefore, she knew who the murderer was?"

"Maybe."

"Well, I can't see Andrew as a murderer."

"Why? Because he's a writer? Really, Oliver, you believe all writers are essentially good people because they are artists? I happen to know they're a crazy, drunken lot, capable of the same kind of behavior as the general population."

"Yes, but Harry, listen to this: Andrew kills his pretend mother because she knows he sent me the shoes? That doesn't make any sense at all. The shoes are frivolous. Killing for a frivolous reason is not a motive—"

"Oliver, what makes you think people kill for logical reasons? Most of the time when people kill it's personal, it's in the heat of a particular passion. Love, hate, greed, anger, jealousy. I'm out of gin."

"So am I. And *Ainslee's*, Edward just informed me, is probably going bust, so they can't pay me for the last two poems I sold them."

"My billfold's in the bloody file cabinet. When Ding Dong gets back I'll have him pick up a couple of bottles."

"Ding Dong's at yer service. Rubber, get Sherlock his gin."

"See what happens when you leave your door unlocked," I mumbled.

Harry laughed. "Just means I don't have to repeat myself."

The room quickly filled with acrid cigar smoke from the weed that Ding Dong had in his mouth. My eyes smarted and

teared. I could have left but I was not about to, not until I heard
what Ding Dong had found out about Andrew Goren. I lit another cigarette in self-defense.

"No one on Moicer anywheres ever hoida him," Ding Dong
said. "Maybe he don't live dere."

"Yeah?"

"Is that all you have to say, Harry?" I demanded. "He told me
he lived on Mercer."

"He told you a lot of things, mostly lies." Harry didn't seem
nearly as upset as I was.

"He wanted me to go with him to his place on Mercer. I refused."

"Good tinkin', Olwer," Ding Dong said.

"Yeah," Harry said. "Good tinkin', Olwer."

I wanted to hose the layer of irony from his face with cold
water.

"Ya want ta look some more, Sherlock? Dis Goren is a guy wit
sometin' ta hide. Wad he look like?"

They both looked at me expectantly. "Late twenties, maybe.
Tall, thin, dark hair, dark eyes. Poetic looking."

"Like finding a needle in a haystack, I'd say."

"Don't hurt ta take anudder look," Ding Dong said.

"Where's dis go?" Rubber demanded. He came into the flat
carrying a distinctively marked case of Booth's gin and set it
down on Harry's desk.

"Direct from our generous Canadian neighbors?" I murmured.

"Jeeze, Rubber, a whole case?" Harry said reverently.

"Why not?"

Harry laughed. "How much I owe you?"

"For you, Sherlock, on da house. Come on, Rubber."

Harry and I exchanged glances. I took a bottle from the case
and caressed it lovingly, then opened it and sniffed. "The real
thing." I gave it to Harry to sniff.

"Mother's milk," he said.

"Would you care for a martini?" I said.

"Just what I need."

"I'll go up and get the fixings. Don't go away."

After going through the ritual of unlocking and relocking my door, I ran up the stairs. "Mattie?"

"In the kitchen."

Where else, I thought. The oven door was open and she was bent over a roasting pan. I counted six crispy brown bird legs. "You never cook like this for me. I'm quite jealous." Jealous, meaning envious, not jealous meaning murderous. Words are so wonderful, are they not?

"Were you able to find the shoes?"

I watched her baste the birds, thinking what a lovely motion it was, what an enchanting color the juices of the chickens were as they glazed the succulent, mahogany birds.

"No. The man who makes them wasn't able to get there. But your nice Gerry Brophy and I did find the murder weapon."

A towel protecting her hands, Mattie slipped the pan back in the oven and shut the door. Straightening, she looked me in the eye and said with determination, "I wish you wouldn't be so flip about all of this, Olivia. Our home has been broken into, we're not safe anymore. Not until this madman is caught."

I set the bottle of gin on the worktable, caught her shoulders and hugged her. "Mattie, honest, I may sound flip, but it's only to keep from being afraid. If I'm afraid, how can I even walk out of this house every day? Your Gerry is doing his best to help us, even as Mr. Walz would like to arrest me."

Mattie shuddered. "Gerry is a good man," she said, hugging me back.

"I'm making us all martinis," I said. "How about it?"

"You sit down. I'll do it." She took the bottle of gin and went into the parlor, where the bar was set up.

"Any mail, Mattie?" I called, hoping there'd be a check.

"I left it on the hall table."

I went through the envelopes, finding only another invitation to read and a fan letter from a young woman at Connecticut College for Women. Alas, the cookie jar was going to have to part with twenty dollars.

Reaching up to the shelf near the window, I took the jar down and counted out twenty single bills. The window sparkled in the

afternoon sunlight. With the advent of cold weather, the backyards were still and peaceful.

As I replaced the jar, something teased my vision. I set the jar
on the shelf and looked out the window again, down at our garden. Something was amiss. Slipping the bills into my pocket, I
went down the back stairs.

"Olivia?" Mattie stood in the hall holding the cocktail shaker.
"Where are you going?"

"To the garden. I'll be right back."

I came out the back door. The erotic stone birdbath lay on the
ground, smashed to bits, leaving no trace of the lovers.

On top of the remains someone had placed the smaller of
Eppie Diamond's funeral wreaths.

Chapter Thirty-six

*Y*ou know that peculiar sensation that someone is watching you? That's what I was experiencing now. I could actually feel the hairs rise on the back of my neck. Slowly, I began to examine the windows of my neighbors' houses. I knew with stark certainty that I wasn't imagining this.

I wanted to shout, who are you? And why are you doing this to me? But I knew I would get no response. I backed away from the outrage and lingered just inside my door, to see if anything, anywhere, moved. From where I stood, my peripheral vision gave me no reward.

"Bloody hell!" Harry said, for perhaps the fifth time in fifteen minutes.

We were sitting in Harry's flat drinking martinis as fast as Harry could pour the gin, and by this time, we had run out of vermouth, of which we took little notice. Harry was sitting at his desk while Mattie, who'd rushed down to view the ruin, was so unnerved she kept bouncing up from the sofa exclaiming, "Oh, no."

I paced.

The precinct had been notified. There was nothing to do but

wait. Upstairs, the roasted birds, rejected, cooled in their pan, for we'd all quite lost our appetites.

Harry said, "I keep hearing Vangie in my head—'piece by piece,' she's saying. 'Even the smallest element counts.'"

"I toast my great-aunt Evangeline," I said, raising my glass.

"To Vangie," Harry said.

"To all great-aunts everywhere," I said.

"To the great Holmes," Harry said. The empty bottle of gin crashed into his trash basket.

"We'd better stash the gin somewhere before the cops get here."

Harry opened all the desk drawers at once and after we emptied the case, I put it in the bathtub, which was already the resting place of a block of ice and a keg of beer.

It's amazing, this Prohibition. It's made us all obsessed with alcohol. None of us would have had this much booze in our homes. We'd never have thought about it. Before, we always drank in saloons with our friends.

Brophy and Walz arrived a few minutes later to find the three of us sitting around, talking and smoking. As soon as I saw Walz with his mean bulldog face, I was sorry we'd called them.

"What's the story this time?" Walz said, his nostrils flaring at the odor of gin. His mouth was set in a grim line. Concern was reflected in poor Gerry Brophy's tense demeanor. When he was satisfied Mattie'd come to no harm, he turned to Harry and me.

"There's been another incident," Harry said.

"What kind of *incident*?" I can only describe Walz's intonation as snide.

"I haven't seen it," Harry said. "Only know what Oliver told me. Someone smashed the birdbath in the garden and dumped a funeral wreath on the rubble."

"Miss Brown." Walz fixed his dead eyes on me. "Will you enlighten us?"

"My beautiful birdbath, Mr. Walz. It's been destroyed—"

"You're talking about that obscenity in your garden?"

An embarrassed flush flooded Gerry Brophy's face. He said, "I don't think—"

"That's right," Walz said. "Don't."

With less grace than I would have liked, I rose, drawing myself up to my fullest height, which is five feet uneven. "You are a rodent, Mr. Walz. And not a credit to the human race."

"Here, here," Harry said.

"Olivia speaks for all of us." The gin and the shock had obviously loosened Mattie's tongue. I squeezed her hand.

"Why don't you go have a look-see?" Harry said. "Sorry I can't join you."

Mattie led and I ushered the detectives ahead of me, surreptitiously casting an eye outside to see if Goo Goo Knox was still warming his hands. He wasn't, nor was there any sign of the fire.

"Oh, Olivia!" I heard Mattie's cry as I came down the stairs behind the detectives.

There was no change. The ruins of my birdbath lay as I'd seen them, the funeral wreath on top. It was Mattie's shock, her feeling of violation that had caused her reaction. I understood. It was what I felt.

"Aye." Brophy, forgetting Walz, or in spite of Walz, took Mattie in his arms. "There's a pity." Then he let her go and kneeled at the carnage.

Walz gave a grunt as if he had something to say, but he didn't follow through.

"You notice, don't you, Mr. Brophy," I said, "that this is the funeral wreath that was on the door to Eppie Diamond's workshop."

He looked up at me and nodded. "So it is."

"Another practical joke," Walz said. "Or, perhaps, you are trying to divert attention from your own culpability."

Mattie's hiss startled me. I touched her arm; she was icy, and it came to me that we were standing in the cold without cover. But I was bursting with fire. "Mr. Walz, as a poet, I confess I believe in the basic decency of people, allowing for the aberration of the murdering mind."

"Miss Olivia—" Brophy put a cautioning hand on my arm. I shook it off with a glare.

I was ready to kill, at least with words, I was, and there was no stopping me. Mattie stood shoulder to shoulder with me.

How I love her. How I'll miss her when she marries Gerry Brophy, for marry him she will.

"You are a crude, judgmental bigot, Mr. Walz." The pent-up
venom spilled out of me. "You have no manners, no sensitivity.
You are full of spite and resentment and therefore cannot see past
the nose on your face."

Walz, his nose and face blossoming a repulsive red, swelling
with anger, raised his hand to do me harm, but Gerry caught
hold and wouldn't let go. I'd already taken a step back so his slap
would not have made contact, but I was raging in a way I never
had in all my life. And it frightened me. Had I had a weapon in
my hand, I might have killed him.

And he might have killed me. I saw it in his eyes. And the
thought crossed my mind, what if he is the culprit here, what if
he—so full of loathing for us, for me—is the so-called practical
joker?

Chapter Thirty-seven

After they left, I asked Mattie to make us a pot of tea. Truth was, I wanted to be alone. If I could ever be alone. Was my tormentor watching me still, from some safe distance?

I sat on one of the garden stools and smoked, my anger so torrid at first I did not feel the cold. Walz and Brophy had taken the funeral wreath away with them. The shattered pieces of my birdbath were thus exposed for all the world to see. Symbolic, it was clear to me, of the shattered pieces of my life since that rainy evening Whit and I had discovered Mackey's body.

Without further thought, I went upstairs, returning with my cloak. I covered the remains, then locked the back door carefully and came upstairs again. Mattie had put a tray of tea things together and was waiting for me.

No speech was necessary. We went down the stairs to Harry's flat.

"Walz rushed out of here like a wounded buffalo," Harry said. "I take it you were particularly hard on the miserable chap."

I gave him a thumbs-up sign. "He accused *me* of doing it, to take attention away from the fact that I'm the murderer. Walz's a nasty beast, and I told him so."

"Ooooh!" Harry shivered dramatically. His color was poor and I could see he was more tired than he would ever admit.

While we had our tea, I said, "I felt as if we were being watched out there. Did you feel it, Mattie?"

Mattie shivered. "I don't know. I'll never be able to go down there again without thinking how easy it is for someone to hurt us."

"You don't have one of the Dusters watching out back, do you, Harry?"

"No. I should have considered it. Anyone could come over those backyard fences." He sagged in his chair; pain made creases in the creases on his face.

Taking Mattie's arm, I said, "Let's go see what Great-Aunt Evangeline has in those trunks in the attic. My cloak is doing shroud duty in the garden." Then, in response to Mattie's confusion, I added, "The poor pieces looked so naked and vulnerable, I had to cover them."

Over Harry's weak protestations, we helped him move back to his bed and left him to sleep off the onslaught of the gin and the unexpected "event" in my garden.

We stopped in the kitchen for another cup of tea and found the turmoil had made us quite hungry. Mattie put together a lunch of cold chicken thighs and generously buttered Italian bread, which we ate, too tired even to exchange a few simple words.

When our plates contained only crumbs and bones, I took out my cigarette case and we smoked. Mattie said, watching me closely, "Are you enjoying this, Olivia?"

I was shocked. "Mattie! How can you say that? This has been a perfect nightmare—our lives have been threatened."

"Yes, all of that is true, but you have thrown yourself into this investigation as if it were a love affair."

"Pshaw, Mattie," I said, but I wondered, was she right? I felt a kind of fever in the back of my eyes, an intensity of spirit that accentuated color everywhere. Fragments of poems fought for expression. I was so very alive.

We set the plates in soapy water in the sink, rinsing off our hands, then in silent agreement, went up to the attic to tackle the steamer trunks. Perhaps, if I was lucky, we'd find me a warm coat.

An exceedingly narrow, curved wooden staircase led up to the attic. The air was close and not unpleasantly musty, somewhat like a library.

"Are there lights up here?" I was leading the way, though I'd only been up here once before, not long after we'd moved in.

"A ceiling light without a shade," Mattie said. "There's a chain."

The attic ran most of the length and width of my little house. A row of small windows was set high on the south wall. I found the chain, or rather, it found me, listing across my forehead like a spider's web. The light was a bare hanging bulb, a stage light. I caught the faint odor of cedar. Two steamer trunks took up most of the space. Squinting in the dim light, I saw an overstuffed easy chair under a dusty white sheet.

"The cedar closet is full of very nicely made clothing, if a little out-of-date," Mattie said, pointing to the source of the cedar smell: a built-into-the-wall closet.

I squeezed past the trunks, leaving them to Mattie, and opened the closet door. "Treasures!" And they were. Heavy woolens, winter things. Men's clothing and women's. I pulled out an elderly racoon fur, very lovingly worn, and tried it on. Two of me could have fit inside, and it was obviously made for someone taller, but what difference did that make? It would keep me warm, right down to my dainty ankles.

"Shirtwaists," Mattie said. "And corsets." She opened the drawers in the steamer trunk. "Look at this, Olivia! Look what I found tucked away among the corsets."

What she held out to me was a photograph in a tarnished frame. I took it from her. Two girls, perhaps my age, maybe a little older, arms round each other's waists, stared back at me with something like amusement. The smaller of the two was full-figured, though not plump. The face under a mannish hat was the same as that of my father, squared jaw and all, whom I'd known only in photographs. I was looking, I knew, at Great-Aunt Evangeline.

The other girl was lovely. Tall, willowy, she had thick dark hair and eyes that spoke volumes. Her sensual lips almost quivered into a smile. It struck me that they looked very happy. Evangeline and Alice.

I clasped the photograph to my breast and tears sprang to my eyes. My emotions were raw. "They are beautiful together, don't you think?" I asked Mattie.

"Why don't we bring them downstairs, where they belong? I'll clean the tarnish from the frame."

She'd read my thoughts. I handed her the photograph. "Are there more of these?"

"Lots." She opened the deep bottom drawer of the steamer trunk. I could see what appeared to be a dense, black leather photograph album.

"Here, I'll take that," I said.

When Mattie lifted out the album, we were surprised to find it was not as thick as it had seemed. Its size was disguised by the curious wooden box it had been resting on.

"What do you suppose this is?" Mattie said.

"The family jewels, no doubt," I said.

She lifted it out. "It's heavy."

"Let's see." I traded the photograph album for the wooden box—and almost dropped it. Mattie was right. It was heavy. I set it down on the sheeted easy chair, undid the latch, and opened it.

Nestled in a bed of velvet, truly like some precious jewel, was a pearl-handled revolver.

Chapter Thirty-eight

I saw you in your grave, love.
Clusters of daisies left my hand,
I thought, as swift as grains of sand.
Someone released a dove,
In memoriam.
White and sure, she soared above,
Then pandemonium.
The sky went red with blood alone
Before we heard the rifle's sound
And rain came down with shattered bone
As you, my love, lay in the ground.

My poems of late have all been about blood and death; a shroud hangs over my mind. Maudlin is not my image of myself. I'm a good-time girl with an intellect.

I pulled the poem from my type-writer and reread it. It had come from some hidden place inside me. I left it on my desk and went over to the window, parting the draperies slightly so I could see down to the street.

Goo Goo Knox and Ding Dong were standing across the way talking, looking up at my house. I had to know what Ding Dong had found out about Andrew, so I threw open my window and called down, "Don't go away. I want to talk to you."

My new coat covered me from chin to ankle and when I stepped out of my house, I saw at first the boys didn't recognize me.

"Oh, lookie, it's Olwer," Ding Dong said.

"Do you like my new coat?" I asked, twirling round for them.

"Nice," Goo Goo said, fingering the fur. "Wad the coppers want?"

"Harry didn't tell you?"

"Da ugly noice is in dere," Ding Dong said.

"Well, someone got into my garden in the back and chopped up my birdbath, then decorated it with a funeral wreath."

"Very funny," Ding Dong said. He wasn't smiling. "Maybe we gotta put Circular Jack out dere."

"Yeah," Goo Goo agreed.

"I don't think so," I said. "I'd feel 'in a wall'd prison.' Besides, it's too cold. He—Circular Jack—won't be comfortable."

"Comfortable, she sez." Ding Dong gave Goo Goo the elbow, and they both howled.

I broke into their entertainment with the reason I'd come down to the street to talk to them. "Did you find Andrew Goren?"

"Naa," Ding Dong said. "He's dere somewhere in dago town. Nobody's talkin'."

"He doan wanna be found," Goo Goo added.

Well, I thought, if I lived on Mercer Street and the likes of Ding Dong came looking for me, my neighbors would probably protect me, too. At least, I hoped they would.

This gave me pause. It dawned on me that one of my neighbors might have caught a glimpse of the birdbath killer. How to pursue this was something I would discuss with Harry.

"Dey ain't seen our butts yet," Goo Goo said, and got the elbow again. He looked at me with chagrin. "Pardon, Olwer."

"Maybe they're afraid of you," I offered.

Ding Dong looked at me with what I can only describe as benign scorn. "Dat's da general idea, ain't it, Olwer?"

"Of course," I said. "How could I be so stupid?"

"'S'okay, Olwer. Youse a goil."

I walked back across the street and listened at Harry's door. Nurse Newberger's strident voice leaked out to me.

Harry swore: "Bloody hell."

I was not going to walk into that. First making sure the downstairs lock was in order, I went up to my flat.

"Mattie?" I hung my coat on the coatrack.

"Up here." Her voice came faintly from way above. She'd gone back to the attic.

When I arrived, I saw her sleeves rolled back, face flushed with the exertion. She had taken all the men's clothing from the cedar closet.

Holding up a suit, she said, "A man of little height."

I took the hanger and held it up under my chin. My height. Great-Aunt Evangeline's height. "Do you suppose she dressed as a man?" If so, Harry had never mentioned it.

"Perhaps." Mattie placed a boy's cap on my head and put another on hers. She took my hand and, with an embarrassed chortle, pulled me in front of the tall mirror so we stood side by side. I held the suit up in front of me again. "Isn't that odd?" My voice trailed off. An idea was stirring in my brain.

"What are you thinking about, Olivia?" Mattie shook my arm, bringing me back to the attic.

I dissembled. "A new poem."

Taking my chin in her hand, Mattie turned my head to her. "Something else, I think."

"The Dusters have been all over Mercer Street and are getting nowhere trying to find Andrew Goren."

"I shouldn't wonder. If I saw one of them, I'd run clear into the next world."

"They're trying to help. Harry, not me. Harry seems to have earned their undying loyalty. I'd love to know how." I stood in front of the mirror and tilted my cap in a roguish fashion. "What do you think?" I rolled my eyes at her.

"Olivia!" She'd read my thoughts.

"What could it hurt, Mattie, dear? Wouldn't you be pleasant to a young lad trying to deliver a manuscript to Mr. Andrew Goren?" I took the jacket of the suit and slipped it on over my dress. "We'll wrap up some newspapers to make it look right." The jacket was roomy, but I could pass for a lad. "What do you think?"

"I think it's dangerous. You can't do this, Olivia."

"Then come with me." I was really getting into the game of it, and my excitement was contagious. "You can take one side of the street and I'll take the other." I placed my hands on her shoulders. "Come, let's find you a costume."

Have I mentioned that Mattie, for all her proper lace-curtain upbringing, is also embued with the spirit of adventure?

Not quite an hour later, as dusk was creeping into the Village, we went out the back door and over the garden fences, through an alley and came out on Grove Street. From here, we trekked down Sixth Avenue to Broome, which intersects with Mercer. It was a long walk and the cold wind set our cheeks ablaze.

With wrapped paper packages under our arms, we looked very much like delivery boys. At least I hoped we did.

We'd addressed our packages to Andrew Goren in bold letters and gave the return address as the publishing company Boni and Liveright. I felt a smidgeon of guilt, playing on a writer's dreams, but if Andrew was hiding, he might be lured out by this, or someone might give him away.

Mercer Street is Italian, the walk-ups crowded with immigrants. Faces stared from windows. Scrawny, olive-skinned children were everywhere. Small garment factories gave them employment, child and adult. Here the texture was suspicion mixed with the grit of poverty.

"I think," I told Mattie, "we must wait for each other from house to house."

"Call me Mike," she said.

I held back a chuckle. She was getting into the game. "Okay, I'll be Pat."

So Pat and Mike shook hands and stepped out onto Mercer Street.

I opened the first door and shouted up the stairs. "Package for Mr. Andrew Goren! Andrew Goren, package delivery!" I went up the stairs in the dingy, onion-saturated tenement and banged on every door.

"No live here," was all I got, even when I asked where he did live. Maybe they weren't hiding him. Maybe it was just a language problem.

Each time I came down to the street, I either waited for Mattie or she was waiting for me, shaking her head.

We crossed Grand Street, working our way downtown. Mercer was coming to an end. On the corner of Canal Street, two burly stevedores were loading barrels of nails into a truck.

"I have a package for Andrew Goren," I said. "Do you know him?"

They looked at each other and shook their heads.

Long spirals of twilight enclosed the city. The tavern next door had a sign in the window saying Dutch and Scottish teas were available. Gin and scotch is what it meant. A group of workmen were already crowding in. I watched across the street for Mattie. No sign of her.

I waited with ever increasing impatience. Where was she? Crossing the street, I opened the door beside the small grocery. The staircase leaned toward me, forbidding.

"Mm—Mike?" I called. Was Mattie braver than I? I stepped outside and looked up and down and across the street. Had we missed each other?

I went into the tenement again. "Mike?" I edged up the stairs a short way and threw caution to the wind. "Mattie?"

No one answered.

Chapter Thirty-nine

*T*here are times in one's life when all clear thought is driven away by total panic. Here I was, standing in a place so feral my only reality was atavistic. Every sense was magnified: my sight, an impressionist's nightmare of the funereal; acrid garlic burned my nostrils. Voices came as babel. Sounds were skittering creatures, eyes phosphorescent. Swaying, I clutched the grimy wall for a brief moment, then plunged out onto the sidewalk. Still clutching my package, I gasped air as a drowning person.

The cold air sobered me. One thing was certain. I would not leave this place without Mattie. I went back into the building. Use the senses that God gave you, I told myself. I saw the staircase. Looking upward into it, I saw nothing but the abyss, upside down, inside out, the eyes of hell's guardians contemplating me.

A door opened above me. Voices charged with anger, fear. The child crying. A light footfall on the stairs. I ducked beneath the staircase.

A boy, a child really, the handle of his big pail moaning in its socket. I saw him in the faintest glimmer of light . . . from somewhere behind me.

The minute he was out the door, I eased my way to the back

of the building, following the trail I might never have seen were it not for the child.

A back door. The light filtered bleakly through the scant opening derived from an improvised horseshoe doorstop. I pushed the door open the rest of the way and stepped outside. And so found a second tenement, probably hidden to all but the residents of the building and, perhaps, the street.

Yet there were many such in the Village. Cottages behind buildings. And this one was somewhat more attractive, with its deep green door and window trim, than its cousin facing the street.

As I contemplated the building in the last sigh of daylight, who should pop out the door, nice as you please, but my missing Mattie.

Well! It was all I could do not to rush at her and clasp her to my breast. I was that joyful. I saw at once she was well. And she was no longer carrying her package.

Catching sight of me, but showing no surprise, she quickened her pace and silenced me with her eyes. I preceded her through the back door of the front tenement, then held up my hand. The boy with the pail had just returned and was mounting the stairs. The heady scent of beer, so sublime, wafted upward over our heads. Then the slam of a door left us bereft.

Mercer Street was dimly lit, pedestrians few. Still, we tacitly agreed not to speak until we were well away from the area.

Finally, we slowed. I still carried my package, which was now obviously *de trop*. I donated it to the fruit and vegetable refuse in a trash basket outside a grocery on Sixth Avenue. "I was so worried about you," I said.

"I knew you would be, but it happened so quickly there was nothing I could do—"

I gave her a ferocious hug. "Mattie, I love you. You found him and he didn't recognize you."

"I didn't see him, but a nice man said he'd see that Andrew Goren received the package."

"At least we know where he lives." You see, I have an optimistic nature.

She cupped her hand and gave me a boost over the back fence, which because of my height I needed, but she didn't. In no time at all we'd crept through the backyards until we came to ours. Our grand adventure was over.

"Bloody hell," Harry said when we finished telling him our story. "You girls don't know how dangerous it is down there. You got Owney Madden in a shoving match with the Black Hand over bootlegging."

"Right, Harry," I said, "and we could have been kidnapped by white slavers." I tilted my head back and blew perfect smoke rings into the air between us. They floated over Harry's head, then lost themselves in the fumes of his cigar.

Mattie giggled. "Dressed like this? Do the white slavers kidnap boys, too?"

Harry snorted. "Boys? Who are you kidding? You two couldn't pass for boys in a million years. You're a dead giveaway."

"But you know us, Harry," Mattie said. She leaned over Harry's desk so he could light her cigarette.

"Besides," I said, "we did one better than the Dusters. We— or rather Mattie—found Andrew Goren."

"Really?" Harry said, drawling. "And how do we figure that?"

"Tell him, Mattie. Harry's being obnoxious. We do deserve credit here, Harry. I insist."

"I found a man who said he'd get the package to Andrew," Mattie said. "He lives in one of those houses behind other houses."

"Sure. And what was in the package?"

"We wrapped up newspapers," I said. "I put Boni and Liveright as the return address."

"Clever, Oliver, but did you consider that the man Mattie gave the package to might have thought it had something of value in it? Something he could sell. And that he had no idea who Andrew Goren was and didn't much care?"

I hadn't, of course.

But Mattie disagreed. "No, Harry. He seemed like an honest man."

"Well, no matter," Harry said. "It was a good try. And who

knows, it could turn into something. I'll have Ding Dong check it out."

Mattie rose. "I'm going up to change. Mr. Brophy is coming to call."

After Mattie left us, I paced, started sentences I never completed, all the time gesturing with my cigarette as if I were talking.

Harry said, "You look like a kid in a costume."

I wrinkled my nose and gave him a fulsome hiss.

"That's a rough section of town and you two are like babes in the wood."

"That's all the more reason why we were a better choice. There's no way anyone down there would talk to a Duster and you know it."

Harry changed the subject. "I'm still thinking maybe we should park one of them out back."

"If we must, Harry. I'm convinced that Andrew is—" I shuddered. "Something evil, and that he killed Mackey and Eppie Diamond. If the police arrest him, everything will go back to the way it was."

Harry nodded. His cigar had gone out and now he was just chewing on it. "You gave him every opportunity to cut your throat, and he didn't."

"True. But it's all in the timing. The timing might not have been right."

We both stopped talking when we heard someone come into the vestibule and ring the bell to my flat. Brophy, I supposed. Mattie's footsteps sounded on the stairs, then the murmur of voices outside Harry's door.

Harry raised an eyebrow. "Is this serious?"

"He introduced Mattie to his mother."

"It's serious."

"If Mattie should take it into her head and marry Gerry Brophy, there'll just be you and me here, Harry."

"I can live with that, Oliver." The corners of his mouth twitched.

I could see he thought the whole thing amusing, so I went

back to business. "I'm thinking my neighbors might have seen who was in my garden."

"Do some real detecting. In a dress."

The doorbell rang. I looked at Harry. "Go on, get it."

Mattie said, "We're going to a lecture at the Ethical Culture Society." She grinned at me, flushed and as happy as I've ever seen her. "Don't wait up."

"Have a good time, children," I said.

"Oh, Miss—Olivia," Brophy said. "Mr. Colangelo can meet with us tomorrow at Miss Diamond's house."

"Mr. Colangelo?" Mattie spun round and stared at Brophy. "You said Mr. Colangelo?"

"Mattie, what's wrong? Mr. Colangelo's the shoemaker who worked for Eppie Diamond," I said.

Her high color vanished. "Oh, dear God," she said, "that's the name of the man I gave the package to."

Chapter Forty

*T*he *Emperor Jones* was sold out for its entire run and we'd dropped the curtain-raiser entirely, so all I had to be was background, which was fine. It's the way we work. Parts one time, walk-ons the next.

I'd arrived at the theatre all right, but could not have told you how I got there. I was having trouble concentrating. What did Carmine Colangelo, Eppie Diamond's shoemaker, have to do with Andrew Goren, who had passed himself off as Eppie Diamond's son?

After our final bows to standing ovations, I was the first to come offstage.

"Wait, Oliver." A hand caught mine, another stroked my cheek. "You're so tense. What's the matter?" Rae Dunbar's breath was sweet on the back of my neck.

I slipped my arm through hers, resting my head against her soft breasts. We were berries in brown greasepaint, tart and mellow to taste, full of stones beneath. Our parting was reluctant. How else to remove all that makeup?

For some reason all the girls were tired tonight. We hardly spoke to one another, eager for the glass of wine or beer, the love.

"How goes it with Whit?" I asked Rae as we, the last to go, left the dressing room.

Her shrug was infinite in what it did not say. "Andrew?" she whispered.

I shook my head. "There is a story to be told."

"I listen well."

"Oliver, come have a drink." Bennett pounced on us. Had he been waiting? "You, too, Rae," he added, giving her his teddy bear smile.

My eyes sent Rae a telegraph and she responded with that magnificent shrug. Hands swimming in fur, Bennett admired my raccoon coat.

"Oliver, stay a minute," Jig said. "I want to hear about Andrew." He waved my companions away. The imperial dismissal.

"Go on," I said. "I'll catch up."

Jig took to the stage, his office, two chairs. "So . . ."

"It is a brilliant play," I said.

"Yes. I want to start rehearsal at once."

"I'm not going to do it."

"What?" He was truly astonished. "But you must. He wrote it for you."

"I can't. He frightens me, Jig. There's something crazy about him. He means me harm."

"Nonsense, Oliver. We're all crazy. He's no worse than Gene. Than any of us."

"Gene is a dear, sweet boy, Jig. He wouldn't hurt anyone. His truth is raw, but he doesn't lie. Everything about Andrew is a lie."

Stunned by my vehemence, Jig faltered. "The play —"

"The play is . . . Someone else will do it."

"He wants to direct you in it."

I got up to leave. "Direct? Have you seen him lately? I don't think he'll be able to direct anyone."

"Please think it over, Oliver. I feel it will be our next big hit."

I knew it was no use, but I promised Jig to think it over. If Andrew would do any directing, it would be in Sing Sing. I left the theatre for the Working Girls' Home, where, alas, Whit had made us a foursome. Suit wrinkled, shirt stained, he looked unkempt, quite unlike himself. Some tragic event had finally struck him and made his hair stand on end.

"Nice coat, Oliver," Whit said. "Sold a couple of dozen poems?" He was drunk.

Why is it that everything Whit said to me now raised my dander? "A new suitor, my dear," said I. "Took pity on me, don't you know, and what with winter on the way." I pulled out a chair and sat down without taking my coat off, feeling more than a little surly.

The saloon was a smoke-filled, noisy den, shades in attendance. The dead among the living. There was no place for me here.

Bennett bought me a beer. I stared into the snowy circle waiting for the foam to subside, the amber to reveal itself. Might I see my future in the bubbles?

"Oliver, come away with me," he said.

I searched deep into his kindly eyes. "One day I'm going to surprise you, Bennett, and say yes, and you'll run for the hills."

"No, I won't, Oliver."

I patted his hand and took a long swallow of beer. Something sub rosa between Rae and Whit was becoming apparent.

"I don't think so," Rae said. Her hand rested on my thigh for a short moment. She didn't look at me.

"Why the hell not?" Whit shouted, "Another round here," grasping the soft part of Rae's arm, just above the elbow.

"I've had enough," Rae said.

"I haven't, and no one is leaving until we have another round."

"What's the matter with you, Whit?" I asked. He'd never as long as I'd known him behaved like this. I'd always thought of him as a gentleman, if nothing else.

"Keep it down, Whit," Bennett said.

Rae pushed his hand away, standing up with such determination, she knocked over her chair. "I'm going home."

When she touched her cheek to mine, I said, "Home?"

"To the Bronx," she said.

"We'll put you in a taxi," Bennett, our chivalrous knight, said.

I stubbed out my cigarette and rose. I draped my arm across Rae's shoulders. "No, you'll come home with me."

As soon as the words were out of my mouth, Whit collapsed on the table and burst into tears, blubbering something about our plotting against him. It was a stunning reaction. A few blank faces turned in our direction.

"You'd better get him out of here," I told Bennett. "Don't worry about us. I have an escort waiting outside."

"An escort?" Rae's humor was lush, lusty, bubbling over.

"Ding Dong," I said, knowing full well she wouldn't understand, but liking the deceptively musical sound of it. How would Rae feel about the Hudson Dusters?

I took her hand, and we wove our way past the shades: evening regulars and the voyeurs who made the rounds of the saloons of a night to catch a glimpse of the bohemians in their native habitat.

We didn't look back. If we had, we might have seen someone separate himself from the shadows and come after us.

Chapter Forty-one

*H*ow late it was, we did not know for sure, but the lights of the city had faded and purple-edged clouds roaming the icy moonlight had no competition. We locked arms as we walked, our murmurings puffing like cigarette smoke on the frigid air.

I felt safe and unexposed. But for two college students, stiffly drunk, and a bum snoring on a stoop, we were alone. Behind us somewhere was a Duster. And Bedford Street was not far. We did not hurry.

As we neared my house, the siren whine of a cat in heat, with all its craving pain, soaked up all breathable air. It lasted long enough to shatter our equilibrium before exploding into the mating shriek.

It was at this moment that Andrew suddenly materialized on the sidewalk in front of us. I stopped short, forcing Rae to do so as well; although, unprepared, she stumbled, and falling, clung to me, as if I were her lifeline.

Andrew, in his shirtsleeves and oblivious to the cold, waved his arms, conducting . . . the dirge. As in my poem. . . . "You have killed me, Olivia," he said, pointing at me, the baton. Death. In the light of the street lamp his face decomposed.

I felt his pain shoot through me. I thought, unexpectedly, "Madness in great ones must not unwatch'd go."

"What's wrong with him?" The fear in Rae's voice brought me back. "What's he doing?"

I squeezed her arm against my side. "Don't speak. Stay behind me." Where was Ding Dong?

My cue came with the creak of Harry's window as it opened and the light that glanced off the nose of the gun.

"Andrew, where have you been?" I projected my voice, as I do well, hoping to wake the street. He looked ill, desperate, skin taut over his cheekbones, eyes wild with fever.

He stepped toward me, a softness passing over him. "I would never hurt you, Olivia."

"Hold it right there, Goren, or whatever your name is. I have a gun on you."

A gun on a madman? I wanted to laugh. The madwoman in me did laugh, I think, which wasn't the smartest thing I've done, although it made Andrew pause.

"Don't kill him, Harry," I said.

"Quiet down there!" someone yelled.

"E-i-i-i-u!"

The cry was not of this earth. I felt the breeze against my cheek as a warm body shot past me in the air and landed fiercely on Andrew, knocking him backward to the ground.

When I got to them, Andrew lay still. His eyes were closed, but I saw he was breathing. He'd had the wind knocked out of him by the tubby cannonball who was sitting on him.

"Who are you?" I said.

He gave Andrew's face a backhanded smack, making sure he was out, then stood up, dusted himself off, and bowed. "Circular Jack. I'd be pleased to make youse acquaintance, Olwer, but not under dese circumstances." A bit of a dandy is what he was, in his red velvet jacket, more so than the other Dusters I'd met. He looked round, spied his hat, a black bowler, and set it squarely on his head.

"Thank you for coming to our rescue." I felt Rae behind me and reached for her hand. "This is my friend, Rae."

"Bloody hell," Harry said, his head and shoulders out the window. "Truss him up and bring him in here."

No sooner were the words out of Harry's mouth than Andrew was on his feet and running. Circular Jack spewed forth a stream of curses and went off after him.

With another "bloody hell," Harry slammed the window shut.

I smiled at Rae. "Welcome to my humble home."

We went inside and had a smoke and a beer with Harry, who was fuming, more I think because he couldn't have given chase himself. The gun lay on his desk. I wonder if he would have used it.

"We've missed you, Harry." Rae smiled at him. "You look like something the cat dragged in," she said.

"You should have seen him last week."

"Thanks for your solicitousness, girls. Walz was here again, Oliver."

"To hell with him I say." I raised my bottle to the absent Walz. "What do you say, Rae?"

"To hell with Walz, whoever he may be," Rae said. She clicked her bottle with mine. "But what of Andrew? He's frightening."

"Yes," I said. "He's fixated on me."

"And who is not?" she said, mostly serious.

Harry snorted, as well he might. He's the only one who sees me with clear eyes, I think. His view is less clouded, less subjective, than anyone else's, even Mattie, and so he's not obsessed with me, and for this I'm more than grateful, for whom would I trust?

I told Rae, "The police think Andrew may have killed Mackey." No sooner were the words out of my mouth than the faint niggle that had been working at me since Andrew first appeared before us utterly mad, grew fierce. I can't explain it, intuition perhaps, but I didn't think Andrew was a murderer.

Rae nodded, looked thoughtful. She took the bottle from my hand and set it on the floor beside hers. "And so, to bed. I've got to teach the pure of heart tomorrow."

Her warmth was my refuge. I wanted more. "We'll say good night then, Harry."

"Get me another before you go, will you, Oliver?"

I did, but now Rae hesitated. "It could have been Andrew at Whit's . . ." She'd spoken more to herself than to us.

I was impatient, at the door. Harry said, "Hold your horses, Oliver. I think Rae has something to tell us."

She looked at me, a slow flush rising to her cheeks. "Whit and I had an argument, which is why I left him. You saw how he was tonight. He's still in love with you, Oliver. And after the break-in, he even thought I was the one who did it, that I wanted to get back at him."

"The break-in?" Harry prompted. I saw respect on his face.

Rae said, "Someone broke into Whit's flat and cut up all his clothes."

Chapter Forty-two

I will not write again of love.
Better, odes to nature's bounty,
Sonnets to wind, or clouds above
And bird and beast and flower and tree.
The simple grace of stream and field
Shall be my inspiration now.
In blank verse 'twill be revealed
My passion for the pastoral.
I leave the moon and stars to men
The pledge of love I give them, too.
I shall not write of those again,
The words of truth I save for you.
Today, I carve my oath in ice,
But summer doth exact its price.

Where, I thought, is that naive child, that Olivia Brown, of a year past? She has gone. Forever, I think. Replaced by Oliver. Oliver knows the way of the world. Doesn't she?

I have become cynical. Well, not really. Perhaps I'm more observant than I used to be. Love is fleeting, is it not?

I removed my sonnet from my type-writer, and rolled in a clean sheet of paper.

It was midmorning. Pedestrians and carts had resumed their passage beneath my window on Bedford Street. Amid the murmur of voices I could now and again catch a word or phrase.

There was something different about me this morning. As if

I'd crossed the Rubicon. I was whole. I stared into the middle distance. My fingers hovered on the keys.

> *Fear breeds incest on itself*
> *Constraining action, thought and reason.*
> *Shackles smother cries for help,*
> *Expression finds a gentler season.*

Yes, I thought. Fear had taken over my life. It had frozen my brain so that it was all I thought about, then it fed on itself. And I had allowed it.

Sometime last night, with poor Andrew facing me in front of my house, I had shaken off the shackles of fear that had been confining me. My soul had reasserted itself and said, that's enough. No more.

"How was your assignation?" I asked Mattie a short time later.

"An assignation, with Elizabeth Cady Stanton speaking stirringly on equal rights for women to over a hundred other people at the Ethical Culture Society?"

"I do believe Mr. Brophy has a soul, quite unusual for a policeman."

"Olivia!" She set a slice of toast in front of me, and as I buttered it, poured the coffee into two cups. "I lent your friend Rae a clean pair of stockings and some sensible shoes this morning."

"She's been living with Whit, but they had a fight."

"I like her."

"So do I."

"Gerry said to remind you about meeting Mr. Colangelo this afternoon. I'm to come, too. He'll call for us at one o'clock."

"He wants you to identify him as the man who took the package?"

"Yes." She looked very unhappy.

I offered Mattie a cigarette and put another into my holder. She moved the kettle and passed her cigarette briefly over the flame. Then I lit mine from hers. Inhaling, I let the smoke out slowly. "Andrew approached us on the street early this morning."

"Harry told me."

"He wouldn't have hurt me, Mattie," I said, in response to the concern she couldn't hide but to which she gave no voice.

"How can you be so sure?"

"I just know." When Mattie sighed, I added, "I'm not afraid of Andrew anymore. In fact, I've given up fear entirely. It's kept me from thinking clearly."

"Oh, dear," Mattie said, raising her eyes to heaven. "Now I'm really worried." She stood up and rinsed the dishes in the sink, stacking them on the drying rack.

"Oh, pshaw! I forgot that I had wanted to talk to Madame Gabori, the hat designer. So if I can find something decent to wear, I'll call on her and meet you and Gerry Brophy at Eppie Diamond's house."

Mattie had altered one of Miss Alice's pretty frocks for me, so off I went in my borrowed finery: Miss Alice's blue silk, Great-Aunt Evangeline's raccoon coat and Ilona Gabori's Eppie Diamond shoes. O la, I felt like a girl right out of the pages of *Vogue*.

"I'm going uptown," I told Red Farrell, who was sitting on his bony haunches in front of Harry's door smoking a particularly acrid cigar. He squinted up at me with his peculiar eyes, scowled, and gave no sign of moving, which was a relief.

In fact, the Hudson Dusters didn't venture far from their own territory. Their appearance on New York's most fashionable boulevards would definitely be cause for consternation among retailers and shoppers alike. And Red Farrell, his pale blue, pin-pupil eyes, partially chewed ear, flame-red hair creeping from his tatty wool cap, would stand out like a boil on a Madonna's face. It would not be tolerated, as in the Village, where almost any aberrant behavior is tolerated for its very sake.

So I was quite alone when I got off the subway on Fiftieth Street and walked to Madison Avenue. Ilona Gabori's atelier was on Forty-eighth, in a squat brick building of two floors. A discreet decoration on the window of the door announced: LES CHAPEAUX DE PARIS, and just beneath that: *Madame Ilona Gabori, Prop.*

I peered inside and saw a small but plush reception area that looked like the drawing room in a mansion. A pretty woman in a hat sat behind a small table. She was speaking on the telephone.

My hand on the knob, I was drawn to the sliver of showroom window to the left of the door. A burgundy drapery, pulled back on one side, revealed the head of a mannequin, whose beautifully painted face was partially obscured by a tight-fitting black-and-white cloche with a tiny rolled brim pulled down below eyebrow level. The whole effect was stunning.

But not half so stunning as the face on the mannequin itself. It was mine.

Chapter Forty-three

$\mathcal{M}$y shock was magnified when I stepped into the shop. The face on every hatted head was mine.

"Are you unwell, Mademoiselle?" The girl who had been behind the table now stood beside me. Her voice was low, intimate, the accent, cultivated French. She was tall, very slim, and wore a black cloche that covered the top of her earlobes and skimmed across her brows. "Oh!" She stepped back when she saw my face.

I sat down on one of the gilded chairs. "I am as shocked as you," I said.

She smiled. "Not shocked. I've never met one of the living mannequin models. It's quite a nice likeness, don't you think?"

Think? What I was thinking was not for civilized ears.

"I've come to see Madame," I said. I patted my pockets, looked in my rarely used purse. I really needed more cards, or perhaps I should take better care of the ones I had. Here was one I'd made a note on. *Ephemeral.* What on earth did that mean? I took my pencil and crossed it out, then handed the card to the girl.

"Olivia Brown," she read from my card. "You're the poet?"

"Yes."

"I'm Violetta. I manage the shop for Madame. I am delighted to meet you. I look forward to your poems in *Vanity Fair*." Her accent had all but disappeared. She obviously donned it for Madame's uptown clients.

"Thank you."

"I am also a writer," she said, modestly. "Of course I have so little time to—"

I think she would have told me the story of her life had not two very fashionably dressed women entered the shop. Violetta slipped back into her exaggerated French and turned away from me to greet them.

"Madame Gabori," I said, seeing that my significance was quickly fading.

"Oh, yes, excuse please, mesdames." She left the room, closing the door behind her.

The women, who already wore cloches in the latest fashion, walked from head to head admiring Madame's work. When they came to me, the hatless, eccentrically dressed girl with the mannequin's face, they stopped.

"Goodness gracious," one of the women said. "You're the mannequin."

"Not at all," I said, uncharitably. "Someone has stolen my face."

They were both staring at me rather unmannerly, I thought. It was a good thing that Violetta returned and held the door leading to the studio open for me.

"Madame will see you now, Mademoiselle Brown. We are sorry to have kept you waiting."

The studio consisted of a line of alcoves in which were set elegant little dressing tables with tall, three-way mirrors and stands of various sizes and design. Hand-held mirrors lay facedown on the dressing tables. Hat trees and seated mannequins, all with my face, were clustered at the far end of the room like guests at a garden party.

"My dear!" Ilona Gabori, formidable in a dark blue mohair costume I recognized as Chanel, greeted me as if I were a long-lost protégé. "You've come for a hat at last. I am joyful." She kissed me on both cheeks, and taking my arm, pulled me toward the garden party. "I see you are wearing the shoes."

"I came to ask you about Eppie Diamond," I said, allowing her to remove my coat.

She frowned at my dress, trying to place it. Then nodding, she said, "Lanvin, I should say, but not from a recent collection."

"Why are all your mannequins wearing my face?" I sat down in the chair she indicated.

Ilona Gabori looked surprised. "I chose from the different styles. You have a face for our time, and for hats. Like this one." She fitted a cloche on my head and smoothed my hair under so that just the tips of red showed on either side, pointing toward my mouth.

"But I did not give my permission to have my face used on mannequins."

"Ah, so . . ." She handed me a mirror and stepped back. "See how you have the look for my hats. Such a long, lovely neck. A sensual mouth. You will wear it, of course."

I admired myself in the mirror. "You're very nice, Madame, but I cannot afford your hats." Reluctantly, I reached up to remove it.

But she stopped my hand. "No, no. It is my gift to you."

"I accept, but only if you'll answer my questions about Eppie Diamond and tell me who sold you the mannequins."

"My next clients are waiting, but I will tell you quickly. The mannequins I get from Glaser on Fourteenth Street." She helped me on with my coat. "What do you want to know about Eppie Diamond?"

"Her son."

"She had no son. She had no children."

"Then who is Andrew Goren? Perhaps her husband had a son from a previous marriage?"

"Sol Goren had no children. He and Eppie were married very young. He died ten years ago. Who is this Andrew Goren you ask me about?"

"He calls himself Andrew Goren. I don't know who he is."

"Is he young and handsome?"

"Yes."

"Eppie had a . . . an interest in young men. They tended to take advantage of her . . . generosity."

Violetta opened the door. "Are we ready, Madame?"

"Yes, yes, indeed. Violetta, will you see Mademoiselle Brown out?"

I walked westward, aware that the hat had transformed me from an eccentric to an original, in fashion terms. Heads did turn as I walked.

Glaser on Fourteenth Street, Ilona Gabori had said. I had the distinct feeling that I should know it.

At Seventh Avenue, as I was about to get on the subway to Eppie Diamond's to meet Mr. Colangelo, it came to me.

Bennett Newman lived on Fourteenth Street. And the building he lived in was owned by Glaser Family Printers. Wasn't it possible that Glaser Family Printers also made mannequins? Couldn't they be the Glaser Company that Ilona Gabori had mentioned?

It went like this: Bennett Newman lived in a flat over Glaser Family Printers. Someone had painted my face on their mannequins. Bennett made his living as a graphic artist. It was basic arithmetic. Two and two are four. Ergo, Bennett had painted my face on the Glaser mannequins.

Chapter Forty-four

A black automobile stood in front of Eppie Diamond's house, and as I passed it, I heard a tapping on the window and saw Mattie motioning to me. A uniformed policeman got out of the car and held the door for me. I slipped in beside Mattie on the backseat.

"I'm sorry if I'm late," I said.

"You're not late, Miss." The policeman had returned to the driver's seat. "But they are waiting for you inside."

Mattie was very agitated. "They didn't want me to confront him, Olivia, so I waited in the car and when he came, I recognized him. It's the same man who took the package for Andrew Goren. What does it all mean?" Her distracted fingers commented on my hat.

I put my arm around her. I could feel her shaking right through the fur of my coat. "We'll soon find out." I tapped the policeman on the shoulder. "Shall I go in?"

"Yes, Miss. I'll be taking Miss Timmons home now."

"No, no," Mattie said, "I'd rather wait."

"It's too cold for you to sit here. I'll be home in less than an hour, I'm certain." I gave her another quick hug and got out of the car before the policeman could come round for me.

Now I saw the house clearly. Still desolate. Still wearing its mourning wreath on the front door. The one on the ground-floor door under the stone stairs was missing. Of course.

As I pondered whether to enter the house from the ground-floor workshop or the parlor floor, the car taking Mattie home pulled away from the curb and drove off down the street.

I decided to try the door to the workshop and gave the bell a quick twist. A dissonant sound came from within. Almost immediately, the door opened. Gerry Brophy seemed relieved to see me, and after I entered, I saw why.

"At last you've deigned to grace us with your presence, Miss Brown," Detective Walz intoned.

He was a thick and stolid presence standing behind the man seated at a worktable almost hidden behind a tower of shoe boxes. The boxes wore paper I'd come to recognize as distinctively Eppie Diamond's—and William Morris's.

"What time is it, Mr. Brophy?" I asked.

Brophy took up his pocket watch. "Ten minutes past two o'clock, Miss."

"I believe we arranged that I be here at approximately two o'clock, did we not, Mr. Brophy?"

"We did, Miss."

Then, as if he was as impatient as Brophy and I to get on with it, the man behind the boxes stood with such haste that the boxes leaned precipitously. With large, deft hands, he stopped them short of crashing. His eyes met mine, and it was so simple. In that glance I had an answer to one of the puzzling events that had recently overtaken me.

"This is Mr. Carmine Colangelo," Brophy said. "He's going to help you find the shoes you left with Miss Diamond."

"These are shoes that are finished, Miss," Colangelo said, in heavily accented English. He was dark-complected and spare of structure, with long arms and large hands like mitts.

He proceeded to open one box at a time and I shook my head each time. We went through all the boxes and I kept shaking my head.

Finally, after Mr. Colangelo opened the last box and I shook my head for the last time, I said, "They're not here."

To which Walz responded in a falsetto, "Oh, I'm so surprised."

If I were not a law-abiding citizen . . . Mr. Colangelo's eyes met mine again.

"Is of course possible," Mr. Colangelo said, "person who murdered Miss Diamond, took shoes away with him."

"Why?" Walz asked bluntly.

"I am not police," Mr. Colangelo said with a shrug.

A sweet man, Mr. Colangelo. I hated to upset him, but the pieces were coming together, at least some of them, and I had to make sure I was right.

"I'll be on my way now," I told Walz and Brophy.

Colangelo took a black, broad-brimmed hat from a hook and set it on his head. "I'm finish now?"

"Go on, go on," Walz said, waving us out. Behind him, Gerry Brophy gave me a most unprofessional grin.

I waited to ask my question until we were on the street. We fell in side by side walking toward the subway. "How is your son, Mr. Colangelo? I understand he's been ill."

His shoulders drooped. "Antonio? He is good sometimes, not good now."

"Your son, Mr. Colangelo. Eppie Diamond was not his mother?"

He turned to me, offended, shocked, eyes afire at last, so I knew without any doubt. "His mama die when he is five. Never, never, me and Miss Diamond."

"Then why," I asked, "does Antonio call himself Andrew Goren?" I'd had no idea what I was going to do once I'd confronted Mr. Colangelo with what I suspected, but somehow I'd ended up accompanying him as he walked. When he didn't respond, I said, "Your son is an astonishing writer." I had to rush to keep up with him: Eppie Diamond's shoes were not made for walking.

"My son is sick boy, but he does not murder anyone."

"I agree," I said. "The police are looking for Andrew Goren. They don't know yet that your son has been calling himself Andrew Goren. They will find out."

He stopped and stared down at me with Andrew's eyes. "You will tell them?" His hands clamped my arms.

"I may have to, if only to clear his name. And mine."

"They will put blame on him." He began to shake me. There was such agony in his eyes that instead of anger, I was moved to tears.

"Please." The whole world was spinning.

He stopped and looked down at his huge hands. As if he'd touched something fiery, he let me go. Mumbling, "Excuse please, excuse," he moved away swiftly.

As I leaned against a fire hydrant to recover and watched him hurry toward Union Square, the seedling of a thought began to germinate. What would Carmine Colangelo do to protect his son? Would he kill?

To avoid the remotest possibility of a meeting with Detective Walz, I walked down to Fourteenth Street first before I turned back toward Seventh Avenue. A dust-laden gust of wind made me pause.

"Oliver!"

This uninhibited shout broke into my meditation and caused the unpleasant sensation of my bones abruptly transforming to pudding. Hand shading my eyes, I surveyed the area.

The call came again. "Oliver!"

I finally saw him, across the street, waving at me like a Navy signalman. Edward Hall, hatless, his thick hair buffeted in the wind, forded Seventh Avenue dancing nimbly through carts and automobiles toward me, the lapels of his coat raised against the cold. A long knitted wool scarf was slung around his neck.

"Oliver!" He clasped me in his arms and tried to find a spot on my face to kiss, which wasn't easy because of my hat.

Laughing, I kissed him on the mouth, which clearly both surprised and delighted him. It was an impulsive thing to do, but he looked so gallant fighting his way across the street to me, I couldn't resist. His lips were sweet and sensitive, until they demanded more and I turned my face away.

"I have wonderful news," he said, undeterred. "Come with me and I'll tell you all about it."

"Can't. Have an appointment."

"Please." *Jubilant* was the best word to describe his demeanor, and believe me, any description of Edward would have had to contain the word *morose*, so I was intrigued.

The Green Dragon Tea Room, a chop suey house, is a block in the right direction, so I let Edward steer me there. A dimly lit, dingy saloon, the GDT, as the Chelsea neighborhood refers to it, is a place for basic cheap Chinese food and watered-down gin disguised as tea in those little Chinese tea mugs.

"What is your news?" I asked, as we settled opposite each other into a booth in the back. I reached over and adjusted the collar of his coat. He was wearing a new shirt and now that I looked more closely, a very good suit. As long as I'd known him, I'd never seen him in a suit.

A wizened Chinese waiter in black arrived with chopsticks and napkins, a China teapot with dragons on it, and two little mugs. Gingerly, I put my fingertips on the teapot. It was ice cold.

"One order of chicken chow mein," Edward told the waiter, brushing aside my protest cavalierly. The waiter's face was impassive, with no sign that he either heard or cared. After he left, Edward filled our cups and lit our cigarettes.

"Okay," I said. "Tell me now."

Edward took a fifty-dollar bill from his billfold and set it down under my cup. "For your last two poems."

"*Ainslee's* debt, not yours."

"I'm making it mine. *Ainslee's* is gone. I've taken the job at *Vogue*, and I want to publish your poems again."

"*Vanity Fair*—"

"I understand you have a relationship with Crowninshield now, but they can't take everything you write."

This was certainly true. I need other outlets for my poems.

"I'll think about it, Edward." I folded the money and thrust it in my pocket. Pride I have little of, when it comes to getting paid for my work.

Rather brusquely, our waiter dropped the covered dish of chow mein down on the table, along with bowls of dried noodles and rice, and a tiny plate of yellow mustard. There was no attempt at communication.

"I'm willing to share you, Oliver." Edward's fawn eyes were moist, absorbing me rather like a predatory sponge. "I can do a lot more for you now."

I took a sip of gin. "I'm happy for you, Edward."

"What do you say, Oliver? Can we have dinner together and talk about it?"

"I said I'd think about it."

"What about dinner?"

"No." I finished the poor excuse for gin, deposited the remains of the cigarette into a chipped glass ashtray, and stood up to leave. But Edward caught my hand. "Don't, Edward. It's no good."

"You've taken a new lover since Whit." His tone was more despairing than accusatory. "Didn't you hear me, Oliver? I said I was willing to share."

I left him in haste, thinking more of getting away than my talk with Mr. Colangelo. I couldn't help but wonder, is there something wrong with me that men react this way? All I want is the freedom to love, the space and time to write my poems, and no commitments that would interfere with either.

It was raining, a light, cool mist, when I came out on Fourteenth Street. I knew exactly where I was going, and it wasn't home. Not just yet. I was going to confront Bennett Newman, the man who had been painting my face on all those mannequins.

Chapter Forty-five

*T*he flat was chilly. The only heat came fitfully, from a riser pipe near the small kitchen.

Bennett had answered my knock yelling, "Quit that bloody knocking and come on in." He stood in front of his slanted table, pen in hand, absorbed in his drawing, his cigarette a long ash on the lid of a paint tin. From the back, in his heavy brown sweater and brown trousers, he looked like a gigantic bear.

"Are you painting my face on every mannequin in New York?" I demanded.

The bear turned into a man, who grinned at me. "Now, Oliver, don't be angry." He set his brush down carefully so as not to disturb his work. "You should be flattered." His face was flushed. When he kissed me his nose was cold, cold as mine.

"I suppose, since it's you." I flopped down on his sofa and took out a cigarette. "It feels a little like being robbed."

"I'll stop then." He came over and sat on the floor in front of me. "Shall I?"

I cupped his chin in my hand. "You're a dear thing."

"Shall I paint Rae's face on them? I don't think that will please the Glasers. They've sold out every one of your mannequins."

"Hmmmmm. Perhaps I should ask for royalties."

He pulled me down on his lap and removed my hat. "You mustn't have anything covering your hair."

"Don't you think it's very stylish? It's an Ilona Gabori."

"I like you just the way you are. I think it's time we went off together, don't you?"

No, I didn't, but to cover the sudden awkwardness, I offered him my cigarette, and when he took it, I crawled out of his lap and back on the sofa. "Wait till you hear the latest," I said, recapturing my cigarette.

Leaning back on his hands, he said, "One day, my pretty."

"Oh, pshaw, Bennett. You'd hate me in a minute."

He put his hand over his heart. "I can feel it coming on right now."

He was such a clown. I stretched out on the couch so that we were on eye level. "Andrew Goren is really Antonio Colangelo. Not the son of Eppie Diamond at all, but the son of Carmine Colangelo. What do you think of that?"

"Who is Carmine Colangelo?" He stood up and got one of his own cigarettes, a sharp-smelling French brand which was not a favorite of mine, went into the kitchen briefly, and returned with two glasses and a bottle of beer.

"Eppie Diamond's artisan shoemaker."

He poured beer into each glass, then set the bottle on the floor. "You mean the Italian guy she keeps locked up in her cellar?"

"What?"

"A joke, Oliver. Just a joke. Not even mine. Mackey's joke, as a matter of fact."

That disclosure seemed to squelch us both. We fell silent, each to our own thoughts. The light from Bennett's skylight had grown anemic. We became dusky shadows to one another. Wrapped in my coat, I was cozy, lying there on the sofa. He sat on the floor, leaning his back against the sofa, so near our breathing blended.

"When I came back from France," Bennett said, "I thought everything would be different."

"How so?" I murmured, snuggling into my coat, my eyelids growing heavy.

"Pure," he said. "Clarity. As it was meant to be . . ."

> *The somber procession left the church,*
> *Six braw pallbearers in black, two women mourned,*
> *While gryphon screamed from her lofty perch,*
> *"'Twas not as if you were not warned."*
> *A pyre awaits, my pages writ are fuel,*
> *The ardent torch extends no charity,*
> *Because, my friends, there is no golden rule.*
> *Fire ends all. Pure is not to be. Nor clarity.*

I groped for my pencil in the dark. The poem had come full blown in my dream. Waking, I wanted to write it down before it was lost.

Suddenly, I didn't know where I was. I sat up. What was that odd smell? Something burning. My funeral pyre. I staggered to my feet. My coat slipped to the floor. The room was alive with a shivering glow.

I was at Bennett's. I remembered now. I must have fallen asleep. Where was Bennett then? Dear God, his drafting table was on fire. I ran into the kitchen and filled his coffeepot with water, threw it into the flames, went back and did it again and again until I had about drowned the drafting table, and what had been a fire was just damp embers.

"Bennett!" I heard the fear in my voice. The darkness settled over me like a pall. "Bennett!"

Chapter Forty-six

The street, in this district of businesses and warehouses, was deserted, the cobblestones glazed from the steady mist. I thrust my arms into the sleeves of my coat, pulled my hat over my ears. The frantic urge I'd felt to get myself gone eased somewhat. The cold was tranquil and innocuous.

What had possessed Bennett to leave without a word? I could have been ash, as the cigarette he'd left to burn out on his drawing board.

My poem loitered on the edge of my mind. I needed a cigarette. Now, yes, and on the street. I searched my pockets for my case. It wasn't there. Damn, I must have left it upstairs. I didn't want to go back, but I did. What is a girl without her cigarette case?

Besides, Bennett's flat was awash in paper. Awash, all right. Bitterness, or something akin, sponged up the charred air. I flicked the light switch. Nothing happened.

I returned to my pockets for matches, which was good, because what my fingers now stumbled on was a folded paper square. I unfolded the square and held it up to the fuzz of gray light coming from a grimy bulb near the stairwell.

Bennett had left me a note after all. He was going up to Lord and Taylor to deliver his drawings and he'd be back, but should I awaken before, he didn't want me to worry.

Well, really! Wasn't there something essentially mad about leaving a note of explanation folded into a square the size of a postage stamp in someone's coat pocket?

Still, unfolded, it was a decent piece of paper, so I used the wall for a desk and with my pencil stub, also from my pocket, I scratched the poem that had roared into being on my waking. I was not entirely satisfied with it. I folded it up on its seam lines and restored it and my pencil to my pocket.

The effort wearied me. I needed that cigarette then and there, but my case was lost somewhere in the morass of Bennett's flat. Leaving the door to the hallway open to cast a trifling light, I moved cautiously back into the room.

The mess was concentrated around Bennett's drawing board where the fire had been. I opened a window. Cold air moved right in, altering the fragile balance in the room, from surreal to real.

I sat on the sofa and felt round and under the pillows, looking for my case. No case, but a handful of coins, a drawing pencil with a broken point, a pair of scissors and some scraps of ribbon, and a lip gloss. *Bennett Newman, you devil, and here I thought I was your one and only.*

When I stood, the toe of my shoe sent my cigarette case spinning. It had been on the floor near the sofa all this time.

No sooner had I retrieved it, shoving it into my less cluttered pocket, than I became aware of voices coming from the street below Bennett's window. Bennett. Who was he talking to? Arguing with was more accurate. My heart threatened to burst from my breast. Stephen Lowell. He'd come back. But what were they arguing about? They were close friends. I'd put a stop to that.

I was about to lean out of the window when Bennett and Stephen suddenly fell silent, looking up the street. I soon saw the reason why. They were joined by that awful Detective Walz and his sidekick, Gerry Brophy. All four stood in the rain, talking.

Bennett pointed up to the window. Was he trying to warn

me? I saw Walz look up, but I knew I couldn't be seen unless I wanted to be.

Would that I were a witch and could utter a spell that would get me from this place. But I wasn't. I was, however, a very smart girl. Or so I thought.

The stairs were not a problem. I almost made it down and gone before they all arrived. But those Eppie Diamond shoes were not made for scampering and I was caught on the stairs.

At their foot I noticed a door leading into Glaser Family Printers. I uttered a silent incantation. The knob turned freely. I ducked in and closed the door just as Bennett and Stephen, and the two coppers, opened the outside door.

It was as if I'd stepped into a coffin and closed the lid. A sweet, almost fruity, smell filled my nostrils. I had no idea where I was, some storage closet perhaps, but what did it matter? Yet I felt I wasn't alone. Was this the lair of the murderer? Would he grasp my throat, raise his fearsome knife and—

I flattened myself against the door and tentatively let my fingers explore what was around me. Something cold and smooth. God help me, an arm. I stifled a scream. Not a living arm. More than one arm. A breast as smooth as alabaster. The hilt of a sword. I snatched my hand back.

The voices of the men faded as they climbed the stairs to Bennett's flat. I waited only until I heard the floor creak above me. I opened the door carefully. My concern stopped me only long enough to light a match. Immediately I saw I was right to think I was not alone. I was in a charnel house, but of dead mannequins, all with my face. My sharp breath killed the match. I made a dash for the street.

My house was full of light when I came up Bedford Street. Too full of light. A man stood at my front door. Though he looked wet and uncomfortable, he wasn't going in or out. I slowed my swift pace.

"Olwer!" The harsh whisper stopped me. Ding Dong stepped out of the boxwood bushes in front of my neighbor's house and pulled me unprotesting into the shadows.

"What's going on, Ding Dong?"

"Da coppers come lookin' for youse. See dere." He pointed to the man at my door. I saw now he was wearing a uniform.

I wiped the rain from my face. "What do they want?"

He shrugged. His beady eyes didn't meet mine. "Ask Sherlock."

"Is that cop going to stand there all night?"

"Looks like it."

"Are they inside my house, too?"

"Not now."

I took Ding Dong's arm. "Come with me."

We went over the back fences, adding our quiet shuffling to the prowling of the cats, the wind through the bare branches of the trees, hardly breaking the winter stillness.

My back door was padlocked.

"I don't understand," I said. "Who did this?"

"Da coppers. But don't youse worry none." Ding Dong took out a leather package from his baggy trousers and unwrapped it, revealing all manner of tools. He made fast work of opening the lock, then he held the door for me.

I went in, but he didn't follow. Rain that had collected in the brim of his hat, spilled over now, drizzled down his face.

"Aren't you coming?"

"If I leave it open, dey'll know. I'll lock up and go back how we come."

"Wait." I touched his sleeve. The velvet was wet, coarse. "Tell me what this is about. I can't go in not knowing."

To my surprise, Ding Dong gave my shoulder a sympathetic pat. "Your friend, da schoolteacher," he said. Then he ran his finger across his throat.

Chapter Forty-seven

I staggered up the back stairs barely breathing, cold sweat breaking out all over me like the pox. Somewhere, I'd shrugged off the burden of my coat and left it. My legs shook so violently I didn't know if I could continue. I gave up, finally, and continued my upward climb on my hands and knees.

My schoolteacher friend. Rae. It wasn't true, it couldn't be. I couldn't accept it.

"Mattie." The words stuck in my throat.

Then Mattie was there, kneeling beside me, holding me, rocking me.

I don't know how she got me to my bed, but I remember hot milk laced with whiskey.

How is it that sometimes, when the silence is so loud, it pierces through the deepest sleep? So it is this time. Breathing is labored, painful. I've been running, terrified, through grand, high-ceiling'd rooms—Lord and Taylor—men's suits and ladies' dresses—always checking behind me for my pursuer. I know it is a dream. I run because I have to. Past elegant girls in evening dresses, who reach out alabaster arms to catch me, call out to me with no sound from their cold lips. They want to make me one with them, for we all have my face.

Then Chopin. I come upon a woman slumped over the keys of her grand piano. The huge, drapery-framed windows beyond the piano look down on a Fifth Avenue glittering with diamonds. The woman stirs herself and turns to me. Eppie Diamond. The gash in her throat drips blood on the beribboned box of shoes she holds out to me. "You are my beautiful boy," she tells me. "All mine."

My feet refuse to move me on. I twist round, and fooling them, break free, rushing head down through a sideways passage. *I am Alice, and I have fallen down the rabbit hole.*

They are coming for me, I know, because I've done something I didn't know I'd done.

"Explain!" I howl at the draperies, the crystal chandeliers, the fine mahogany counters strewn with silk lingerie.

The Jack of Hearts is Ding Dong in velvet, his peaked cap flopping in front of his mashed nose. He has brought me a gift wrapped in William Morris paper on a red satin pillow held up high. "Take it, Olwer," he says. He gives me a reassuring smile.

The mannequins crowd round me.

I stand on tiptoes and take the gift, tear off the wrappings. True and sure, it finds my hand. The trench knife that killed Eppie Diamond is still stained with her blood. My scream shatters the dream into a million piercing shards.

"I want every detail," Harry said like his old self. "Everything you did from the minute you left here. Don't skip anything."

Numb, I stared at Harry. "I don't care," I said.

"Olivia." Mattie squeezed my hand so tight, I winced. "You do care. That's why it hurts so much."

"I do care." The tears were hot pellets on my cheeks. "It's my fault she's dead."

"It could have nothing to do with you," Harry said.

"You don't believe that, Harry."

He sighed. "No, I don't." His fingers edged the pencil back and forth, top to bottom, bottom to top. A cigarette burned in an ashtray. "I liked her," he said.

My feet were cold. I curled them up under me. Where were

my shoes? Shoes? I am thinking about shoes when I should be thinking about Rae. I said, "You must tell me how it happened."

Mattie said, despairingly, "We've already told you—twice. That's enough." Her teeth pressed hard on her lower lip. She sent a pleading look to Harry.

"I don't remember it at all." I didn't. "I'm sorry. Tell me again."

Harry said, "Someone must have followed her into the subway this afternoon when she left the school. He caught her from behind."

I groaned and put my face in my hands.

"She bled out in a minute. Never knew what hit her."

I shot up from the sofa in a fit and threw myself about the room. I couldn't stand the thought. "A minute! Harry, a minute is eternity. She must have been so frightened. Harry, think of it. Think of it!"

Mattie tried to comfort me, but I wouldn't be comforted. She asked, "Olivia, where were you this afternoon—after I left you?"

I fell back on Harry's rumpled Murphy bed and lay staring at his ceiling. The paint was separating from the plaster in crisp, loose feathers. "Your ceiling needs painting," I said.

"Olivia." Mattie's worried face peered down at me. She lit a cigarette and handed it to me. Lit one for herself.

"You went to Eppie Diamond's house to find the shoes you left with her," Harry prompted gently.

"They were in the workshop. Carmine Colangelo, Gerry, and Walz. The entrance is under the stairs." I pushed myself up on my elbows. "Andrew Goren is Carmine Colangelo's son, Antonio."

Harry whistled through his teeth. The cigarette in the ashtray flared.

"I don't understand," Mattie said.

"I guess Andrew felt he'd be accepted more readily as Andrew Goren. He knew Eppie Diamond, knew she didn't have a son. He writes fiction. It was easy for him to make up an identity."

"He's a nut," Harry said.

"Yes," I agreed. "But he didn't kill anyone."

"He had the motive—for Mackey at least. Mackey made a fool of him."

"And Eppie Diamond?"

"Maybe she found out he was using her name and her life and told him to stop."

"Now no one is left to tell him to stop," Mattie said.

"But why Rae?" *Why Rae?* My fists came down hard on the bedclothes.

Harry shrugged. "Where did you go from Eppie Diamond's?"

"After about a half hour, when we didn't find the shoes, we gave up. Mr. Colangelo and I left together. I walked with him for a block trying to get him to talk about Andrew, but he was recalcitrant. We parted and I walked down to Fourteenth Street and then back toward Seventh Avenue and the subway."

"But you didn't come home till near seven o'clock," Mattie said.

"I ran into Edward Hall and kept him company over lunch at the Green Dragon."

"Till seven?" Harry said.

I shook my head. "There was something I needed to do. I'd gone to see Ilona Gabori at her atelier when I left here. Every mannequin she owned wore my face."

Harry was staring at me as if I'd lost my mind.

"I mean, my face was painted on every mannequin."

"How can that be?" Mattie said.

"I asked the same. She told me the mannequins came from the Glaser Company." I lay back again. Harry's bed smelled of cigarettes and beer, mixed with perspiration. It was reassuring. "I remembered that Bennett Newman's flat is above the Glaser Family Printers. It was Bennett who had painted my face on all the mannequins. So when I left the Green Dragon, I went off to berate him."

"What did he say?"

"Harry, your cigarette!" He grabbed his nub of a cigarette before it could burn the papers on his desk. Another fire would not please me.

"Go on, Oliver. You were going to tell us what Bennett said about the mannequins."

"He was not at all remorseful. He said I should be flattered and if I didn't like it maybe Rae would."

"Were you there till seven o'clock?" Mattie stopped drifting and sat down on the bed beside me. I held her hand.

"Bennett had to deliver some drawings to Lord and Taylor, and I fell asleep. I woke up because he'd left his cigarette burning and it had started a fire. I put out the fire and was on the street when I realized I'd left my cigarette case in the flat so I went back to get it. And that's how I saw him and Stephen Lowell arguing under Bennett's window. I would have called down to them, but Gerry came along with Detective Walz, so I hid downstairs in the Glaser Family's storage closet until I could get away."

Harry was making frightening noises. "The coppers think you killed Rae."

"What is the matter with everybody? I couldn't. I loved her."

"They found a letter to you in her purse."

I sat up, moved again to tears. "Did you read it? What did it say?"

Mattie put her arm around me. "She said she was going to marry Whit."

"No! She wouldn't." I looked to Harry for a denial.

"She did."

I felt betrayed. "No more now, please, Harry." I stood up.

"I'm sorry, Oliver, but I have to—" He stopped dead, exchanged a glance with Mattie I couldn't fathom.

"Have to what? Tell me."

"Oliver, Mattie's been scrubbing up the trail you left on the back stairs when you came home. And your coat—"

"What trail!" I screamed. "What about my coat? What are you talking about, Harry, damn it all?"

His face was blank. I couldn't read anything in his eyes. He said, "Oliver, how did you get all that blood on your coat and shoes?"

Chapter Forty-eight

*M*y attorney, Thomas Jenner III, Esq., is tall, pleasant-faced, not much older than I, but truly a generation apart in the way we look at life. He arrived for lunch, which Mattie served in our tiny dining room. He had already spent an hour with Harry, who had told him all the particulars of my troubles.

I'd inherited Mr. Jenner, as he had me, from my great-aunt Evangeline. Thomas's late father had been Aunt Evangeline's attorney.

Proper person that he is, and I am not, he would have waited until we were having our coffee to begin talking business. But my concerns overrode the niceties of convention and certainly overrode the soup. I said at once, "What are my legal rights in this, Thomas?"

A thoughtful, if provoking man, he finished his soup, while I, impatiently, tickled my plate with my spoon in my effort to get him moving.

His attire was formal: suit, vest, coat, tie. His shirt had the stiffest of collars. A pocket watch with a Phi Beta Kappa key for a fob was strung across his middle. The whole picture was quite out of tune with the Village. I wondered if that was precisely why Great-Aunt Evangeline had chosen his father to handle her affairs.

After Mattie served those wretched cucumber sandwiches, he asked her, "What have you done with the shoes and the coat?"

I looked at Mattie, aghast. My God, I had never even thought to ask her.

"They are in the attic, drying. The rain had soaked through everything."

"Let me have a look at them. Then I want you to pack them together in one parcel and leave it with Harry Melville. Be discreet. I will send a boy to collect it. I want them out of here before the police arrive."

"The police! No, Thomas," I said. "I'm trying to avoid them."

"You can't, Olivia. My design is to keep you from being arrested. I've arranged for them to interview you here at five o'clock. I could not put them off. We must prepare a statement and a strategy." He nodded to Mattie, who rose and left us.

I lit a cigarette from the stub of my other. My hands shook. "I'd be grateful for more wine," I said, offering Thomas my empty glass.

He filled it scantly, saying, "No more for now. They will ask you questions. You will tell them only where you were between the hours of two and five yesterday. Nothing else."

"I was with them for part of the time, from two, I think, for at least a half hour."

"Fine. And afterward?"

"I walked toward Union Square a short way with Mr. Colangelo, then started back and ran into a friend, Edward Hall. He's an editor with *Vogue* now. He wanted to eat lunch and talk to me about sending my poems to him, so I sat with him awhile."

"How long?" He was making notes with a very pretty fountain pen.

"I don't know, Thomas. I don't pay much attention to time. Perhaps less than half an hour or a bit longer."

"Then what?"

"Since I was in the neighborhood, I went to see Bennett Newman." I didn't bother with the whole story about the mannequins. It had nothing to do with Rae's horrible death or the blood on my coat and shoes.

"You knew he'd be home?"

"Bennett's almost always at home, painting. He's an artist. He has no hours either. But he does come out at night with our Provincetown Players. That's how I know him."

Hearing Mattie on the stairs, we both stopped and waited.

My coat had dried with the smell of the veldt, or as I imagined the veldt. Primitive and wild. The right sleeve and down the right side were stiff, and mildly sticky to the touch, stained black with what I, unknowing, would have guessed to be tar. I pulled my hand away, allowing Thomas to inspect the coat.

The shoes were in a cloth bag, still damp. I lifted them out, ruined, not by blood, but by the rain and my backyard climbing, unwearable. Not that I would ever have worn them again.

"I don't see any blood."

"Look at the soles," Mattie said.

The leather soles were ingrained with an uneven rusty color, would become more so as they dried. I didn't want them near me.

I was truly beleaguered. Punishment from the gods for some wrong I had committed, in another life. Of course, what hurt the most was Rae.

Was it her blood on my coat and shoes? And whether it was hers, which was insupportable, or someone or something else's, from where could it possibly have come?

I lay on my bed in the dark, smoking, listening to the winter thunder growling rings round my house. The siren, my typewriter, gave no call. Every few seconds came a sharp flash of lightning, then the supreme crash, a thousand angry waves magnified. I was afraid of the dark now, so hadn't drawn the draperies. Outside, Rae was in the wind.

When the rains came, so did I mourn.

Toward morning I fell into a fitful sleep beset with dreams of mannequins in my pursuit, calling my name. I awoke in a pool of sweat, struggling with the bedclothes.

"Oliver."

I did not move or open my eyes. Had they come to get me?

"Oliver."

I lay perfectly still, trying to make some sense of the murmuring voice that seemed to have come out of my dream.

"Oliver." Now the murmur was accompanied by a hand on my shoulder. "Oliver, wake up."

I opened my eyes. Bennett, the huge teddy bear, was kneeling beside my bed. He gave my shoulder a shake.

"Bennett!" I sat up so quickly his hand fell away. "What are you doing here?"

Such a sad smile. "It's Whit. We must go to him."

"Whit? My God, now something's happened to Whit?" I swung my legs to the floor so that now I looked down on him.

He clasped me round the waist, head against my breast. I stroked his bristly hair. "He's taking Rae's death badly. Stephen says he may take his own life."

"We must stop him!" I stepped back. I was still in my nightdress. "Wait downstairs and let me put myself together."

Bennett heaved himself up and stood over me. "Don't be long." He turned to go.

I suddenly remembered the fire. "Yesterday," I said, "you left your cigarette burning."

He brushed my words aside. How strange, I thought. But everyone's behavior had become strange. It came to me then, how had he gotten in, how had he gotten to my room? I put my hand on his arm. "Bennett, wait. Where's Mattie?"

"I don't know. Your door was open. I called but no one answered, so I came on up."

"She must be with Harry, though it's not at all like her to leave the door open."

"Hurry, Oliver."

In haste, I washed my face. My eyes were red and swollen, sensitive to soap and water. My mouth was dry, my tongue thick from too much wine. I brushed my teeth.

When I came downstairs in my bulky green wool sweater, ready to leave, Bennett was sitting in the parlor with a cup of coffee, my last poem, the poem that had come to me in his flat, on his lap. The sense of urgency he'd conveyed to me earlier seemed to have subsided.

"Mattie's back?"

"No, but I found the coffee, and"—he flapped the sheet of paper at me—"this. It's very good, Oliver. I swear, you get better and better."

"I do." My mail was on the hall stand. I scrawled a note for Mattie on the back of a bill and left it there, then remembered I was not free to leave my home. "Did you have any trouble getting past the police guard at my door?"

"Police guard? There was no one standing at your door." He took my hand.

"There wasn't? That's odd." The fear, that girdle across my chest, eased somewhat. "Maybe they've found the person who killed Rae."

"Good God, Oliver, they don't think you did it? I thought I took care of that."

"They're coming to talk to me at five," I said. "I think they're going to arrest me." I shivered, took my hand back. "What do you mean, you thought you took care of that?"

"When they questioned me this morning. I told them we'd been together all afternoon."

"You are a good egg," I said. Standing on tiptoe, I kissed his cheek. "Maybe that's why they removed my guard."

"You couldn't have killed Rae," Bennett said, following me down the stairs.

"I loved her." Where was the key? It should have been on the hall stand where we keep the spare. Mattie must have taken the one in the lock.

"Of course you did, but you couldn't have done it anyway," he said. Hands on my waist, he lifted me down the last few stairs and held me tight against him. "I wouldn't let any harm come to you, Oliver."

"I know that." Were the Dusters across the street? If they were, I wouldn't be concerned about leaving my door unlocked.

He set me on my feet. " . . . So don't you think it's time we gave up this crazy life and went off together? What do you think? My grandfather left me enough money in trust for us to live peacefully in the country, a little village on the Hudson, I should think. You will write and I will paint . . ."

"You're a dear, but I don't want to go off with anyone, not even you. Let's see if Mattie's with Harry." I knocked on Harry's door. "Harry?" I tried the door. It was locked. "That's really strange."

"Maybe Mattie took Harry somewhere."

"I suppose . . ." That didn't make any sense. I looked out the window in my front door and saw that Bennett was right. There was no uniformed guard in front of my door. As I watched, to my relief, Red Farrell came shuffling down the street, a cigar between his teeth.

Bennett's hand on my elbow pressured me. "Come on, Oliver, I don't want to leave Whit on his own—"

"I thought you said Stephen was with him."

"Stephen was on his way."

"Okay, let's go," I said, giving Red a casual wave.

It had gotten warmer after the storm last night and streamers of fog hung suspended in the still moist air.

"Who is that?" Bennett asked. "He looks disreputable."

"A friend of Harry's." I tucked my hand into Bennett's reassuring big paw, and we rushed off, my feet barely grazing the sidewalk, to Washington Square South, where Whit had rooms.

I was grateful to Bennett for giving me an alibi. It only occurred to me as we climbed the stairs to Whit's flat, that in giving me an alibi, Bennett had also given himself one.

Chapter Forty-nine

Stephen met us at the door, his eyes brimming with compassion. Behind him, the haunting whine of a harmonica.

I'd been in Whit's flat many times. He'd furnished the two small rooms with a few antique pieces that his ancestor, a royal governor, or tax collector, or something appalling like that, had brought from England in the eighteenth century. Books, though, were everywhere, filling shelves up to his ceiling, stacked on the floor. Although he wrote smart, witty reviews for journals and the *Tribune*, he lived in genteel poverty.

Sitting, legs splayed, in his big old easy chair, Whit played "It's a Long Way to Tipperary" on the harmonica, with more feeling than he'd ever revealed to me. His hands clustered round his mouth, hiding the instrument. The timbre grated on my nerves.

He wore nothing but a singlet and a dingy pair of shorts under an open robe, a state of undress that was so unlike him it was alarming. His eyes were a bit glassy, but he didn't look in any danger of harming himself, unless being drunk could be construed as harming oneself. If this was the case, we were all guilty.

"See who's here, chappy," Bennett said, his words layered with a disconcerting tenderness.

Whit stopped in mid *Tipp*. His eyes were puffed and bloodshot. "She wouldn't have left me, Oliver," he croaked, giving no notice to Bennett. "Like you." He raised the harmonica to his lips and finished the song. That was it. That and the tears that suddenly appeared. He was lost to us, wandering in some kind of no-man's-land of grief.

I knelt beside him. "Not like me, Whit." But I received a glance filled with such hatred that I flinched. I rose, poised for flight, looked up at Stephen. He had the most arresting eyes: light blue with a dark blue outer edge. I felt their tug in the pit of me. Whit groaned, drawing me back to him. "Where are his shirt and trousers? Why is he sitting half-dressed like this?" He was not himself. Whit never sat round in his underclothes, not even with friends. Not even with lovers.

"Why?" Whit glared at me. "Ask me, Oliver. I'll tell you." Stephen moved closer, so to defend me. His scent was intoxicating. I shook my spirit free. Not now.

"Okay, Whit, where are your clothes?"

His belligerence faded. "I had a nosebleed, blood all over my shirt and trousers. They took everything away. As if I could do anything to hurt her. She was human and real, Oliver, not like you." He began to sob.

Stephen and Bennett exchanged a glance, then Bennett reached down and lifted Whit. "Come on, chappy." Between them, his arms over their shoulders, they carried him to his bed.

I followed, covered him with a blanket. He had been my lover, briefly, now I felt only pity, and a tiny stirring of resentment.

"The police took them, he said." Stephen put a pillow under Whit's head. So gentle. Elegant hands with tapered fingers.

We stood in Whit's front room, nonplussed, passing a cigarette round to light the other two, all thinking our own thoughts. It would have been nice for each of us to shed a tear of two for Rae at this moment, but I wasn't sure I wanted to share that intimacy with either Bennett or Stephen or even Whit.

"They think he killed her?" Bennett was pale. "Why would he?"

"I left him and he took it badly. If Rae was planning to . . ." But she hadn't been, at least not according to the letter the police found, which I hadn't yet seen. I would reserve judgment.

"What should we do?" Bennett said.

"About what?" Stephen's response was to Bennett's question, but his eyes spoke to me. It was disconcerting.

"About leaving him alone," Bennett said, giving Stephen a sideways look.

"You have a deadline, Bennett. I'll stay with him," Stephen said. "Oliver, will you stay, too?"

"She can't," Bennett said.

"Don't speak for me, Bennett." My nerves were getting the better of me. Still, Bennett was right. I couldn't stay. "But," I smiled at Bennett to soothe the hurt I'd put on his face, "Bennett's right, of course. Whit needs his boys right now."

In the next room Whit began to sob. It was the most awful sound. I headed for the door before I did the same.

"I wish we could do something for him," Bennett said. "After all, we're his friends."

I don't know what came over me then. "Perhaps you can give him an alibi as you did me . . . and yourself," I said.

When I arrived home, Harry's door was open and he and Mattie were standing nose to nose, having what looked like an agitated conversation. They stopped when I walked in.

Mattie shrieked, "Olivia, thank heavens! Where have you been?"

"Bennett came and told me Whit was going to kill himself. Didn't you find my note?"

She shook her head. "Where was it?"

"On the hall stand. Where did you go, Mattie? You left the door unlocked and Bennett came right up to my bedroom."

Mattie clapped her hand to her mouth.

"Bloody hell," Harry said.

"I made sure to lock the door when I left. I was only gone a half hour to do the marketing."

"Bennett said we had to go over and be with Whit. Stephen was with him when we got there."

"It was a false alarm, I take it?" Harry asked.

"He was drunk, playing the harmonica and sitting in his underclothes. The police had taken away his shirt and trousers because he said he'd had a nosebleed."

"Well, well, well," Harry said.

"Did you notice the policeman is not at our door anymore?"

"I did," Mattie said.

"It's because Bennett told them I was with him all afternoon. If I have an alibi, how can they arrest me?"

"Depends on any other evidence they've collected."

"I didn't do it, Harry."

"I'm not saying you did."

"Where were you about an hour ago? I knocked. Your door was locked."

"They dragged me over to the hospital to take a picture of my leg."

"Did Thomas's boy pick up the package?"

"Yes."

"The police are coming in a little while, Harry. What am I going to tell them?"

"Sit down, Oliver. Let's talk about it."

They arrived a short time later, Walz and Gerry Brophy.

Cigarette in hand, having had a biscuit and just enough wine to ease me, I was composed, as much as I could be. When Mattie presented our visitors, Thomas, who'd arrived just before them, stood beside me.

Mattie's manner was stilted with anger. Gerry Brophy looked miserable. Walz, on the other hand, was enjoying himself. I had the distinct feeling that they were going to arrest me.

"Miss Brown," Walz said. As he paused in my arched doorway, his face a map of menace, I suddenly thought, there's no truth in him. He's playing a role. But then, so am I.

"May I present my attorney, Mr. Thomas Jenner? Thomas, Detectives Walz and Brophy."

I watched them all shake hands, this primeval male thing of circling, feeling each other out.

"What can we do for you, Detectives?" Thomas said. He sat down on the sofa beside me, while the detectives sat opposite us.

No one said anything. I smoked.

At last, Walz said, "We have added Miss Rae Dunbar to the list of people you have associated with who have been murdered."

No one spoke. Thomas rose. "Is there anything else, gentlemen? If not, we bid you good day."

Walz turned crimson. "We want to hear how you spent yesterday afternoon, Miss Brown."

"I spent a good deal of it with you, Mr. Colangelo, and Gerry, Mr. Walz," I said.

Walz looked at Gerry, who said, "We're not questioning the time you spent with us. From two o'clock to two-thirty, isn't that right?"

"I'm not certain, Gerry. I left with Mr. Colangelo, and walked a way with him."

"Why did you do that, Miss Brown?" Walz said.

Thomas put his hand on mine. "My client doesn't have to answer that question, Detective."

Walz leaned forward, his belly swelling over the waistband of his trousers. "It would be better for her if she did."

"Let's move it along," Thomas said. He drew out his pocket watch, opened the case, then snapped it shut, presenting the image of a man whose time is very valuable.

"What time did you leave Mr. Colangelo?" Gerry Brophy asked.

"I can't say. Perhaps a few minutes after we left you."

"Then you went up to Eighty-first and York and killed Miss Dunbar!"

I could have wept, but I did not. "I met Mr. Edward Hall for lunch," I said. "At the Green Dragon Tea Room. On Fourteenth Street."

Walz could not hide his disappointment. "What time was that?"

"I don't know exactly. About quarter to three. We spent a least half an hour together. You might ask Mr. Hall. You'll find him at *Vogue* Magazine, where he is an editor."

"I think it would have been impossible for my client to have gotten from Fourteenth and Seventh to Eighty-first and York at the time Miss Dunbar left the school," Thomas said.

"Really?" Walz's voice had a frightening undertone, implying he knew something we did not. "Miss Dunbar was seen leaving the school after four. If your client had gotten in a cab, she could have made it."

"I think not," Thomas said. "A fifteen-minute luncheon? It takes that long just to get tea at the Green Dragon."

"And after your lunch?"

"I went to see Bennett Newman."

"What time could that have been, Miss Brown?" Walz nodded at Gerry Brophy, who was making notes on a pad.

"I don't know. Half past three, perhaps."

"Very interesting, Miss Brown."

"I believe we have been cooperative, Detective Walz," Thomas said, "so I'm going to call this meeting to a close. Do you have any direct evidence against my client?"

"The case is building, Mr. Jenner. We'll have fingerprint evidence from the knife later this week."

"Fingerprint evidence? That's ridiculous. I don't own a trench knife and I've never even had one in my hand."

Thomas's stare was disconcerting. What had I said?

A triumphant smile flooded Walz's bulldog face. "How did you know it was a trench knife that killed your friend, Miss Brown?"

"Don't answer that, Olivia," Thomas said, his hand on my arm.

"Nonsense, Thomas. I want to answer. I have nothing to hide." But I did. I had the coat and the shoes. And what else? "Mackey and Eppie Diamond were killed with one, so I assumed. What's wrong with that?"

I'd grown to loathe Detective Walz's smile, and there it was again. "Well, we're making our own assumptions, Miss Brown," he said, getting to his feet and motioning for Gerry to come along. "You should be aware that we have a sworn statement from Mr. Newman that you arrived at his flat close to five, in a state of distress."

Chapter Fifty

*T*homas wouldn't let me say another word. In fact, he insisted that Walz and Brophy either arrest me or leave our premises. They left.

I was sure there had to be some explanation. "Bennett Newman would never have lied about this," I said. "It's Walz who's lying."

"You're too trusting, Olivia," Mattie said. She was not a hand-wringer, but she was doing just that.

"I'm going to have someone check out this Bennett Newman. Too bad Harry's incapacitated."

"Bennett's my friend. If he said it, it's because Walz rattled him. You saw what Walz tried to do with me. The truth is as I told you, I got to Bennett's around three, then fell asleep and he went over to Lord and Taylor to deliver some drawings. The next time I saw him he was with Stephen Lowell."

"Who is Stephen Lowell?"

"A poet. A very good poet. He and I have been exchanging mutual-admiration letters for the last few months, and then one day Bennett turned up with him. It seems they are friends from Harvard."

"Did he know Rae? Or the others, Mackey or Eppie Diamond?"

"I don't know. Stephen lives in Chicago. He's got a family there. He'd told me he doesn't get to New York very often, so I was surprised to see him again so soon."

Thomas made a note in his book. "I'd better do some checking on Lowell as well."

"Thomas, these are all nice boys, veterans, even Whit. They are not murderers."

"They were soldiers. They learned how to kill, Olivia."

"Pshaw, Thomas. That was the War. This is the Village and we're not mediocre people. We don't lie and we don't kill. We're all living the only true seriousness."

Thomas actually smiled. "That's what you all say."

He folded up his papers and departed.

And I, the most truly serious suspect? I bathed and changed my clothes and went downstairs to talk to Harry.

His door was open and I heard him before I saw him. Along with the thump, thump, thump. I thought he was talking with someone so I waited, but couldn't make sense of what he was saying over the thumping sound, nor did I hear another voice.

When I walked in, Harry was pacing round his flat on one crutch, which accounted for the thumps, talking to himself. He looked at me and, I swear, growled.

"Come to any interesting conclusions?" I asked, settling on his couch and fitting a cigarette into my holder.

He bent and lit mine from the one wedged between his yellowed fingers. "It's your story, Oliver," he said.

"What do you mean, my story?"

"You have the key. It's no stranger doing these murders. It's someone you know. Someone we both know, say from the Players, from the saloons. We have to find a way to smoke him out."

"How?" I had very little energy for this. Rae's death had left me drained and dispirited.

"Ding Dong's outside. Take him and go see Andrew Goren, or whatever his name is."

"And do what?"

"You don't have to do anything, just see him and talk to him about what's happened."

"All right."

"Then drop in on Bennett. Same thing. Are you going to the theatre tonight?"

"Yes."

"Talk to Jig and Susan. See if Edward Hall comes round, and Stephen Lowell."

"I think it's time you told me what went on between you and Whit about the time you were attacked."

"Crap," Harry said. "Nothing to do with this." A slow blush spread across his face. And all the while he was clumping and pacing.

I was suddenly very interested. "You're embarrassed! What is it? Come on. Tell me."

"Christ, Oliver, he figured I was the reason you threw him over." He sat down at his desk.

"You, Harry? Really?" I smiled. "You and me? Did you laugh?"

"I did. Couldn't help it. But he didn't take it kindly. He told me he'd bash my head in if I didn't stay away from you."

"What was he doing in St. Vincent's that night?"

"Swearing he didn't do it."

"Did you believe him?"

"I don't believe anybody about anything. Can we get back to you now?"

"Sure." I tried to swallow a hysterical chuckle, and near succeeded.

"I want you to promise me you won't go anywhere without Ding Dong." Giving me a stern look, he shook his finger at me as one would an incorrigible child. I shrugged. I would behave myself. I didn't have the energy or the will not to.

So now I was knocking on the door of the house behind the house on Mercer Street, confident that somewhere in the shadows of the tenement hallway lurked my formidable shadow.

The door was opened by a frail old woman, tiny, dressed in

black from head to foot. A black shawl covered her white hair
and her narrow shoulders. She stared at me and I at her.

"Andrew—er—Antonio?" I said.

"No here," she said. She moved to shut the door, but my foot
was there first. I was unmovable. She was frightened. I felt ill. I
hadn't meant to frighten her.

"I only want to talk with him. He knows me. Tell him,
Olivia."

She backed away from the door. I started to follow.

"Olwer!"

I saw Ding Dong come into the sunlight and had the immediate perception that the sunlight might shrivel him into a pile of
ashes. But I was wrong. "What?" I said.

"Don't go dere."

"Pshaw," I replied, and went in.

There was a door on each side of the hall. I was wondering
which one when the one on the left opened and the old lady
beckoned to me.

Poverty here was not so genteel. Makeshift furniture, with a
few dark oversized pieces, their surfaces covered with intri-
cately crocheted doilies, made for little walking space in the
small room. The old lady sat down at a worktable and went
back to shelling peas. I had ceased to exist. I stood and watched
until I heard coughing in the next room and followed the
cough.

I saw at once that Death had made himself at home in this
room. Andrew lay on a narrow bed, his cough weak. His eyes,
set deep, were two burning holes in the white of his face. Under
the thin blanket, his body made hardly an impression. He held
his hand out to me and I kneeled beside the bed.

"Olivia," he whispered. I could barely hear him. Holding my
hand tight, he brought it to his lips.

His condition shocked me. Tears welled up before I knew it.
"You didn't kill anyone, did you, Andrew?"

A death's-head smile was all I got. Releasing my hand, he fell
into a shallow sleep. I rose and went back the way I'd come.

"What's the matter with him?" I asked the old woman.

"The romantic fever," she said.

She meant, of course, rheumatic fever. I couldn't help but wonder, then, were we all dying of romantic fever?

When I stepped outside, Ding Dong was leaning against the side of the building, chomping on his cigar. "Youse oughtenta go dere alone," he said.

"It was only an old lady and a very sick man."

"Youse oughtenta."

"They won't talk to me if you're there, Ding Dong."

"Why not?"

After a moment of trepidation, I said, "You're too scary."

He burst out with a high, squeaky laugh. He wasn't at all upset. "Good," he said.

"Our next stop," I said, "is Fourteenth Street near Eighth, and Bennett Newman."

"We'll get a ride." Ding Dong signaled the air on Mercer Street, and what do you know, an ice wagon stopped. The driver, a gimlet-eyed fellow with the stubble of a beard, greeted Ding Dong with respect.

We climbed onto the back of the cart and rode, our legs dangling—it was a new experience for me—to Fourteenth Street, where we disembarked. Not waiting for Ding Dong to take leave of his pal, I strode right off to Glaser Family Printers.

What I came upon stopped me dead in my tracks.

A sawhorse stood outside the door leading to the printing establishment. I peered inside. They seemed to be closed and it was the middle of the afternoon.

There was yellow tape across the door leading to Bennett's flat, but I saw immediately that someone had cut it. I had my hand on the doorknob when Ding Dong caught up to me.

"I'm goin' wit youse."

"You can stand by the stairs."

I opened the door and would have gone right up the staircase, but I saw something odd. The storeroom where I had hidden from the police yesterday was closed tight and sealed with yellow police tape.

Why?

I suddenly knew why. I ran up the stairs and burst into Bennett's flat. "Bennett! The room downstairs, the storeroom full of mannequins, why have the police sealed it?"

He stood at his easel, his palette in his hand, a cigarette dangling from his lips, a surprised expression on his face. "I thought you knew, Oliver. They found the murder weapon there, stabbed in a mannequin's breast."

Chapter Fifty-one

My knees shook so, I grabbed onto the edge of Bennett's drafting table to keep from falling. The result was, I knocked over a pot of India ink. It smacked the floor and cracked like an egg, a black egg, which left a picture not unlike the color and shape of a spatter of blood. An avalanche of pens and brushes followed.

To my disgust, the whimper I heard was mine.

Bennett threw down his palette and caught me before I went the way of the ink and the rest. He carried me to his couch and kneeled, arms round me.

"You see," he said, "it's all too much for you. That's why we must be together." He lit fresh smokes for both of us.

"Oh, Bennett." I patted his cheek. He had a single-track mind. "You don't understand. I was there yesterday." Unbidden, the sweet, cloying smell filled my nostrils.

Bennett paled. "There? You mean when Rae was killed?"

"Oh, no. I mean in the storeroom in the dark with the mannequins. I saw you and Stephen and the two coppers and hid in there." Oh, Lord, I had even touched the hilt of the knife, though I didn't realize it at the time. It would have my fingerprints. I was going to be arrested for Rae's murder. I saw this very dispassionately, as if I were outside the story, looking in. Bennett lifted my chin. "Oliver?"

"They're going to arrest me, Bennett. Will you still love me if they do?"

"They're not going to arrest you. I won't let them."

"You told them I didn't get here till almost five o'clock and when I came I was upset."

"Never said that. Told them the truth, Oliver." He sat back on his heels. "You got here about three and we were together all afternoon."

"Well, not exactly. You did go off to deliver your drawings."

"Much later." He sighed. "But I haven't told the whole truth to anyone." He rose and picked up the broken ink bottle, the pens and brushes, setting them back on the drafting table.

"You haven't?" I shivered. Could it have been Bennett all along? I studied him as he brought a towel from the kitchen and wiped up the spilled ink. Perhaps he hadn't heard me. Instead, I asked, "Will you be at the theatre tonight?" I was chattering. Of course, he would. He had a small part.

"I don't have an understudy," he said.

"Will Stephen be there tonight?"

His face crumpled when I mentioned Stephen. He came over and sat beside me, taking my hand between his two huge paws. "I want you to promise me you'll never be alone with Stephen."

"What?" I sat up. "Our Stephen? Stephen Lowell?"

He nodded, eyes downcast.

"Why?"

"I can't say."

"But you must."

"Oliver . . ." He looked so unhappy I gave him a hug. "Oliver . . . I saw Stephen kill a girl in France."

Chapter Fifty-two

Stephen. My Stephen with the sensuous eyes.
Not true. I said, "In the War, accidentally."

"It was no accident. He cut her throat with his trench knife."

"My God, Bennett. Who else knows?"

"No one. He's my friend. I helped him hide her body and we threw the knife into the Seine."

"You must go to the police."

"I can't. He's my friend."

"Anyway, why on earth would he murder Rae?"

"Because he's in love with you, Oliver, and he thought he could never have you so long as Rae was alive." His voice broke. "If he murdered Rae, they will send him to the electric chair."

"But if they arrest me, Bennett, I will go to the electric chair." And all these men who love me will be so unhappy.

"That will never happen. I told you I won't let it."

"Well, thank you for that, my Galahad," I said, stabbing out my cigarette. Oh, yes, I was testy. And I was angry. I had a right to be. I got to my feet, swept past Bennett, who tried to hold me.

I ran down the stairs and practically fell over Ding Dong, who sat at the foot of the stairs eating an apple. Without a word, he stood up and dug into his voluminous pockets. He brought out another apple, which he first polished on the side of his mangy coat before handing to me.

What me, look a gift apple in the mouth? I bit into it, and the juices sprayed me. Sweet, white apple juice. It was clean.

"Where to now?" In preparation, Ding Dong hiked up his baggy trousers, threw the fringed tail of his silk aviator scarf over his shoulder.

"The theatre, sir," said I.

If you think I was flip and frivolous, I wasn't. It was all subterfuge. The news that Stephen was a murderer had unnerved me. How would I ever again be able to trust my judgment in people?

Jig was sitting in the basement on a low stool that totally disappeared under the volume of person and clothing. I presented Ding Dong, who had insisted that he sit backstage to watch over me, as my bodyguard.

In his long velvet coat, Ding Dong drew himself up like an English peer. "How do," he said.

Jig tugged at his forelock, somewhat amused. He stood, producing the hidden stool, and graciously offered it to Ding Dong. Thus the leader of the notorious Hudson Dusters sat in the wings this night for the performance of *The Emperor Jones*.

Before the curtain, his booming voice dripping with pathos, sincere pathos, Jig announced that the Provincetown Players were dedicating the evening's performance to one of our own, who had died tragically.

Ah, Rae.

Then we went on because the show, as a microcosm of life, always must.

When the curtain came down and we'd taken our bows, I saw Ding Dong frozen on the stool, a most peculiar look of awe on his face. "So what did you think?" I asked. Out of the corner of my eye I saw Bennett moving toward me.

"Jeeze, Olwer, da Kid wrote a nigger play and it ain't half bad," he said. The Kid is what the Dusters called Gene O'Neill, whom they knew from the saloons and dives as an okay guy.

"What have we here?" Bennett was staring at Ding Dong. I put a restraining hand on Bennett's arm.

"May I present a friend of Harry's, Mr. Ding Dong? This is Bennett Newman."

Ding Dong glared at Bennett and neither of them shook hands.

"Will you come have a drink, Oliver?"

I shook my head. I didn't much like the thought of sitting round with my friends and the menacing Ding Dong hovering over us. "I'm tired."

"I'll see you home."

"I'm seein' Olwer home," Ding Dong said. His tone made argument impossible.

"Rae's funeral is tomorrow morning." Bennett spoke softly to me, his back to Ding Dong. Ding Dong's fury was palpable. "It's in New Jersey, but you'll want to go."

"Yes," I said.

"I'm arranging a car. I'll come for you at nine tomorrow."

I stood on tiptoe and kissed his cheek. "Okay."

A short time later, I was home. All was well. I locked the door and climbed the stairs.

"Olivia." Mattie was standing on the stairs in her nightdress.

The air grew thin around me. I couldn't breathe. "What's wrong?"

"Where were you?"

"At the Players. It's performance night. Why?"

"Oh, dear me, of course. How could I have forgotten? It's just that he was here four times looking for you. He was so concerned. He had something to tell you that was very important, he said."

"He? Who? You mean Detective Walz? They're going to arrest me?"

"No. No. A nice young man named Stephen Lowell."

Chapter Fifty-three

I was beside myself, cleft in two. I threw my pencil down. I clasped my neck with both hands. Sweat, cold and oily, flushed from every pore. Stephen intended to cut my throat, as he'd done Mackey, Eppie Diamond, and Rae. As he'd done the girl in France.

I kept my fears to myself until I was sure Mattie was sleeping, then I went downstairs to talk to Harry.

He looked up from *The Hound of the Baskervilles*, and set it aside.

"Research?" I asked.

"Anything new?" He was propped up in bed, leaning on two fat pillows. All he needed was a few animals to complete the peaceable kingdom.

I went into the bathroom and took two beers from the tub, then came back and set them down in front of him.

Squinting at me, he opened both bottles. "You have something to tell me?"

I sat down on the bed near him. "You should have seen Ding Dong take to the theatre."

"I told him to stick with you come hell or high water."

"He did. Not everyone was happy about it."

"That poet friend of yours must have been here a dozen times looking for you."

"Stephen Lowell."

"Yeah."

I tilted my head back and took a big swallow. "Bennett says he killed a girl in France. Cut her throat with a trench knife."

"Bloody hell!"

"Bennett helped him hide the body."

Harry brought the bottle down with a thump. "Bloody hell."

"Bennett's not going to tell, either. He just wants me to stay away from Stephen because he's afraid—"

"That does it. You're not going anywhere until the coppers get him."

"Pshaw, Harry, I'm going to Rae's funeral tomorrow morning in New Jersey. The Dusters have been all over me. Tomorrow will be fine. Bennett's driving me." I took off my shoes and settled myself beside Harry on the bed. After each crisis, I'd begun to notice, all I wanted was to sleep. So it was now.

"Damn it all, Oliver, you don't know how to protect yourself. I'll get Ding Dong to go with you."

I snickered, laid my head on Harry's shoulder. "Blood will spill, Harry, if that happens. Bennett and Ding Dong did not hit it off."

"Then I'll go."

"Mmmmm."

"Hey, don't you go to sleep on me." He gave me a gentle shake. Very gentle. My eyelids were glued shut. His breath was moist and beery. "Did you find what's his name, Andrew, Antonio, or whatever he's calling himself?"

"He's got rheumatic fever. He couldn't even lift his head from the pillow. Not our murderer . . ."

A shout, then another.

Someone was in the room.

"Let go of me. Who do you think you are?"

Sunlight stung my eyes.

"Bloody hell," Harry mumbled, throwing the pillows from the bed.

"Glory be to God!" I couldn't believe it. Red Farrell and Rubber Shaw were holding a fiercely struggling Stephen Lowell. His collar was awry and he looked as if he'd slept in his clothes.

As for me, I had done the same, and in Harry's bed, no less. My poor heart was ready to explode. I swung my feet to the floor and felt frantically for my shoes. It didn't matter that they had hold of him—who could think logic at a time like this—I was terrified. My brief glance at Stephen told me he was quite mad.

"Oliver," Stephen said, trying to shake off his captors. "I have to talk to you. Privately." Something in his voice caught my attention. I don't know what it was. I stared at him now. Could I be wrong? In the light of day he didn't seem murderous, just upset. After all, he was a poet. No. What do murderers look like? Remember, I told myself, you are no judge of anyone's character.

"Youse wanna talk to him, Olwer?" Red Farrell gave Stephen a violent shake, so violent I thought I heard his teeth click.

"Go see if you can shake out a copper," Harry told Rubber Shaw.

"Dere's one hangin' out da front."

"Get him in here." Harry moved his hand from under the bedclothes. He was holding a gun, pointing it at Stephen.

"What the hell is going on here?" Stephen Lowell demanded, tugging his arm away from Red Farrell. "Oliver, I have to talk to you."

I closed my ears to his plea. "What time is it? I've got a funeral to go to." I slipped past the Dusters and Stephen and out into the vestibule. No one called after me. Relieved, I unlocked my door, relocked it, and took the stairs in an unladylike fashion.

"Get dressed, Mattie," I yelled. "Bennett's driving us to New Jersey to Rae's funeral."

Bennett arrived, a giant bear in somber pelt, a short time later. He was surprised to see Mattie in her mourning clothes, with her almost saucy little black hat and veil. "I didn't know you were coming with us," he said.

"Of course, Mattie's coming. She knew Rae also."

"It's fine, girls, come along. We don't want to be late," he said briskly. "I've left the motor running."

I touched his shoulder as we followed him down the stairs. "Bennett, Stephen's been here many times since yesterday, trying to talk to me."

He stopped on the staircase, so short that I ran right into him, and Mattie right into me. "No, Oliver, you mustn't—"

"There's no worry." I gave him a little nudge. "He should be on his way to the police station right now." Though I wasn't quite sure, since I heard loud voices coming from Harry's flat.

Mattie and I stopped to admire Bennett's shiny black Packard automobile. A bouquet of blood-red roses lay on the front seat, their flagrant perfume a seduction.

Bennett leaned into the front seat, searching for something, then he straightened and patted his pockets. "I've done it now," he said, chagrined.

"What is it, Bennett? It can't be all that bad."

"I've forgotten the gin."

"Oh, dear, that's perfectly dreadful of you," I said. If you think that by my flippancy I had ceased to suffer over Rae, you would be wrong. I knew I couldn't get through it without juniper support. "What do you think, Mattie?"

"I think we might have half a bottle in the liquor cabinet upstairs."

Bennett beamed at us. "Well, run along and get it, there's a good girl."

Mattie said, "I'll be right back."

I smiled at Bennett. "The roses were a sweet idea. Rae would have loved them."

The sky was overcast but it wasn't as cold as it had been. It began to rain. "No point in getting wet," he said. He gave me his hand. At what seemed the very same moment, who should come out our door but Walz and Gerry and Stephen Lowell.

I didn't want to see them take Stephen away, so I grabbed Bennett's hand with some haste and climbed into the automobile. Bennett got into the driver's seat and shut the door.

"Oliver!" The scream was chilling. Suddenly, Stephen was at the window of the auto, clawing at it. "No!" Walz grabbed him, tried to pull him away. I heard the rumble of the motor, the sound of the brake releasing.

As we pulled away from the curb, Stephen screamed again and I heard him very clearly. "Don't go! Oliver! He killed a girl in France!"

Chapter Fifty-four

$\mathcal{B}$ennett! What are you doing?"

He'd pulled away from the curb while I was still trying to absorb what Stephen had hollered at me. *He—Bennett—had killed a girl in France.* Who had told the truth? I had a sinking feeling in my stomach. From under the front seat a bottle rolled with the movement of the automobile. A bottle of gin.

I shook Bennett's shoulder. "Stop at once, Bennett, right here, and tell me the truth." Did I really want to hear the truth while I was trapped in the rear seat of an automobile?

We drove slowly downtown. Bennett was humming. I stared at the back of his neck where his hair clustered in thick curls just under his cap. Stephen's words rang in my ears. The scent of the roses filled my veins with lethargy. I wanted to sleep. I rested my forehead on the back of the seat.

"Bennett? Answer me!" I tore off my sandal and hit him with it, knocking off his cap. The automobile swerved sharply, tires shrieked. His hand caught my wrist, wrenching it. Pain shot up my arm. I dropped my shoe.

He righted the auto and kept his attention on the road. The rain glancing off the roadway made everything dazzle. I rubbed my wrist and tried to make out where we were. We were traveling east, away from the ferries to New Jersey.

I tried another tack. "Bennett, where are we going?"

"We're running off together, Oliver." He said it matter-of-factly, as he'd always said it.

"I thought we were going to Rae's funeral. The ferries are on the Hudson, aren't they?"

"We're going by way of Brooklyn," he said. "Don't worry. It's much faster this way."

"Why didn't we wait for Mattie to come back with the gin?"

"Poor Stephen," he said. "I don't want you to suffer."

Suffer? My lips formed the word, but I had no voice for it. The sky had grown dark and thunder rolled over us. We passed City Hall. I knew the truth now in the depth of my soul. "Bennett, I'm concerned about Mattie. We shouldn't have left her like that. I think we should turn back and collect her."

"You are a beautiful person, Oliver. You care for people and they hurt you. She is going to hurt you, too. I'm the only one who truly loves you." He recited this without once turning his head to look at me. "We're going to be together now."

I saw I was trapped. In order to get out of the car I would have to be sitting in the front seat, where the roses were. "Bennett, please stop the car. I want to come sit in front with you."

"Soon enough, Oliver. Soon enough." He negotiated a turn and there was the Brooklyn Bridge, in all its magnificence, ahead of us.

The realization hit me like a bolt of lightning. I was not going to get out of this alive. I was going to be that poet of the Village, you know, the one with so much promise? Too bad she died so young.

I saw Mattie in her mourning clothes, marrying Gerry Brophy. And Harry. He would certainly miss me. And all my lovers. Stop, I told myself. All this romantic fever is making you lame-brained. Maybe I just had to keep him talking. With Mattie's help, Walz and Brophy would figure out what had happened. I was depending on Stephen to talk sense. But they thought Stephen was a murderer. I was lost.

Perhaps I could keep him occupied, distract him, and figure a way out. "Bennett, you killed the girl in France, didn't you? Bennett?"

"She said she loved me, but she didn't."

"I love you, Bennett."

"I know that, Oliver, but you always let other people get in the way."

We sailed right onto the bridge along with a line of other automobiles. I had no heart for its beauty today. Rain fell in torrents. Traffic moved slowly. The trolley in the center of the bridge had its lights on.

"Mackey wasn't obsessed with me, was he, Bennett?"

"Not at first. I designed him, Oliver. I saw how much he resembled you. Then he betrayed me."

"With Andrew? And with Eppie Diamond?"

"She would have told you I ordered the shoes. I said they were for my mother."

"You say you love me, but you did all those things to scare me. Help me understand. Why did you hurt Harry?"

"If you were frightened and alone, I knew you'd turn to me." He hunched forward over the wheel, trying to see ahead of him. Suddenly, he turned the wheel, sharply, and I was thrown to the floor. When I raised myself I saw he'd brought our automobile into a horizontal position. He turned off the motor, grabbed the roses, and jumped out. The honking was a cacophony in my ears.

Bennett moved the front seat forward and reached in back for me. "Come out now, Oliver."

What was I to do? I could make him drag me out, or I could get out docile as a lamb and then try to run. I decided that I had a better chance if I got out of the automobile. We were not alone on the bridge. Someone would come . . .

In the end, I had no choice. Bennett was a huge, powerful man. The roadway was wet under my feet, and I had only one shoe. I stood in the deluge, a tiny element among the towers and the steel cables of the bridge. Rain washed my face, clung to my eyelashes, soaked through my clothing. I had no words for the occasion.

Bennett shoved the drooping roses into my arms and tried to pull me to the railing. I resisted, but I knew I wouldn't be able to for long.

I made myself limp, then jerked away, shouting, "Help!" But I didn't get far. People were getting out of their automobiles now. Bennett's arm went round my waist. He lifted me with one arm, high off the ground. I punched and kicked like a churlish child.

"Bennett, stop! You mustn't do this." The thunder came down on us so loud, I couldn't hear my own scream.

"Stand back!" Bennett shouted at the circle of people watching us. He made a waving gesture. Lightning slashed across the sky, catching something in its field. A knife. I stopped struggling.

Someone separated himself from the crowd and walked toward us.

"Bennett, please, you don't want to do this." My tears mixed with the rain and there was no beginning and no ending.

We stood at the railing and I looked down at the furious water far below. Taking the roses from my unresisting arms, he dropped them one at a time into the black water. I knew he would cut my throat and my blood would mix with the flow of the river . . . He held my chin in his hand and kissed me. "Don't be afraid. We'll be together," he said.

The death of a poet with promise, I thought. No! I lashed out at him, felt a sharp blow, heard him scream. Then I was on the ground, crouched. Someone had thrown himself on Bennett and saved me. Someone was fighting him now. My savior. I jumped up. Bennett would kill him, this brave man. Bennett was choking him, bending him over the railing. The rain made it difficult to see clearly. But I saw the knife where it had fallen. I picked it up and moved forward. I raised my arm. I couldn't use it. Opening my hand, I let it go.

I threw myself at Bennett, pounded on him with my fists. He flung me away, but in doing so, he let go of his opponent, who came at him. Confused, Bennett backed away, slipped, paused for a moment to spread his wings, and went backward over the railing.

His scream was swallowed by the clap of thunder.

I lay sobbing, huddled on the roadway, stunned. Somone bent over me, lifted me and held me tight against him. He smoothed the wet strands of my hair. "It's all right now, Dorothy," he said in a voice I recognized.

It was my nemesis, Detective Charley Walz.

Chapter Fifty-five

$\mathcal{B}$ennett had a breakdown in France," Stephen said, holding my hands between his. "There was a girl—her throat'd been cut."

"Bloody hell, Lowell. You could have said something."

We were in my parlor, Stephen beside me on the sofa, Harry, seated in Great-Aunt Evangeline's chair, his plastered leg propped on the footstool. Mattie, having brought us tea and cakes, sat on the piano bench, listening.

I asked, "Bennett and this girl, Stephen, were they lovers?"

"I don't know. He implied they were, and I had no reason to doubt him. But she was a barmaid. I daresay he wasn't her only lover. You have to understand, I've known Bennett for years, since we were boys. He would become obsessed with certain things, like stamps, lead soldiers—"

"Girls?" Harry offered.

"Yes," Stephen said, reluctantly.

I pulled my hand from Stephen's embrace, and took a cigarette from the box on the table. Stephen lit it for me, even as Harry fumbled in his pockets for matches.

Harry said, "You should have warned us. Oliver was almost killed."

Touching my cheek, brushing back an errant curl, Stephen

said, "I didn't think you were in danger. I'd put myself there first. And I didn't know for sure that Bennett was having a relapse. He had made a life for himself here."

"What happened to Bennett after his breakdown?" Mattie said.

"His family placed him in a sanatorium in Switzerland, and I lost track of him. Then I heard he was living here, so when I came to town, I looked him up. He seemed fine, happy."

"But surely you had some sense he was growing obsessive about Oliver," Harry said tersely. He tapped his fingers on his cast.

"It's okay, Harry," I said. "It's not Stephen's fault. He tried to tell me and I wouldn't listen. And Bennett said it was Stephen who killed the girl in France . . . I knew Bennett and hardly knew Stephen at all." I looked into Stephen's tender blue eyes and melted.

"It's not as if Chicago is around the corner, Melville. I admit I was worried . . . " He paused, embarrassed. "I have obligations."

> *Shall I give my heart to you,*
> *When you will likely it betray?*
> *Since you have promised others, dear,*
> *I'll lend it t'you for just the day.*

A week had passed since they'd brought me home in a state of near collapse, feverish, sick at heart. At first I'd refused to talk about Bennett, about what had happened. Whenever I closed my eyes, the scene on the bridge appeared and played out like a moving picture, with me as Pearl White.

I felt fragile, as if my bones would break should someone touch me, but I was very much alive.

"There's only one thing troubling me," I told Gerry Brophy. As time went on, more came back to me from that terrible night.

"What would that be?" Gerry had his arm round Mattie, she with the adoring expression on her face. She fingered her en-

gagement ring as she had since he'd put it on her finger a week
ago.

In a few days it would be Thanksgiving, and we were at the
Working Girls' Home. It was Harry's party tonight. His coming-
out party, he said. He was out of the cast, free of crutches.

"When Detective Walz saved me, I'm sure he called me
Dorothy."

"Dorothy was his daughter," Gerry said. "She wanted to be a
writer and live in Greenwich Village. He wouldn't let her. She
was too young, only seventeen."

"Seventeen is not necessarily young," I said. I was twenty and
felt ancient.

"One day she just disappeared."

"Just disappeared? You mean that story Mr. Santelli told me
was true?"

Gerry nodded. "She was never seen again."

"The poor man," Mattie said.

He saved my life, the poor man.

I wandered off. Harry was at a nearby table surrounded by
friends. I took my glass of gin and sat down at the far end of the
bar by myself. I was in full retreat.

"Well, Oliver, where are all the usual bees?" Harry took the
seat next to me.

"I've given it up, Harry."

"You have?" He hung his arm over my shoulders and whispered in my ear, "Not you."

"Yes, me. Love is not really free. It comes with a great price
tag."

He laughed. "Well, let me know when the price is right."

I spun round and stared at him, but Harry was shaking hands
with a tall, broad-shouldered man with light hair, greeting him
like a long-lost pal. His eyes met mine while he talked to Harry.
I felt an ever so slight tremor.

I wonder if Harry felt it, because he suddenly turned to me
and gave me a slow, quizzical smile. "Paul, you two ought to
know each other," he said.

I couldn't have agreed more.

The History Behind Free Love

Since before the Great War, the Village had been the beacon that drew young artists and writers to New York. After the Armistice, it became the place to be, for women as well as men.

Flats, food and wine were cheap, ideas and talk were rich, love was free. Genders blended.

Women had just gotten the vote.

What a wonderful time to be alive.

I chose Edna St. Vincent Millay as my spiritual inspiration and made my protagonist, Olivia Brown, a poet. I steeped myself in Millay's Greenwich Village, in the glory days of the Provincetown Players, where Eugene O'Neill's work was first performed by enthusiastic amateurs, Millay included.

Millay's letters and poetry were invaluable, as were Allen Churchill's *The Improper Bohemians* and Ann Douglas's *A Terrible Honesty*.

The setting of *Free Love* is the Village in 1920, with its bars and saloons and coffeehouses, with the Provincetown Playhouse. The places I've used existed, as did Prohibition, which only served to enhance the romance of alcohol.

I found the Hudson Dusters (I've used their real names) in Arthur and Barbara Gelb's biography of O'Neill, and I made them mine. They did take O'Neill under their wing, but the rest is fiction.